Praise for
THE KNOTTED STRINGS

By Jake Page
Published by Ballantine Books:

THE DEADLY CANYON
THE STOLEN GODS
THE KNOTTED STRINGS
THE LETHAL PARTNER

THE KNOTTED STRINGS

STRINGS

Jake Page

BALLANTINE BOOKS • NEW YORK

Copyright © 1995 by Jake Page

All rights reserved under International and Pan-American Copyright Conventions. Published in the United States by Ballantine Books, a division of Random House, Inc., New York, and simultaneously in Canada by Random House of Canada Limited, Toronto.

Library of Congress Catalog Card Number: 95-94903

ISBN 0-345-38783-X

Manufactured in the United States of America

First Hardcover Edition: March 1995
First Mass Market Edition: February 1996

10 9 8 7 6 5 4 3 2 1

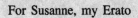
For Susanne, my Erato

author's note

Out of respect for the privacy of the Pueblo people who live along the Rio Grande in New Mexico, the pueblo herein, like the characters and events throughout, is imaginary. But the history is pretty accurate, thanks in part to the published work of Joe S. Sando, pueblo historian, and William deBuys, chronicler of New Mexican land use. Others who, wittingly or unwittingly, provided technical assistance are Peter Stelzer of Anasazi Productions; Conner Daly of the Albuquerque Police Department; Tasha Mackler of Murder Unlimited in Albuquerque; Michael Lieder, Washington lawyer and chronicler of Indian law; and, in ways that he would not have imagined, Abbott Sekaquaptewa, Hopi statesman.

beginnings

THE KNOTTED STRINGS
A Screenplay

by Joseph Drew Hill

Screen is dark. Sounds of Pueblo village life heard all around—children playing, scuffling, occasional scold from mothers, fire crackling in outdoor oven, and so forth. Quiet Indian voices in brief snippets of conversation. As if sound man moving around plaza of a busy pueblo.

          VOICE-OVER *(heavy Spanish accent)*
Señor: The Guardian and Discreets of the Apostolic Order of San Francisco of the city of Santa Fe in New Spain present themselves with the submission and respect owed to the sovereign and royal person of Your Majesty, and I say . . .

EXT. PLAZA

Screen brightens, revealing busy pueblo plaza, naked children darting about like fish in an aquarium, women in black woven dresses (see Exhibit A) going about their

1

chores, making baskets, grinding corn. A few old men
sit in the shadows of a two-story building, conversing
sporadically.

VOICE-OVER

The wise and lofty dispositions of the Laws of the In-
dies were dictated by the experience dating from the
beginning of the conquest of America. As long as
they are respected and practiced, they will be a
source of spiritual and temporal good and will keep
the vast dominions of Your Royal Majesty in the
most flourishing state. . . .

EXT. HILLS BEYOND PLAZA

Camera rises to show hills beyond plaza. Dust cloud re-
solves itself into a group of horsemen. A Spanish detail
of five, armor and weapons (harquebuses) gleaming in
late-afternoon sun accompanied by a brown-cloaked
friar. They are riding at a slow gallop toward the
pueblo with a calm and grim determination.

VOICE-OVER

Señor: The Indians in this region of your dominion
have compliantly taken the vows of the Holy Church
and sworn their fealty to Your Royal Person, yet they
persist like children in many of their heathen rites.
They are like children, led into insubordination by a
handful of men, witches to be sure. . . .

EXT. PLAZA

Horsemen enter plaza. Children, fearful, run to their mothers. The Spaniards draw up in the center of the plaza and dismount. As a unit, they stride toward one of the houses around the plaza and enter it.

VOICE-OVER

Along the Rio del Norte, in every village, it is the same. Idleness, distrust, instability, even rebelliousness, are characteristic of them. Their perdition must follow, several thousand souls lost after nearly seventy-five years of patient service in behalf of Your Royal Majesty and our Mother, the Holy Church, unless more stringent measures are taken . . .

EXT. PLAZA

Two soldiers drag a middle-aged Indian out of the house and into the plaza. Women shriek. Other soldiers exit the house bearing various artifacts—masks and other ceremonial paraphernalia. They set the pile on fire in the plaza as the Indian man, held by soldiers, watches in horror.

FADE TO:

EXT. STOCKADE IN SANTA FE

Six Indian men, some quite old, have been stripped of their breechclouts and stand naked, with their hands tied high on poles. We see them from the viewpoint of the soldiers ringed around one end of the stockade. A late-afternoon sun glints copper from their backs and buttocks. Before them stands a grim-faced friar. Six sol-diers move toward them, each carrying a whip.

VOICE-OVER

And so, Your Royal Majesty, we guardians of the Apostolic Order of San Francisco, with the concurrence of His Excellency, the Governor of this province of New Spain, have undertaken to punish the sorcerers who have been so unwise as to lead these, your children, astray . . .

EXT. STOCKADE IN SANTA FE

We see the six Indian men's faces, see them wince with the first lashes. Focus in on one face, a relatively young one. This is PO'PAY, a religious leader from San Juan pueblo. His face is set as if in bronze, black eyes burning with unalloyed hate and a growing contempt. We hold on his face for an agonizingly long time, watching him lurch with each blow, as we see

OPENING CREDITS

one

T. Moore Bowdre reached out a hand and let it rest on the round haunch. He caressed it with a touch surprisingly light in such a large man, his paw almost dancing over the well-muscled surface, fingers exploring.

"Well, damn, if that isn't just about right," he said. "Get their head and their ass right and everything falls into place."

The old stone mill house in which Bowdre now stood was no longer functional since some landscape architect diverted the stream out from under it. The room was lit only by the fading day outside a north-facing door. Bowdre stepped back from the clay, as if to contemplate it. In his mind's eye, he held the stop-action picture of a bighorn sheep, a ram, perched on a ledge, alert, the eternal truths of mathematics found in its horns curled back on themselves, the magic of the spiral, nature's perfection, just like a spiral of seeds in a sunflower, the winds of a hurricane . . .

What the hell was the name of that boy? Mo thought. The one who worked out that math? Italian fellow.

Brain's goin'. Gone. Skull full of porridge.

He heard footsteps outside his stone studio. A tap on the wood frame of the door.

"That you?" he said.

"It's me," said Connie Barnes.

"Come on in. I'm done for this day."

"Oh, Mo, it's . . ."

"Nowheres near done, but can you see a. . . . ?"

"A mountain sheep. A ram."

"Yup. U.S. Fish and Wildlife Service commissioned it. They released some of these guys in the Ladron Mountains down near Soccoro. No sooner than you could look at your watch they found two of 'em dead. Shot. By poachers. They're gonna do a big education program, make sure everyone knows the penalties. Wanted a bronze ram—you know, a symbol of the campaign. 'Shoot a sheep in the Ladrons and we gonna cut off your cojones.' That sort of thing. You want to have a look at this old boy's cojones? This is a *ram*. I took a little artistic license." The big man emitted a snare-drum laugh. "Hah—hah—hah."

"That's okay, Mo. I'll wait till it's done."

"I can tell you are grinning ear to ear."

"How?"

"Your voice is different when you pull your lips back that far to the sides. What's so funny?"

"They're here," she said.

"Who's here?" he said, ushering her out of the studio onto the lawn.

"They're filming the Pueblo Rebellion."

"The what? You mean those boys are upset again? What's their problem this time?"

"No." Connie laughed. "The *movie*. They're making a movie about the Pueblo Rebellion. In 1680."

"Well, that's nice, but I don't see what's so funny about that."

They walked a few paces toward the old, one-story adobe house, the big man facing straight ahead as if staring through his dark glasses.

"Well, see," she said. "I'm going to be in it." She giggled the high-pitched giggle of Indian women.

"You watch out there, woman. You'll get lockjaw if you smile any wider than you're doing. A part? In a movie?"

"Well, it's a nonspeaking role."

"Sorry. A role."

"I'm going to be Po'pay's wife. You know, the leader. I guess she just stands around in the background while he's planning everything, and kind of scowls a lot."

"And you're good at scowling?"

"He seems to think so."

"He?"

"Andrew Pindaric. He's the director. I met him in the Wheelwright. He was wanting some jewelry, an old turquoise bracelet. Navajo. I was working in the back, appraising a new shipment? And they asked me to come out and help him, you know—choose. And I could feel him watching me, real funny, and I guess I was concentrating, and he said I had a great scowl, did I want to be in his movie."

"Did you tell him you're Hopi, not one of those Rio Grande people?" They went into the house. "I could sure use a beer."

"Mo, are you jealous?"

"Of what?" He made his way into the kitchen and to the refrigerator.

"He's handsome."

"Well, why should I worry about that? Hah—hah—

hah." Mo took a bottle of icy-cold Negra Modelo from the shelf. "You've already proved you prefer ugly men."

"Anyway," Connie said. "The Hopis took part in that rebellion. They killed the priest at Oraibi and threw him over the side of the mesa."

"Ah, yes," Mo said. He drank hugely from the bottle in his big paw. "Hopi, the Peaceful People. What's for dinner? Is there anything in this fridge?"

"Maybe we should go out."

"Okay, go to Tiny's. Maybe run into some movie stars."

"Not at Tiny's. They don't hang out at places like that," Connie said.

"Oh. Well, now that you're gonna be a star, maybe we better move up. Like Santacafé? Oh, mercy, imagine. An ol' country boy dining with the swells."

"Tiny's is okay."

He put the empty bottle in the sink. "Fine. And you can tell me about the Hopi role in the Pueblo Rebellion. I thought you folks were kind of off the beaten track way over there in Arizona. . . ."

Connie smiled and stuck her tongue out at him, but of course he didn't see that.

Buddy Foreman, with his wife, Alicia, seated beside him, nosed their Toyota Celica into the parking lot of the Best Western Motel and stopped.

"Will ya look at this!" he said. "This place is jammed. Lookit all those pickups. Jeezis, there gotta be more pickups in here than in the entire state of Delaware."

Buddy Foreman owned and managed two Fit-Rite

shoe stores in Dover, Delaware, and was a member of the board of the Dover Chamber of Commerce. In Dover, the chamber of commerce was trying to encourage visitors with more upscale wheels than pickups.

"I hate it when you use bad language, Buddy."

"What, what? What bad language?"

"I'm not going to *repeat* it."

Buddy Foreman looked at his wife, a round woman with brown hair going to gray, and wondered what on earth she was talking about.

"Why don't you calm down, Buddy? This is our vacation. In Santa Fe."

"Well, where am I supposed to park, for ... ? The place is full. Look! There's a bunch of Indians getting out of that truck. Look at them. They're all dressed up."

A short, dumpy woman with shiny, long black hair and a black dress that covered one shoulder, leaving the other one bare, hoisted an infant out of the cab while two young boys vaulted out of the back. The driver, wearing a bright green shirt, a lot of turquoise beads, and a red band around his head, stepped out of the cab with a nearly eerie gravity and looked from squinted eyes at the motel.

"That's what Indians wear, Buddy. They're very traditional people," Alicia Foreman said knowledgeably, suddenly breaking into a smile. "I know what it is! It's that movie! I read about it in *People*. They're making this movie about some revolt or something, when the Indians out here fought the Spanish. They must be— this must be the casting place. They said they only wanted real Indians playing Indians. C'mon, Buddy, park the car. C'mon. Maybe we'll see some stars.

Maybe we'll see Andrew Pindaric." The woman beamed at the thought. "He's directing, you know."

"Park. Sure, park. Where? Hey, we're surrounded by Indians." His witticism brought a smile to the normally turned-down corners of Buddy Foreman's mouth. He couldn't wait to have a drink. He frowned again at the premonition that here in the Best Western Motel on the outskirts of Santa Fe out in this hinterland, they might not know how to make a manhattan. He put the car in gear and said, "Maybe around back."

The hallway to the Desert Rose Room was lined with Indians, some standing, leaning impassively against the walls, others—mostly women—sitting on the orange carpet with children, baskets, thermos bottles, baby bottles, and plastic coolers from the K mart. Expressionlessly and wordlessly, they awaited fame and glory as extras in the multimillion-dollar Sweetwater Pictures production of *The Knotted Strings*, their own historical moment in the sun when their ancestors had ejected thousands of Spaniards—soldiers, friars, rancheros— from their land up and down the Rio Grande, and burned churches along with forts and government buildings.

Gerry Baca, the up-and-coming manager of the Best Western, had been delighted when the Sweetwater people asked if they could rent a meeting room in his motel for casting the extras—the publicity value alone was worth whatever disruption it might cause—but he had had no idea how many of these soft-spoken people would turn out for their chance at the limelight. The hall was mobbed. How many more, he wondered, were jammed into the Desert Rose Room? He picked his way through the crowd, followed by Mona Friedman, the assistant casting director for the film, an angular blonde—maybe late thirties—with long legs and very expensive clothes of bright, primary hues that seemed flamboyant even in Santa Fe. She in turn was followed by a short, stout young man in a navy-blue suit with a mop of brown hair that kept falling over his forehead regardless of his nervous attempts to push it back. He had not caught the young man's name.

The manager looked back over his shoulder and said, "It looks like a lot of them plan to stay for the duration."

Mona Friedman merely raised her eyebrows skeptically.

They reached the doors of the Desert Rose Room and Baca twisted the door handle and pushed the door open. He bowed. "Here you are, Ms. Friedman. Good luck with your search." He smiled.

"Thank you," the woman said, and strode through the door.

"Señor," Baca said to the back of the short, stout man as he followed her closely into the room. Though he knew it was an unfashionable thought, Baca couldn't imagine himself working for a woman.

The two motion-picture professionals stood in the middle of the sea of people and looked around them.

"My God, Arnie," the woman said in a whisper. "It looks like the London tubes during World War Two." The large room was filled with Indian families sitting on the carpet, lone Indian males leaning against the gilt-colored walls. Maybe two hundred Indians, counting the ones strewn out in the corridor.

"You were there?" Arnie said archly.

"Let's cut the shit, okay, Arnie? We've got to find thirty presentable people out of this cattle drive."

Arnie looked around the room and pushed his hair back. "Mona, see that woman over there? The one with the beads?"

"They've all got beads."

"Over there. In the corner. Sitting. God, what a face. Like a Mongol. Maybe for the wife of Po'pay."

"Forget that. Andrew's already found that one. Found some woman in a museum and offered her the job. I mean, they give Eleanor and me the job of casting this thing and then he just snaps up Indians off the goddamn street."

"Director's prerogative," Arnie said.

Mona Friedman glared at her overweight subaltern, then looked around at the sea of brown faces.

"Look at these people," she whispered. "Where are the thin people, like in the old photographs? Most of these people are . . . fat. We can't have a lot of fat people milling around in this film."

Under his breath, so quietly as to be inaudible even to himself, Arnie said, "Bitch."

"Okay, Arnie, tell 'em the procedure."

The short, stout man pushed his hair back and crossed to a table that had been set up at one end of the room. He cleared his throat with an elaborate flourish and, in a loud voice, said, "All right. People? People . . ."

"Yeah, yeah. Sure. Yeah. Of course I—"

The brawny young man jammed the receiver down on the tabletop.

"Shit!" he said. "Everyone is a goddamn editor. I

mean every goddamn pencil-necked pantywaist in this whole operation is a fucking *editor*." He thought to himself that he didn't like these cordless phones. Slam 'em down on the table and they make a dumb clunking sound, nothing like the ear-shattering clatter and ding of hanging up a real phone. The receiver began to wail. He picked it up and glared at its button-ridden belly with contempt. He jabbed the off button with a stiff forefinger and the little red light went out, the siren silent.

Joseph Drew Hill, sitting in bright green briefs at the combination desk-bureau in a room on the third floor of the Best Western Motel, was twenty-nine years old and famous—at least in certain circles. A product of a small town in upstate New York, he had wound up in the city stalking the grubby streets, writing terse and pointless short stories about the mean-spiritedness of urban man, and lifting weights in a run-down gym in Queens. He tried a little boxing, flattened some black guy with a lucky roundhouse right, and the black guy hadn't gotten up from the canvas. They'd carried him off with a stretcher and Joe Hill never waited to find out what had happened to him. He left for upstate New York, found himself a cabin in the hills, and wrote a short, ugly novel about hunting, fathers and sons, and an old woman who was an Onandaga Indian. Joe's grandmother had been an Iroquois.

The novel was a *succès d'estime*. Robert Bly had eaten it up and a lot of people found the mysterious connection between the boy protagonist and the strange old Onandaga woman "the seeds of a modern mythology" and so forth. "Raw power," said *The New York Review of Books*, and Joe Hill had started reading up on Indians, getting more and more pissed off that they had all gotten such a rotten deal, and also that his connection was so distant from the roots of native America (his grandmother had been a thoroughly assimilated head nurse in a provincial hospital, married to a mechanic named O'Toole) that he couldn't honestly claim it. Joseph Drew Hill prided himself on a complete, even destructive honesty.

To be honest, he hadn't known anything about Indians when he wrote his *succès d'estime*, but then, he realized, neither did the assholes in New York who reviewed books. He concluded, a bit hastily, that there weren't any real Indians in the East, so he concentrated his researches on the western tribes. He soon came across the Pueblo Rebellion of 1680 in his reading and set out to write a screenplay, which, by one of those accidents that later seem to be fate, had finally found a sympathetic reading. It was an authentic, historical screenplay, the events seen from the viewpoint of the rebels, not the Spaniards, and the Sweetwater vice-president had guaranteed to maintain its historical integrity, though he oleaginously cautioned that "a movie isn't a screenplay, heh, heh. They grow organically."

So here was the first sign of organic growth, Joe Hill thought, like a wasp gall on the tender shoots of fucking truth.

He reached out and snatched the cardboard-bound screenplay off the table. He riffled the pages, and sent it spiraling through the air. It landed with a clunk in the wastebasket.

"Assholes," he said. "It's history. *History*. You can't fucking repeal history." He looked in the mirror that hung above the table in his motel room. Round face, dark eyes slanted. Like one of these Indians around here, he thought. But no cheekbones. Upturned nose. Very non-Indian. Can't fucking repeal genetics either, he thought.

The bathroom door opened and a young woman stepped into the room minimally wrapped in a small white motel towel. Her black hair was lank from her shower, water dripping from its ends onto her shoulders.

"Did I hear you talking to yourself?" she said. She had large black eyes, a heart-shaped mouth, and a wondrously thin Roman nose, giving her the look of a Middle Eastern patrician, an appearance that belied her small-town origins in eastern Iowa.

Joe smiled, glanced up at her, then frowned. "Frigging ducks are already nibbling." He smiled again fleetingly. "And I wasn't talking. I was shouting. To myself."

"Isn't it crazy people do that?" She sat down on the bed and crossed her legs modestly. He stared at the crotch that had been.

"I'm crazy about you," he said.

"You're just crazy. What do they want?"

He stood up, shot one hip out, and dangled a hand from his thick wrist. "They want me," he minced, "to *think* about—just start *thinking* about what Father Pio says when the warriors from Tesuque pueblo go after him. You know, when the rebellion actually starts? He's on his horse and these guys come out of an arroyo, they're all painted with red, and the soldier, a guy named Hidalgo, is with him, saw the whole fucking thing. And the old friar says, 'What is this, children, are you mad? Do not disturb yourselves; I will help you and die a thousand deaths for you.' I mean, that's what he fuckin' said. Hidalgo went back to Santa Fe and reported that. Verbatim. I got three sources for it, three! What, am I supposed to change the goddamn historical record?"

"It does sound kind of stilted. Did they really talk that way?" Joe Hill glared at the woman. "Anyway," she went on, "what does it mean, he'll die a thousand deaths for them?"

"Jesus Christ!" Joe exploded. "It's like—it's—he's a fucking friar. He's Christ's representative here on earth. *He*'ll take all their sins. All those guys thought like that. Bunch of nuts."

"Well, maybe . . ."

Joe's brows gathered together in suspicion. This Clarissa Long with her big eyes and patrician nose and her tanned legs and grapefruity tits—she was part of the production team. Junior but part of it, some kind of continuity clerk, helping see that everybody wore the same outfit in successive shots, stuff like that. Maybe she was a spy.

"Whose side are you on?" he asked.

She smiled at him. "Sit down here, Joseph Drew Hill, you hard-assed country boy with quill and parchment." He sat down beside her. "I'm not on anyone's side. I just help my bosses make movies and I like screwing the roughneck screenwriter on this gig. So calm down." She paused, glancing at Joe Hill's lap. "Or for that matter, don't."

Sergeant Anthony Ramirez of the Santa Fe Police Department stared morosely, as he often did, into the opaque yellow-green margarita that sat before him on the table in Tiny's. Over at the bar a couple of men were talking about *beisbol*, and at a few of the tables nearby, young couples talked quietly and gazed into one another's eyes, their faces lit from below by candles— one to a table—glowing from red jars. A white-haired woman materialized next to Ramirez's table.

"Everything okay? You haven't touched your drink. Something wrong, Sergeant?"

Ramirez looked up at her and smiled. "It's fine, Emma. I was just thinking."

"That's not allowed when you're off duty."

"I can't help myself."

"I just want everyone to be happy. Oh, look, there's Mo Bowdre and Connie. I'll go tell them you're here."

"Bueno," Ramirez said, and took a sip of his margarita. He watched as the big man with the blond beard made his way unerringly through the obstacle course of tables—familiar ground. Connie stopped by one of the tables and talked animatedly to the couple seated there.

"Hey, Tony," Mo Bowdre said, pulling out a chair. "Emma says you been sittin' here for twenty minutes staring into your cup. Thinking. What's the matter? Man's inhumanity gettin' you down?"

Ramirez looked at the big man, candlelight glinting off the black lenses of his glasses, big teeth gleaming behind his close-cropped beard, thick forearms lying poised on the table. A man of great self-assurance, and bombast, an oddball, a *tipo rara*, a blind artist, and his friend.

"It's woman's inhumanity tonight," Ramirez said.

"Oh, hell. Stood up?"

"Not that. My friend is gone to see her parents in Las Cruces. No. We pulled in a woman today. She thought her old man was cheating on her. They were broke, stone broke. When he came home—he was playing cards at the firehouse, for chrissake, and he was out of work, s'posed to be looking for a job—when he came home she hit him with an ax."

"Jeez."

"Six times. With an ax. Then she just sat there, waiting."

"That sounds more like the world's inhumanity to people."

"Yeah, I think that's it. People snap. Maybe I should've stayed in school, been an archaeologist."

"You'd still be mucking around with dead people," Mo said.

"Yeah. I guess it's my morbid Spanish heritage." Ramirez grinned.

Mo heard a beer bottle being placed on the table.

"Thanks, Emma," he said.

"It's me, Mo," Connie said, sitting down. "Hi, Tony."

Ramirez bobbed his head in an oddly elaborate bow and smiled at her. "You look, what? Especially radiant tonight."

"Tony's girlfriend is out of town," Mo said, "and he's been pondering the psyche of female ax murderers here tonight. The criminal mind is a fallow field for thought, isn't it? Maybe we should try and cheer this boy up. Let's see. . . ."

"Melinda over there? She's going to have a baby," Connie said. "That's cheerful, isn't it?"

"How many is that? Twelve? Why don't you tell Tony about your new career? See, she's gonna be in the movies. Larger than life on the silver screen. Well, I suppose it's going to be color, isn't it? Wife of the leader of the Pueblo Rebellion, fellow named Po'pay. A woman of great power and even greater taciturnity. Hah—hah. Tell him about it, Connie."

"You just did."

"Oh, yeah. So I did. Well—"

"It's a nonspeaking role," Connie said. She beamed and told the policeman about her meeting with Andrew Pindaric in the Wheelwright.

"And the Pueblo Rebellion. That's when they threw the Spanish out, right? Ran 'em all the way to El Paso," Ramirez said.

"Uh, well, yes."

Ramirez smiled and took a sip of his margarita. "And twelve years later they were back."

"Does it—uh—bother you, this film . . . ?" Connie said.

"No, no. Those were different times. The Spanish probably deserved it back then. They came back wiser. That was way before my people came up here anyway. All of us Hispanics, we're mestizos. Part Indian, you know? Though some of the guys up north forget that. No, I don't have any trouble with that old story. Water over the gate."

"Dam," Mo said.

"What's the matter?" Ramirez asked, looking around.

"It's water over the dam, Tony."

"Right."

In the mission church years ago, how many years? Seventy, seventy-one. Whatever. Then he had been given the name of Luis Rodriguez, but his own people had given him the name Jonva and that is what they called him when speaking in the old tongue even to this day. Jonva.

He was a tired old man. He felt himself slowly bending toward the earth. The days would soon enough pass

him by, lift him up, leaving his husk to go back to its
mother like a cornstalk. If he were deserving. If he
could bring peace and tranquility back to his people. He
scowled at himself for entertaining the thought that it
would have been better if his people had not asked him
to serve yet another term as governor. Governor of the
Pueblo of Santo Esteban. A white man's idea of a job,
with all the parliamentary procedures they had invented
over the years and insisted that the People follow, with
all of what they believed to be authority vested in him
now by virtue of the canes with the silver tops. Mr. Lincoln, the Great White Father, had handed out such canes
to all the pueblos on the river to reassure them of their
sovereignty and freedom. The Spaniards had done the
same thing much earlier, but they had somehow managed to overlook the pueblo they called Santo Esteban.
Mr. Lincoln, the man with the sad face like an Indian
face, had ordered a silver-crowned cane for each pueblo
governor, inscribed with the name of the pueblo, the
year 1863, and his signature, *A. Lincoln*. Since then, in
this century, the New Mexico governor, the King of
Spain, and a descendant of Christopher Columbus had
each awarded the governors similar canes, and most of
the Pueblo people took these more recent gifts as harmless tokens of the white man's curious, on-again, off-
again feelings about the Indian people in their midst.
But the cane from Mr. Lincoln was highly regarded as
having some kind of magical legitimacy—as do many
things that are old. The canes did indeed, in some manner, reaffirm the sovereignty of the Rio Grande govern-
ments. A strange white man's notion, Jonva now
thought. Sovereignty over what? Freedom from what?
Want? The people had rarely wanted in earlier times

and had always been sovereign, if that meant free to follow their own light, to roam their ancestral lands, and to consult with their own gods. Ah.

In his lifetime, Jonva had seen his world trans-figured—automobiles, tourists, cash money, alcohol, food stamps, welfare—all making his people *less* sovereign over even their own bodies and minds, even less free. There were some bitter old men, as acrid as smoke from coal, who still railed against all this, demanding a return to the old ways. They had cataracts in their minds, could not see that it was impossible. One could only hold on to those old ways that could be remembered while taking now from the white man's world that which was least harmful. One had to adapt. One had to accept some of the white world's rules in order to survive, even to retain some things.

Keep the language alive. Hold on to the language as a man clutches a rock in a windstorm.

Jonva sat in the governor's office in the new building that housed the tribal headquarters. It was a small building, five rooms only, to serve the hundred and twenty-seven members of the tribe. Still a sufficiently foreign idea, this government, that the People had insisted the government building be erected just outside the pueblo proper, behind some old cottonwood trees that had grown from seeds inundated here before the river's course had shifted slightly to the west.

A tributary river shifts and this does not become history in the white man's books, Jonva thought. History—what is that? Events that some people remember, and because they remember them, the events are important. How much is forgotten?

This movie about the Pueblo revolt. What do we re-

member of that except what the Spaniards wrote down
in their books? A few stories, a few heroes. But do we
remember what happened afterward—to our heroes, to
the rest of us? The leader himself, the prophet from San
Juan, the strange genius who persuaded all the People
up and down the river to cooperate—discredited a few
years later for too much pride, for claiming more authority over the People than they thought was his due.
And some of the People fleeing from their ancestral
lands for fear of the reprisals of the Spaniards when
they returned, as they surely would. Tewa-speaking
people, akin to Jonva's own, leaving to live among the
Hopi. Others going north to intermarry with the Navajo. How many people were sundered from their traditions, their lands, their gods as a result of that great
triumph?

But then, how many new traditions were begun? New
people formed? Didn't the Navajos take on some Tewa
gods then, as well as Tewa mates, creating a new people
from their Apache past? So it is said. Some of these old
men here, Jonva thought, forget that the river can
change its course . . . of its own accord. One cannot
stand on the banks and make it stay. One can drown in
the effort.

Thus did Jonva, Luis Rodriguez, Governor of the
Pueblo of Santo Esteban, review yet again his decision
to allow the film people from California to use the plaza
for what they called *location* for their movie about the
Pueblo revolt. They would, they promised, be gone by
the annual feast day, and they would restore anything
they had to change. They were paying a generous
sum; they would employ many men and women of the
village as extras, laborers, even caterers. The tall man

with the yellow hair and deep-set eyes, the one who was in charge—he was a sincere man, Jonva could tell. He spoke with a soft voice.

And it would be a good thing, he thought, for people to know about that event. Whites, he knew, generally thought of the Pueblo people up and down the river as—what was the word?—quaint. It would be good for them to see that there was more to us than that.

But there were those men who opposed his decision, and others in other pueblos, people who did not understand that rivers change their courses, that such things as the climate can change, that the world can realign itself. His job was one of continual persuasion, like urging the corn to grow and transform itself, but this time . . . he didn't think the old men and some of their young adherents could be persuaded. They would simply have to grumble, but this did not bring peace to the village, and controversy, though inevitable, was not healthy. He would consult his old uncle.

He turned around in his swivel chair and looked at the two flags standing pretentiously on poles—the Stars and Stripes and the flag of Santo Esteban. He felt caught in a force field that flickered waywardly between them like an electric current. He fell asleep sitting in his chair and didn't hear the door to his office open behind him.

Gregorio Velasquez looked at six of himself, different angles in the different mirrors artfully arranged around the hexagonal bathroom. He noticed that all the Gregorios were canted a bit to one side and he felt a bit sick to his stomach. I am standing, he said to himself, in the leaning tower of pizza. He laughed. That is funny.

His stomach lurched. Too much pizza. Makes a man sick.

He put his hands on the tiled counter, blue and red tiles from Mexico, very pretty, and steadied himself, righted the six Gregorios. He leaned forward and peered at his image in the mirror nearest him. A few lines, a little baggy under the eyes, but still a handsome man. He straightened up, thrust out his chest, and turned sideways—still magnificent. Irresistible. He reached out, grasped a glass carefully in his hand, and took a large sip of bourbon.

"Aahhh."

He looked again at one of the Gregorios, standing sideways, and sucked in his stomach.

Antonio de Otermin, he intoned to himself. Governor of the entire northern province of New Spain, master of all that could be surveyed north of El Paso, ruler of thousands of savages. A grand role, a grand man, even in defeat. His bare foot slipped on the tile floor and the six Gregorios lurched, grabbed the counter, and regained their composure.

His temples, he noted for the hundredth time in as many days, were graying. Nicely. A mature man. Very attractive to a right-thinking thirty-year-old type of woman. He examined the hair on his chest, peeking through the maroon silk bathrobe. Also graying. Suddenly he was quite sad. This, he opined, could be his last role of this kind. After that ... nothing romantic, heroic. Character roles. Ah, shit. He gulped a bit of solace from the glass of bourbon. So this role, Antonio de Otermin, would be his last grandee.

And it was his first in several years.

Yes, a bit of a problem there. But now he was fine.

Under control. His voice was strong. The time in the gymnasium ... magnificent. The body of a forty-year-old, maybe a thirty-five-year-old. He smiled at himself and the six Gregorios smiled back. He polished off the bourbon, set the glass down with a clank on the cheerful Mexican tiles, and allowed his maroon bathrobe to slip from his shoulders. He stood admiring his taut naked body, seeing six Gregorios, six angles. Magnificent, he thought. Magnificent. What mighty loins. He turned to the door and there were twelve Gregorios, twelve now—imagine, he thought, the woman who gets twelve Gregorios. ...

He took a step, slipped, righted himself, and opened the door into the dimly lit bedroom.

"My dear ..." he said, and fell over on his face.

"Goddamn it, Greg, you fucking lush." A naked woman leaped out of the bed, stomped over to the now unified Gregorio Velasquez, lying prone on the carpet, his soft white buttocks pale and sickly against the rest of his artificially suntanned body. "Get up!" the woman snapped. "Get up, you stupid drunken son of a bitch."

Gregorio Velasquez did not move. He didn't seem to breathe. Then he uttered an apneic snort and gasped in some air.

The woman stomped back around to her side of the bed and, cursing, jerked and thrust her way into her clothes. With a final "Christ!" she stormed out, slamming the door behind her.

It was not until eight o'clock the next morning that a tribal secretary found Jonva, Luis Rodriguez, Governor of the Pueblo of Santo Esteban, in his swivel chair, evidently dead from a heart attack in the night. And it was

26 Jake Page

not until eight-thirty, after repeated wake-up calls, that a hotel employee was dispatched to the room of Gregorio Velasquez, the celluloid governor of the northern provinces of New Spain, and found him lying naked on the floor, the back of his head smashed in. Blood and vomit had erupted on the carpet, on the wall, on the dust ruffle of the king-size bed. The employee immediately threw up, thus making matters all the more confusing.

two

A nude couple writhed discreetly in the deep shadows, and a grinning Mary Hart appeared on screen, wearing a bright red jacket over a fluffy blouse.

". . . and that's the second in *Entertainment Tonight*'s series on the double standard in nudity in Hollywood. Now"—her delighted smile was turned off as if by a rheostat—"there is tragic news from Santa Fe, New Mexico, where producer-director Andrew Pindaric is just getting under way with a Sweetwater Pictures film, *The Knotted Strings*. John?"

John Tesh, wearing a navy-blue jacket, a light blue shirt, and a striped tie, looked positively presidential.

"Yes, Mary," he said, staring into the camera, "tragedy has struck in Santa Fe. Just days before shooting was to begin on the set of Andrew Pindaric's film about the Pueblo Rebellion, veteran actor Gregorio Velasquez was found dead in his hotel room. Police who arrived at the scene this morning called the death a homicide."

The screen showed a studio portrait of Gregorio Velasquez, his limpid black eyes giving him a Valentino look, followed by the scene of a phalanx of reporters thrusting microphones under the nose of a man in plain clothes with black hair.

"When questioned further by *ET* correspondent Martha Zwick, Santa Fe police had nothing further to report," Tesh said as he reappeared on the screen. "Asked if there were any suspects, Detective Anthony Ramirez of the Santa Fe Police Department said, 'No comment at this time.' Sweetwater today released a statement calling Velasquez's untimely death a tragedy and an outrage. They expressed confidence that the Santa Fe police would mount a thorough and successful investigation into the matter. And, they said, the filming would go on as the studio sought a replacement for Velasquez. The actor was slated to play the role of the Spanish governor of New Spain in the Pindaric-directed epic of repression and revolt in the early days on the southwestern frontier."

For another twenty seconds brief clips of Velasquez in other roles sped by on the screen—a younger Velasquez as a pirate, a somewhat more mature Velasquez on horseback as Mexican revolutionary Pancho Villa, a yet more mature Velasquez staring soulfully at a flamenco dancer—and then John Tesh reappeared, looking solemn. "A grand career," he commented. "Gregorio Velasquez was fifty-eight years old. *ET* will follow up on this tragedy as events unfold."

The rheostat turned Mary Hart's expression back into a smile and she said, "Now *ET* takes you to . . ."

But of course, a number of events had already unfolded throughout the day in Santa Fe prior to *Entertainment Tonight*'s fifty-three-second memorial for the fallen star.

Sergeant Anthony Ramirez had arrived at La Posada de Consuela fifteen minutes after the distraught manager called to report to the Santa Fe Police Department that an apparent homicide had taken place in a room on the fourth floor. The room of Gregorio Velasquez, the actor. When Ramirez pulled up, with a uniformed officer sitting in the passenger seat, another squad car was already parked in the semicircular drive next to a massive stone urn filled with yellow cinquefoil. The huge brown adobe structure rose up—six stories of neo-pueblo architecture four blocks north of the city's plaza, dominating the otherwise low skyline. The hotel, only three years old, was owned by a consortium of six of the northern Pueblo tribes. For the most part, it was also staffed by well-trained members and decorated thematically by artists and artisans of those tribes, and with this unquestionably authentic Indian ambience, had been successful from the start. And with a fine sense of diplomacy, the major members of the crew of *The Knotted Strings*, including the key figures in the production team and those members of the cast who were not local, had been billeted there in spite of the extra costs. The rottweilers in the corporate finance department of Sweetwater Pictures had growled menacingly about this extravagance, but Pindaric's office had simply been adamant.

"It's the Indians' story, after all," Pindaric had said, "and it's not as if Sweetwater were going to share the profits with them." An inside joke. By various accounting procedures, Sweetwater, like the other majors, never made a profit, even on its most successful films. The rottweilers continued to growl until it was pointed out that it was good PR, which, however vaguely, they could compute into something akin to dollars.

Ramirez stopped behind the squad car, repeating the

thought that occurred first when he got the call: what a mess this will be. The town was already host to a handful of paparazzi and those pushy reporters from the Hollywood press and the supermarket tabloids, nosing around like stray dogs in a garbage dump. Ramirez had told the hotel manager to say nothing about it to anyone else until the police could investigate the scene, but he was sure that someone from the hotel staff would not be able to contain himself—or herself. Yet the expected pack of scavengers had not yet materialized by 8:52 A.M. He stepped out of the car and motioned to the forensics in the car behind to follow him. The manager, a thin man with graying black hair and the face of an Indian, was standing in front of the large carved wooden door. He wore a gray business suit, a white shirt, and a bolo tie that Ramirez figured was worth about a thousand dollars, inlaid with about seven different kinds of semi-precious stones including a couple he couldn't identify. Unnecessarily, Ramirez took out his wallet and flipped it open to show his badge.

"Sergeant Ramirez," he said.

"Yes, Sergeant, thank you. I am José Montana. I am the manager. This is—"

"Can you take us to the room, Mr. Montana?"

"Immediately. An officer is already there. Officer Gutierrez, I believe. Nothing has been touched, I assure you. Except the door. I instructed the staff to say nothing about this."

Six cops, four in plain clothes and carrying an assortment of cases and satchels, followed José Montana into the high-ceilinged lobby, where a few people stood at the reservation desk and a few others browsed in a shop full of Indian artifacts and paperback books, dominated by a long shelf of Tony Hillerman mysteries. It all looked normal as could be.

No more, Ramirez thought to himself. A celebrity murder. The city was already jammed with tourists. He wondered where all the other sharks of the press would stay when they got wind of this. "You're from . . . ?" Ramirez said to the manager.

"San Juan pueblo," the man said. "This way." He gestured toward a bank of elevators, the doors of which were adorned with designs reminiscent of Anasazi pottery. Above one of the doors, an arrow glowed red. Presently the door slid open and a short woman with blonde hair and a familiar face stepped forward, stopped, and looked quizzically at the assembled cops.

"Gracious," she said, and clicked past the official phalanx on stiletto-thin high heels.

Inside the elevator, all seven men studied the floor numbers as they successively lit up. The manager said, "That is Melanie Moreno. One of the actresses."

"Playing one of the many blondes of Spain?" Ramirez said.

"Perhaps she'll wear a hairpiece," the manager said.

Outside Room 403, the manager gently pushed open the door and said, "There you are, gentlemen, just as it was found. You—uh—you need me?"

"Not for now," Ramirez said. "We'll want to talk to you later, of course, and the person who—"

"Alonzo Ortiz," the manager said. "An assistant manager."

"And, of course," Ramirez went on, "the night staff. Later this morning, perhaps."

"I'll let them know."

"*Bueno.*" Ramirez entered the room, followed by the

forensic men and the medical investigator, and nodded at Officer Gutierrez, who was standing uncomfortably with his back to the naked corpse lying amid blood and vomit on the carpet. Ramirez dismissed him, and the large officer left with a look of profound relief on his face. "Check the windows first," Ramirez said to his men. "If there's nothing, then open one. It stinks to heaven in here."

Ramirez took in the room, the corpse yellowing on the floor next to the luxurious king-size bed with stylized red, blue, and yellow rain clouds painted on the hand-carved headboard. A white cotton bedspread with myriad little tufts, little balls of cotton in a geometric design, had been neatly turned down, and the covers, a white sheet and a multicolored Pendleton blanket on the far side of the bed from where the corpse lay, were thrown back. One of the pillows on that side was mussed, indented.

The room was large, the bed taking up only a small part of its generous floor space. Two large easy chairs flanked a sofa at the other end. There were two bureaus and a large cabinet along one wall. On the opposite wall were three windows, the curtains drawn.

The medical investigator, an Anglo nearing retirement age, stooped beside the body on the floor. "Fucking mess," he said. One of the cops began dusting a window and the others stood by waiting for orders. Ramirez crossed over to the other side of the bed and bent over, sniffing. Faintly, he smelled perfume on the pillow.

"Do you suppose Señor Velasquez wore perfume?" Ramirez asked.

"Yeah," the MI said. "An exotic fragrance like Jack Daniel's. He had pizza last night and what looks like a lot of booze. Two guys barfed here, it looks like. The other guy had a shrimp salad."

Ramirez's stomach recoiled. Shellfish made him ill under the best of circumstances.

"Nothing on this window," the fingerprint man said.

"Open it, for chrissakes."

The MI stood up. "Pretty straightforward. The guy was killed by repeated blows to the back of his skull by a thin round object, like a fire poker but thicker. Like a broom handle or something. I'd guess about midnight to two last night. I'll know more when we get 'im on the table. You guys want to take your pictures? I'll call downstairs for the ambulance boys to fetch him." He went out into the hall.

Ramirez nodded and the forensic men began their methodical puttering. "I'd be real interested to see if you pick up some hair from that side of the bed," Ramirez said. He went into the bathroom, stood in the middle of the room, and was unnerved to note that there were six images of him ranged around the walls. There was a large oval sunken bathtub in the floor rimmed with red and blue tiles like those on the sink. A maroon silk bathrobe lay on the tiled floor.

This isn't a bathroom, he thought. It's a shrine.

The toilet was raised off the floor, sitting on a marble plinth. A throne, in truth. Gold fixtures. He thought of his mother's house, with the little carved wooden *santos* lovingly placed in small niches in the adobe walls— each a little shrine unto itself, to be prayed to when the particular saint's talents were needed in the lives of mankind. Into how many grand houses in Santa Fe had misfortunes of one kind or another brought him, to look into the elegant and often tawdry affairs of the inhabitants, to see these elaborate shrines called bathrooms. Would future archaeologists see the remains of such a thing as that raised toilet and assume it was an altar of some sort, a place of purification and worship? And worship of what? A place where certain elevated priest-hoods performed a cabalistic ritual. The People of the Sacred Dump.

Ramirez shook his head to clear away foolish thoughts. He saw a glass on the sink and bent over to sniff it. Bourbon, indeed. He walked into the bedroom.

"You done that thing over there?" he asked the cop with the dust.

"What thing?"

"That." Ramirez pointed. "The cabinet or whatever."

"Yeah."

Ramirez crossed the room and opened the double doors. On one shelf was a television set and a VCR. On the shelf above was a selection of whiskeys, vodka, gin, tequila, brandies, and soft drinks. There was a bottle of Jack Daniel's, a half-liter bottle that was two thirds empty.

The MI, thought Ramirez. The old guy's got a nose almost as good as Mo Bowdre's.

A few minutes past nine o'clock, Ramirez left Room 403 to the forensic people and took the elevator down to the lobby, where he was accosted by a young woman with mousy hair, a mostly orange shirt probably from Central America, blue jeans, and black jogging shoes.

"Sergeant? I'm Samantha Burgess—"

"Yes, I know. With *The New Mexican*. What are you doing here?"

"I was going to ask you that."

Ramirez sighed.

"I was walking by the hotel," the woman said. "Saw you and the forensic guys come in here. So what's up?"

Ramirez sighed again.

"Homicide, right? Otherwise—"

"For now," Ramirez said, "that's your story. A homicide in this hotel."

"C'mon, Sergeant. Who?" The woman's eyes—a nearly colorless hazel—took on a gleam.

"So far as I know, it was no one who is related to you, Ms. Burgess, and one of the procedures in such things is to notify the next of kin before—"

"Was it one of the movie people?"

Ramirez regarded the young woman, thin, intense, cocky. Two years ago she had been a freelancer, writing stories about local artists for promo magazines. A nobody. Now she was a full-fledged reporter for *The Santa Fe New Mexican*, a kind of investigative reporter. Better to deal with a local, he thought, than the alien vultures.

"Ms. Burgess . . ."

"Sam."

"Ms. Burgess, it is too early to let you know about what has transpired here. Call me at about noon. You will be the first to know."

The woman smiled. It was a nice smile, Ramirez thought: a smile is a transforming thing.

"Thank you, Sergeant." She turned and walked across the lobby. Her jeans, the policeman noticed idly, were about half a size too small.

Like a computer program activated by a tap of the finger, a list of questions and people to be questioned scrolled through Ramirez's mind. The dry diet of standard procedure, he thought, and so useful a way of

functioning without having to dwell on the depressing
sights and smells of a dead man lying on a carpet, naked as the *niño* he had once been when he entered this
world, now with his brains spattered. . . . Ramirez
sighed again and looked around the lobby for the manager's office.

By nine-thirty, two physicians from the Indian Health
Service—one from Santa Fe, the other from the San
Juan pueblo to the north—had converged on Santo
Esteban and jointly pronounced Luis Rodriguez dead
from a massive heart attack. The doctor from San Juan
pueblo perfunctorily signed the death certificate in the
dead governor's office as the sounds of lamentation
could be heard distantly through the open windows. The
widow and her son, Martin, sat in the adjoining office,
silently, their eyes vacant. Small rivulets ran down the
old woman's face, following the arroyos and canyons
etched into her cheeks by eight decades of life. The two
physicians appeared in the doorway.

"Mrs. Rodriguez, we are profoundly sorry."

The old woman, Marta, looked up at them. "He is
free now," she said, and looked again into the distance,
the past.

"Our sincere condolences . . . of course, you are . . .
you're free to make your arrangements."

"Yes," the woman said. The doctors left and four
men from the village entered the room. Marta merely
nodded and they filed into the governor's office, carrying blankets in which the old man's husk would be
wrapped, prayed over that afternoon in the house he had
lived in for more than a half-century, his name never
mentioned again lest he be drawn away from his new

journey. He would be buried before sundown. And by the time the sun rose again between the peaks the white man called Elk and Grass mountains, the site of her people's emergence into this world, in the range called Sangre de Cristo, Blood of Christ, he would be well along his new path.

"The priest will want to pray," Marta said.

"This afternoon?" Martin asked.

"No. Soon. Tell the nephews to take him to the mission. For the priest."

"Yes, Mother," he said, using a term denoting as well her spiritual role in the tribe. He stood up, sighed, and walked out of the room, leaving the old woman to her lonesome prayers. Standing in the governor's office while his relatives silently wrapped his father in blankets, Martin took a deep breath. It was now his office. The people had voted a year ago not only for his father as governor but for him, now that he was of age under the tribal constitution, as lieutenant governor. To take up his duties, he had left his studies in public administration at the University of New Mexico, and his white friends in the master's degree program had chided him about what they called nepotism. But they did not understand such things—the old ways of Amu kwa, the place of the ants, what the Spanish had chosen to call Santo Esteban.

Mona Friedman strode from the lobby of La Posada de Consuela into the Rio Grande Coffee Shop, ducked around the wooden sign in her way that said PLEASE WAIT TO BE SEATED, and searched the tables for her boss, Eleanor Frank, a black woman with a cap of short-cropped hair. She spotted her in a corner booth, dressed as usual in a black suit with a minimum of gold jewelry. One of the most-sought-after casting directors in the business, Eleanor Frank had a photographic memory—not just for faces—combined with total recall of every piece of gossip about even the most obscure members of the acting profession, as well as a nearly extrasensory ability to see into the inchoate visions that lurked in the minds of film directors. She was forty-six years old, so she said, but looked older in spite of a few trips to the plastic surgeon, and Mona Friedman was more than happy to be learning at the feet of the master.

Mona waved at the black woman. Eleanor had called her only fifteen minutes before, summoning her to the coffee shop, and Mona Friedman liked to take longer than that to rise and proceed through her methodical rites of ablution and embellishment. What the hell is the rush? she thought again as she crossed the roomful of tables. She felt unassembled and gritty. At least, she noted with relief, a thermos of what had to be coffee was on the table. Eleanor Frank had already crushed two half-smoked cigarettes in the ashtray and the blue haze from her third hung over her head like an L.A. inversion.

"So what's up?" Mona asked as she sat down and reached for the thermos.

"It's back to the drawing boards, Mona baby."

"What's that supposed to mean?"

"Production called," the little woman said, directing a lungful of smoke into the cloud above. "We need a new governor."

"What? What? What happened?"

"Gregorio Velasquez, the man from La Mancha, our Latino muchacho on the white horse—"

"Oh, Christ," Mona said, alarmed. "He fell off the wagon."

"Farther than that."

"Eleanor, cut the crap. What's going on?"

Eleanor Frank exhaled more smoke, looked to her left and right, and in a lowered voice said, "Velasquez is dead."

"Dead?"

"Someone killed him."

"Jesus H.—"

"It hasn't been announced officially yet, but Production called. They don't want to lose days on this, so we've got to—"

"But that's awful," Mona said. "How? Where?"

"Someone bashed his brains out last night. In his room."

"A burglary?"

"How the hell would I know, Mona? They just said to find another Antonio de Otermin. Fast. They're juggling the boards but—"

"He just got here. Yesterday afternoon," Mona said. "How awful. He was just right for the . . . damn."

"Look, Mona, you're right, he was perfect. In spite of the fact that he was a lush—a recovering lush—and an insufferable super-macho pig, thought the world revolved around his dick. Like most men. It's a shame he got killed, but we've got until tonight to come up with a replacement. We can mourn his ass tomorrow. See if you can crane your head around and catch the attention of that waitress."

Mona looked around and saw the thick-necked figure of Joseph Drew Hill approaching them.

"Oh, God," she said, turning back to face Eleanor. "I caught the eye of that writer."

"Good morning," he said, stopping at their table with a vulpine grin. "A casting director's job is never done, huh?"

"What are you talking about?" Eleanor Frank said, blowing a column of smoke in his direction. He was a short man encased in slabs of muscle, wearing old jeans and a T-shirt that advertised a wild predator rehab farm in Oregon.

"Hey, the word is out. Old Velasquez got croaked. Everyone's talking about it."

"Jesus," Eleanor Frank said. "It's like a girls' dormitory."

"I never had the pleasure," Joe Hill said amiably. "Who've you got in mind for the role now?"

The little woman regarded Joe Hill as one might briefly examine a roadkill.

"Oh, I get it," Hill said. "None of my business. I just wrote the screenplay."

"You got it, sonny."

"Well," he said. "I hope you ladies can come up with someone this time who's a little more suited to the role than that superannuated bantam *gallo*." The woman in black looked blankly at him. "That's Spanish for rooster," Joe Hill explained with a nasal giggle. "Christ, Otermin was a *man*. He was a prick, but all those Spaniards were. But the character is big. Big, you know? It needs more than a lush with a Latin accent and big brown bedroom eyes. You ladies blew it on that one. Velasquez was about as much like a territorial governor as a gerbil is like a German shepherd. Good hunting."

He turned with a smirk and set off across the room in a rolling, muscle-bound gait.

"That guy's got real class," Eleanor said.

"Never met a writer you couldn't hate," Mona said, craning her head around. "Waitress? Miss? Oh, God. There's that sleazeball from *The Enquirer*. Headed our way."

"It's no-comment time," her boss said, lighting another cigarette. "Oh, Jesus. There's still about fifty Indians coming to the Best Western today. How the hell do we head them off?"

"Arnie can handle them."

"All Arnie can handle is—" .

"Eleanor Frank," said the sleazeball in a low-class British accent, like the early Michael Caine. "Mistress of thespian fate. Good morning. May I join you ladies for a minute?"

"No."

Mo Bowdre sat in his house in an enormous wing chair made from various roots and bits of driftwood liberated from the washes and arroyos of northern New Mexico by a young guy named Ben who lived in Algodones, down near Albuquerque. Mo was whistling an old song his father used to play on a Victrola when Mo was a kid. His father had been what the locals down in Lincoln County called tight. Never threw anything away that either worked or might somehow come in handy—he had boxes of string in his closet, various lengths in various boxes, including one labeled *string too short to use*—and he didn't see any sense in trading in a perfectly good RCA Victor 78-rpm record player manufactured in 1946 and his collection of prewar jazz

on those big heavy records with labels like Decca for
the newfangled 33⅓-rpm long-playing discs.

"This is the music I like," his father would say.
"Don't see no reason for trading it in for the same damn
music on some other gizmo. Then they'll make you
trade in for an even newer gizmo, then another, and all
you got is the same damn music and you spent a thousand dollars on gizmos." He ran his hardware store in
Ruidoso with much the same philosophy, which is why
it hadn't been the most profitable retail business in
town. But its clientele had been loyal enough. It was the
only place in town where you could sometimes find replacement parts for appliances made in the 1930s.

Mo had always thought his father had invented this
eccentric sense of probity because he was embarrassed
to be the nephew of Charlie Bowdre, a fairly flagrant
outlaw who had died ignominiously in the Lincoln
County Wars in the 1880s, a sidekick, however briefly,
of Billy the Kid. Both Mo's parents had long since died,
and the old hardware store was now a ski-equipment
emporium with a lot of flashy neon lights and dazzling
action filmstrips blaring from TVs mounted on the
walls—the derring-do of acrobatic lunatics amid pow-
dery eruptions of snow. Ski à go-go.

Mo was fighting off a distant cloud of gloom that
lurked on the periphery of his mind like those invisible
creatures that haunt the corners of a child's bedroom.
He knew the cloud well, and called it Sculptor's Cramp,
though it had nothing to do with too much manual ac-
tivity. It was, instead, a hollow restlessness, as if his
idea, the notion behind his current work, had been vac-
uumed up by a demonic house servant employed by the
wayward landlord who rented this world to each of us

on an unspecified short-term lease. Sculptor's Cramp—
the arthritis of the soul. Otherwise called lassitude.
Boredom.

Long ago he had known a stained-glass artist, an
elfin man who had said that the real reason for an education was to avoid boredom in those times in a life
when nothing was going on. Mo reflected on this ax-
iom. His own education had been full and eclectic, an
embarrassment of sorts when he would return from the
university, or from his brief stint at medical school, and
realize that his parents didn't have the faintest idea what
he thought about. It had put an unspoken barrier between them, and one that had not been breached. Before
his accident in the mine, they had both died, one after
the other, puzzled if vaguely proud that their third son
had turned out so strangely different than most of the
youngsters in their circle in Ruidoso. His mother had
gone off so quietly, not more than a few months after
his father. Mo had been a witness in the white cubicle
with the get-well cards and flowers as she suddenly began to shrink. The old song's words echoed in his brain,
rattling insistently like a TV jingle, like an unwanted
knocking at the door: "She was stretched out on a long
white table, so clean, so white, so fair."

Mo sighed.

What had started him on this? What triggered this
funk, this bout of incipient Sculptor's Cramp?

Maybe it's this movie, he thought. A whole new
world thrust at me. Well, nobody is thrusting it at me.
But here it is.

Connie. Connie's got herself a part—nonspeaking
role. She's all excited. Hell, why not? Damn sight more

interesting than sorting through beads for an insurance company doing appraisals for museums. She's thrilled.

Damn.

Mo knew exactly what it was.

Routine messed up. Familiar ways changing. It's the way of the goddamn world, isn't it? The tape is always running. So why do we try and stop it at some convenient place?

Damned mortality.

Mo whistled a few more bars of the old song and then, just as Connie came into the room, gave forth part of the chorus in a nearly tuneless baritone: "She'll never find another ma-an like me."

"What's that? Who's she?"

"That's 'Saint James' Infirmary.' "

"You sick?"

"I'm restless. You know, bored?" Mo said. "My creative enzymes have taken the day off. It's a terrible thing to see an artist in the doldrums, I know. A terrible thing. I apologize. You gonna go down to mess with those movie people? Maybe I'll come along."

Connie sat down on a red sofa in front of the fireplace. "I called in to see if they needed me today, you know, the way they said, and they said no. They're taking a day off. In memoriam, they said."

"Memoriam? What the hell for? Some industry holiday? Let me guess. It's David O. Sleaznik's birthday."

"One of the actors. He died last night. A Latino guy. Gregorio Velasquez. He was going to play the governor."

The phone rang and Mo reached out and picked up the receiver.

"Bowdre ... Yeah, hi, Phyllis ... What? ... Oh,

damn, that's a real shame ... Poor old guy. Yeah, sure. About eight-thirty. Want us to pick you up? Okay, see you there, I guess."

He hung up the phone, frowning. "That was Phyllis, down at the herbal magic emporium. It was a bad night," he said. "Old Jonva, over at Santo Esteban. Died last night. Heart attack. Family wants us to come over after they bury him."

"Oh, that's sad. He was so wise."

"Yeah," Mo said. He shook his head. "And an actor died, too, huh?"

"He was killed."

"Killed? How?"

"They didn't say any more than that."

Mo put his head back and remembered the sound of the old pueblo governor's voice the last time they had met. He'd been complaining with his usual blend of humor and real concern about the oddly inefficient ways of the white world, this time about how slow lawyers were. "All that education," he had said, "and it still takes 'em a week to read a piece of paper." Something about land, Mo remembered, old tribal lands they were trying to get back. The eternal quest. Over now for old Jonva.

"Let's go snoop around," Mo said.

"Why?" Connie asked suspiciously.

"Well, it'd be more interesting than sitting here in this chair feeling guilty about that half-baked ram. We can check out Tony Ramirez, see if he's discovered a pattern in events. I don't mean to sound callous. Tonight we'll go be part of the mourning for Jonva, but there's nothing we can do about it till then."

"We can pray for his journey."

"Well, yes. That, too."

There were a total of twelve people on the night staff of La Posada de Consuela, from five different pueblos north of Santa Fe, and one Anglo. Sergeant Anthony Ramirez looked again through the sheaf of forms filled out that morning by himself and two other officers. One had left that morning for an Indian craft show in Sedona, Arizona, and would be home in three days. Nine had been reached and had returned to the hotel that morning to explain that, no, they had not noticed anything unusual, besides the usual raucous crowd of movie people in the lobby and the two bars, had not seen Mr. Velasquez with anyone, no, no one had had occasion to go to the fourth floor, even the room-service waiter. Ortiz, the night manager, had not seen Mr. Velasquez after about ten o'clock, when he had been sitting at the bar alone. Ortiz had noticed that Mr. Velasquez kept looking at his watch, like he was waiting for someone. The bartender, an Anglo kid who identified himself as a ski instructor who, out of necessity, worked bars most of the year, had confirmed that Mr. Velasquez seemed impatient. He had tossed off three double bourbons and gone out into the lobby.

That left three employees still to be interviewed, two from San Juan, including the craftsman, and one from Santo Esteban, the latter being tied up with the village-wide ceremonies and mourning for the pueblo's governor, who had died last night of a heart attack. It was a nonhoper, Ramirez thought grumpily to himself. No one would have seen anything in the hotel except the usual melee of movie people, and who notices *any*thing else when movie people are around? Even in Santa Fe, where people pride themselves on being above ogling at celebrities, so many of them now having homes here. But routine needed to be followed, and there were other lines of pursuit. He wished the MI would hurry up, and the other forensic guys. The phone on his desk rang.

"Ramirez ... Oh, damn." He looked at his watch: noon. "Put her on." He sighed.

"It's like everybody in the world press is on their way to Santa Fe. Everyone in the fourth estate knows," Samantha Burgess said. "Including me."

"Not from me, they don't know anything."

"Yeah, I trust you, Sergeant. A man of honor."

"People gossip. I guess I owe you one."

"I'll take it."

"I'm still waiting for the medical investigator's report. Call me in an hour."

"Suppose I come down to the station?"

"Suit yourself," Ramirez said, and hung up. A large figure loomed in the doorway of Ramirez's cubicle of an office. It had a black cowboy hat perched on its head, a hat maybe one size too small, and a cowhide vest over a blue workshirt. "Don't tell me. . . ." Ramirez said.

"Just happened to be in this crummy neighborhood. Tony, are you ready for the limelight? The lasers of fame seeking you out in this rat hole of an office? The celebrity sergeant, sleuth of the stars."

"I am busy doing the people's work. Get lost."

"Lunch?"

Ramirez smiled. "In the doughnut shop. In twenty minutes."

"Yes, good. A man must eat. International fame nourishes only the ego."

"Will you get out of here?"

By noon, the murder of the actor had been announced in breathless bulletins on local television and radio. Even the classical-music station interrupted its third playing of Ravel's *Bolero* since Saturday to announce the homicide in grave and orotund tones usually reserved for pointing out musicological subtleties. The announcer said the Santa Fe police would be making a statement to the press at four o'clock in the afternoon. Word of the homicide spread like a wildfire in California chaparral throughout the city—the country's oldest capital city and what some of its inhabitants took to be the most sophisticated provincial city in the nation if not the world.

Santa Fe's hoteliers were happy: there would be an additional influx of press, people who spent a lot at the bar. On the other hand, the mayor felt personally insulted when he had heard about it only a half an hour earlier, and took out his pique on the police chief in a spray of sputtering outrage and stupid questions that had crackled through the phone for five minutes of the chief's valuable time.

The director of the city government's department of tourism undertook a careful assay of the situation: locally made movies were a *good*; homicide was a *bad*, especially the homicide of a celebrity. Santa Fe, recently dubbed the world's single most attractive destination by a prominent travel magazine, did not need to be known also as a dangerous place—a *bad*. At least, unlike the problems of his counterpart in Miami, it was just a visiting movie actor who had been killed and not a bunch of tourists. *That* sort of thing was very bad.

The director of tourism pondered the peculiarity of his role. His efforts had been so successful that Santa Fe, some now said, was being overrun with tourism, was at risk of "terminal chic." And this was not merely sour grapes from Taos and Albuquerque, where local pundits always smirked about the City Different. Santa Feans themselves were beginning to grouse. An anonymous saboteur had pasted posters on several gallery windows, telling people not to spend their money in Santa Fe lest it become an adobe Disneyland. The director of tourism simply hated that sort of thing. In response to the general grousing, he had only recently sent out a new series of newspaper ads, especially to Texas papers, carefully advising visitors to Santa Fe about how to honor the city's indigenous cultural richness, the human traditions that underpinned the city's *meaning*.

Though why, he thought to himself, anyone believed that Texans could understand, much less honor, anything without a price tag on it was beyond him. Face it, Texans with fat wallets didn't come here to goggle at admission-free and inexplicable ethnic dances and street festivals.

In any event, the director concluded, the very luridness of a filmdom murder would attract even more tourists to the City of Holy Faith. Motion pictures are artful illusion, and the illusory quality would carry over: people didn't associate real blood with movie stars. On balance, he determined, it was a break-even.

Alicia and Buddy Foreman of Dover, Delaware, got wind of the tragedy in a small shop off the plaza asso-

ciated with the United Nations and cluttered with an assortment of crafts, clothes, and knick-knacks derived
from every third-world country on the planet. Alicia
was behind a curtain struggling into a silk shirt from
Colombia painted with red-and-purple macaws when
she overheard one of the two middle-aged salesclerks
mention the murder.

"Gregorio Velasquez," the clerk said. "You know, he
played Pancho Villa in that film . . . uh . . ."

"Him?" said the other clerk. "He was in here yesterday. I'm sure it was him."

"He was?"

"Yesterday morning. While you were out. It must
have been him. God, he was gorgeous."

Alicia Foreman, stymied by the shirt, which was too
small and cut all wrong anyway, replaced it with her
own blouse and bustled over to her husband, who was
disdainfully eyeing a gaudy papier-mâché skeleton sitting in a wagon. Some morbid piece of crap from Mexico, he judged. His wife whispered, "Did you hear that?
Gregorio Velasquez was murdered last night."

"Who the hell is Gregorio Velasquez?" Buddy Foreman said.

"Augh," Alicia snorted impatiently. "The *movie* star.
I think I saw him yesterday. At that big hotel. It must
have been him."

"Let's get out of here," Buddy said. "This place gives
me the creeps."

In his sparsely but elegantly decorated office in an old
adobe building several blocks from the plaza, Allen
Templeton, Attorney-at-Law, picked up the phone and
dialed a number. Templeton's mother-in-law had been a

Catron, granddaughter of the leading member of what local history books called the Santa Fe Ring, the group of high-rolling Anglos and old Spanish who had managed to sop up most of the available range and mineral-bearing land in the territory back in the 1880s by means of a few outright purchases but mostly by explaining to the nearly illiterate holders of land grants from the Spanish crown that, since they weren't sure of the exact borders of their land, they couldn't properly fill out the papers now required of them. The members of the ring could then grab these old holdings out of the bureaucratic murk for a song, or less, relieving their elected friends in the territorial legislature of a series of knotty and time-consuming legislative considerations.

For a time there, the members of the ring had owned, among other vast tracts, almost all of Lincoln County, which at the time comprised the entire southeastern quarter of present-day New Mexico. The good old days, Templeton thought as he listened to the phone buzz in his ear. Catron County, in western New Mexico, had been named in honor of his great-grandfather-in-law. It was a hopeless county today, he thought, nothing but a lot of national-forest land populated by a thousand or so rubes who still thought shooting an elk out of season was mankind's highest goal. It was commonly said that there were eight elk to every human in Catron County, and Templeton didn't doubt it.

Back in those early days, the U.S. Forest Service had paid good money to acquire the old land grants from their new owners. And the cycle had, of course, not stopped there: the Forest Service proceeded at once to lease timber and grazing rights back to the very same families, the former landowners, for peanuts. It was a hell of a lot cheaper to cut timber or run cattle on the taxpayers' land, after all. But now, what with the environmentalists raising hell with the ranchers and the miners, even hamstringing the developers, Templeton mused, owning land and leasing federal land were no longer where the easy money was. The real money, he smiled to himself, was in being helpful to people who didn't know that yet. There were still plenty of ways to stay rich from the eternal human greed for land. Old Tom Catron, a lawyer himself, would certainly agree.

A voice came on the phone.

"Yes, I heard. It's on the news," Templeton said smoothly. "A tragedy." He listened. "Yes, of course, the papers have been filed." The voice buzzed. "Calm down. Judge Waddell will take it into consideration . . . Yes, I'm sure . . . No, nobody buys Judge Waddell. I know you can't understand that . . . Sure. We'll just let events play themselves out. Stop worrying."

Templeton gently recradled the receiver and smiled piously at his small but valuable collection of hand-carved and hand-painted nineteenth-century *santos* arrayed on the mantelpiece across the room. Wooden saints and angels, with their dolorous faces turned to heaven, so innocent and primitive, fashioned by devout old Hispanic craftsmen before the railroads brought new and garish materials and opened up new markets for their pious creativity.

In a niche in the white wall to his left were three expensive kachina dolls—two from the Hopi, one from the Zuni—awkward figures with beaked masks and feathers, carved from cottonwood roots by men of faith and piety equal to the Hispanic craftsmen. He had bought them from his old friend and client Walt

Meyers, now deceased. Meyers had always liked to point out—though not to the customers in his gallery—that the local Indian religions, with all their kachinas, weren't even half as old as the one the Franciscans hauled up the Rio Grande from Mexico on mules. "These people," Meyers would say. "These Indyinns're always talking about their ancient roots and all that. Hell, I can trace my own lineage back to twelfth-century Sussex. On my mother's side. I know the man's name. Been to his house. Now, you find me an Indyinn who can do that."

Poor old Walt. Templeton had made a quick hundred thou when they'd put the murdered man's gallery on the block and the IRS had gotten done with it.

Templeton looked again at his collection. Here it all was, the symbols of ancient superstition from two of New Mexico's vaunted three cultures, residing here among the weapons of the third culture—the law. *Dolls v. Words on Paper*. No contest. No wonder the Indians and the Hispanics hate us Anglos, Templeton thought. We invented this most powerful weapon of all, Anglo law. And they, with their *santos* and kachinas, they will never understand it, truly understand it.

He looked fondly at the locked cherry-wood filing cabinet that sat gleaming below the niche where the kachinas stood in their stance of perpetual surprise. It was a fine thing, Templeton thought, that the Catron family had been such careful recordkeepers, stowing away the old man's papers, writing diaries in spidery script, names, dates, maps, documents that had accidentally been "lost" in the fires that occasionally erupted in the state archives—the family memorabilia so lovingly preserved, the very stuff of the law.

                       * * *

At twenty-five minutes past noon, Sergeant Ramirez crossed Cerrillos Road, dodging through the traffic, and entered the doughnut store across the street from the SFPD. He spotted Mo Bowdre and Connie Barnes in a booth near the front, and got in line to order what would be both breakfast and lunch that day, a large Coke, a hot dog with everything, and a doughnut that looked as if it had been glazed in a pottery kiln. He carried his tray to the booth by the window.

"Sorry I'm late," he said, sitting down.

"Celebrities often are," Mo said.

"Cut the crap. Why are you here?"

"Tony," Mo said, fondling a large cardboard cup of black coffee. "We have a direct stake in this film. Connie's role and all. Just curious." The sculptor's big white teeth gleamed through his blond beard, and the sun glinted from his dark glasses. "Anyway, I like gossip. Hah—hah."

"They're getting a replacement for Velasquez. The show will go on. So you don't have to worry. Your new career is secure, Connie." The Hopi woman looked uncomfortable and Ramirez smiled at her as if to apologize for his insensitive joke.

"So what happened, huh, Tony?" Mo asked.

"A homicide."

"Come on."

Ramirez glanced again at his big friend, sitting erect at the little plastic table, as stolid as an outcrop of rock. What the hell.

"He was bludgeoned on the back of the head with a wooden implement of some sort, about the thickness of a broomstick. Six blows. Skull smashed. Between midnight and about two. The MI says that was the cause of death."

"Well, that must've taken some time to figure out."

"It wasn't all that obvious."

"A man with his skull broken open?"

"There was some question if he wasn't already dead when he got hit. Had enough alcohol in his blood to kill a lot of men. Point-two-three. MI says he was practically comatose when he got killed."

"So now what?"

"We rounded up the usual suspects," Ramirez, a fan of old movies, said.

Mo smiled obediently. "So what was the weapon?"

"Don't know. The killer took it with him. Or her. Whatever it was, it broke. The MI found some splinters in his head."

"Splinters? Now, there's a splendid clue for the supersleuth of the stars."

"Jesus. Will you—"

Mo held his big hands up, palms forward. "Never again will I allude to your fame." He took a sip of coffee. "God, that's awful stuff. How can you drink it?"

"I don't. I'm spoiled by the coffee in the station. But the hot dogs are A-number-one," Ramirez said, and bit off about a third of his.

"I can imagine. So what about these splinters?" Mo asked.

Ramirez chewed and swallowed.

"We cross-sectioned one, microphotographed it, faxed the picture to the UNM biology department. We're very high-tech these days. Guy there said it was ash wood."

"Hey, don't they make baseball bats out of ash?"

"A lot are from aluminum. They go *plink* instead of *whack*. Anyway, it was no baseball bat did this guy in."

"Did the guy say what kind of ash?"

"It's ash. An ash tree. You know, ash. What the hell."

"There are lots of different kinds of ash trees," Mo said. "What do they make broom handles out of?"

"I got a man checking that," Ramirez said. He put the remaining hot dog and roll in his mouth and chewed. "I gotta go. You guys want my doughnut? Special glaze on it."

"This place puts a glaze on my appetite. See you."

Late in the afternoon, clouds of various shades of purple-gray swept in low up the Rio Grande rift valley and obscured the ancient volcanic crags of the Jemez Mountains to the west. The lowering sun cast a saffron light over the rolling sage lands of the Santo Esteban Reservation and lit the adobe buildings of the pueblo a matte-finish copper, the west-facing windows gold. At the base of a hill about ten miles away in the eastern part of the reservation near the border with the neighboring lands of the Tesuque people, most of the population of Santo Esteban began to collect amid a small sea of pickups that had made their way along a winding dirt track across the high desert, bouncing through two dry washes lined with low cottonwood trees and willows.

On some imperceptible signal, the people of Amu kwa, now assembled below the hill, began a procession up to its windy top, a mournful procession to the high place where Jonva's husk would be returned to the earth. Behind a group of four nephews, the widow and her son, his arm around her shoulders, walked with their heads erect. The people trekked slowly upward in small silent groups, and the clouds above turned gunmetal gray. As so often happened at this time of the year, distant thunder groaned, and here and there on the horizon, lightning made lavender flares behind the clouds. Low-angle shafts of amber sun lit the clouds that hung above the foothills of the Jemez Mountains, filling the canyons with an apricot glow, as though the light were emanating from the earth.

The grave had been dug earlier, a dark pit surrounded with four mounds of loose dirt. The people gathered around it in a circle, twelve or so deep. The nephews lowered their cumbersome burden. Marta Rodriguez stood impassively at the grave's edge and listened as three old men stepped forward and, one after the other, in voices loud enough to be heard by those in the outer ring of mourners, said the prescribed things. The nephews put the dead man's belongings in with him— jewelry, blankets, clothes, a toolbox—and began hastily, almost frantically, shoveling the dirt back into the grave. Other men came forward from the crowd to take turns with the shovels, and when the dirt was mounded up over the old man's remains, they placed flat rocks over the mound.

The light on the Jemez foothills flared red as Marta circled the grave, sprinkling cornmeal on it from a leather pouch. Her son followed suit, and others did the same in the silence, and presently the sun winked out behind the now black clouds in the west. A collective sigh, like a breeze, arose from the assembled tribespeople who turned and began to drift down the hill to their pickups in the fading glow of the still-cloudless eastern sky.

Helped by her son, Marta Rodriguez climbed up into the cab of his pickup and sat looking through the windshield. Her son got behind the wheel. He looked at his mother and she turned her head, gazing in the direction of the Sangre de Cristos, east of the hill and obscured behind it.

"He is gone now," she said. "We must go feed his friends."

"Yes, Mother." The next governor of Santo Esteban turned on the engine, pulled out the switch for the headlights, and eased onto the dirt track that led back across the highlands to the pueblo, where the great river slipped noiselessly between its banks before plunging into White Rock Canyon.

three

Ramirez woke with a start and first light showed in the patch of sky visible through the window in his small bedroom on the second floor of a recently thrown-up apartment building a few blocks from the police station. He rolled over on his back, thinking about the press briefing.

Mobbed. Mobbed with people he had never seen before, never imagined, more television cameras than he had ever seen in one room, everybody shouting unanswerable questions in angry, self-righteous voices even before he had finished reading the official statement. The reporter, Samantha Burgess, sitting in the front row primly taking notes, had looked up and smiled at him wryly while he dealt with the feeding frenzy that had erupted. Finally he had simply clamped his mouth shut and stood motionless, staring at the raucous band of inquisitors until they fell silent.

"The Santa Fe Police Department has nothing further to report on this matter at this time," he had said. "On another matter," he went on, "there were three vehicles parked illegally in an emergency zone in front of the police station as this briefing began. They were all rentals. They have been towed. A regrettable necessity under the laws of this city. If any of them happened to belong to any of you members of the press, you may ask the officer at the desk about the procedures for retrieving them. Thank you for your attention."

He had smiled graciously and walked out of the room to a chorus of groans and a smattering of applause, which, he assumed, was the work of the outnumbered locals.

Ramirez slipped out of bed and, in the kitchenette, flicked on the coffee machine. He tried again to imagine how a woman could have entered Velasquez's room, no doubt ushered in by the actor, presumably taken off her clothes, gotten into the far side of Velasquez's king-size bed while he finished off a glass of bourbon in the bathroom, and then in due course left the room—all without leaving any sign of her presence except for a few strands of dyed blonde hair on the pillow and one black pubic hair on the sheet. He tried to visualize it, shamelessly observing the faceless woman dropping her clothes on the floor beside the bed, lifting the covers. . . . It didn't seem likely that she wouldn't have touched anything receptive to fingerprints.

More logically, she had touched something—maybe the lamp on the bedside table—and wiped away her fingerprints before she left. He wondered how many women with dyed blonde hair had been in La Posada de Consuela last night after ten o'clock. And he tried to imagine how he might find the one who had kept Gregorio Velasquez waiting in the bar while he soused himself with three double bourbons. And who presumably—what else could be presumed?—had beaten his skull open with a broomstick-size, ash-wood object as he lay drunk to the point of near coma on the carpet.

But with what ash-wood object? Certainly not anything one finds in a hotel room. Certainly not the sort of thing a woman carries around in a purse.

Of course, his report to the press had mentioned none of this.

Further forensic analysis would probably let him narrow it down to women with dyed blonde hair who were of an approximate age. Like between twenty and thirty, thirty and forty. Maybe. He wasn't sure just what stories a strand or two of dyed hair could tell.

The coffee machine belched and groaned, and Ramirez thought sardonically that it would be a big help knowing the age set he was looking for among the small sea of women from Hollywood, not to mention the dyed-blonde-female population of Santa Fe itself.

And it could have been a woman who dyed only a few hairs here and there blonde—what did they call that kind of hair job? Icing? And dyed hairs are more likely to fall out than the ones left natural color? Maybe. He'd have to ask about that. More sorrowful lessons of the dead.

And, of course, it could have been another man in the bed, a long-haired dyed-blond *maricón*. He'd have to ask about that, too. Did Velasquez have any preferences in such matters?

And, of course, it could be that Velasquez passed out on the floor and the woman (or *maricón*), thus denied the actor's favors, simply left and someone else came in later and beat the sodden man to death where he lay in his own vomit. And left no fingerprints. Nor did the disappointed lover leave any prints, even on the door as she or he left. Or the paramour did leave prints on the door and the murderer wiped away those prints along with his or her own. It all seemed terribly opaque.

The coffee machine uttered a final groan and Ramirez poured the aromatic elixir into a mug. He set it down on the table and crossed to the apartment door, returning with *The New Mexican*. Samantha Burgess's article was the lead story, under a three-quarter-page-wide headline. There was a recent studio shot of Velasquez, looking somehow both soulful and slick. Ramirez sipped at the mug and read the story, turning as instructed to page eight to finish it. The mousy little reporter had gotten it all right, including the fact that the victim had last been seen by two members of the hotel staff at about ten o'clock in one of the two bars in the lobby. She had gone on to quote a few members of the film crew about how fine a man Velasquez had been, his generosity and devotion to Latino causes ever since the days in the Sixties when Cesar Chavez organized the migrant workers in California. She had quoted the mayor's pompous statements about bringing the perpetrator to justice, and also the governor of the state, whose comments she had no doubt tactfully edited into complete declarative sentences.

Ramirez yawned, stretched, and headed for the shower, wondering how long the police chief would leave him in charge of such a glamorous homicide, one that had so caught the attention and piqued the pride of the city's and the state's highest officials. Waiting for the stream of water to warm up, Ramirez thought bleakly about the woman who reached the end of her rope the other day and now sat silently in a jail cell, the one who had dispatched her husband with six blows from an ax. She and her husband's story had appeared on page three, about two and a half column inches. The paper had misspelled the couple's last name.

The simple constitutional procedure had been followed, the piece of paper countersigned by the first woman to hold the position of secretary-treasurer, and Martin Rodriguez, age thirty-one, officially became the governor of the pueblo of Santo Esteban at 9:32 A.M. Mountain Daylight Time. The simple ritual was witnessed by the other seven members of the tribal government's office staff, who shook the new governor's hand without a word and returned to their desks.

Martin sat in the governor's chair, behind the governor's desk, swiveled around and looked at the two flags, and wondered what he was supposed to do. He heard the secretary-receptionist say, "Excuse me," and swiveled back to find three men entering his office. His heart sank. It was Antonio Tupatu, an oppositionist, a bitter man of middle age from the Red Ant moiety of the pueblo. He was followed by two younger men of his persuasion. The three men stood just inside the door, and Martin uncertainly said, "Yes?"

"The door was open," Tupatu said. The secretary appeared behind the men, her mouth agape.

"It's all right," Martin said, and she ducked out of the office. He looked at Tupatu. "Yes," he said again. "What can I do for you, Antonio?"

"Your father was an honest man," Tupatu began.

"He trained me to be the same," Martin said.

"Your father was honest, but he fell away from the path of Amu kwa."

"Antonio, I have heard—" But the man had begun to rehearse the familiar litany of grievances, going back generations, whereby the ancient meanings and ways of life of Amu kwa had been traduced by acceding to the blandishments of the white world. Each grievance had to be remembered, spoken on each occasion, the matters of the past thus achieving a lasting reality in the present. Martin sighed and listened with half his mind, certain of where Tupatu was headed. And after five minutes, during which Tupatu's two lieutenants stood nodding, their arms folded across their chests, Tupatu arrived at the current transgression, the leasing of the pueblo to the film people. Tupatu spat out a word that meant, approximately but more forcefully, *apostasy*.

Tupatu was a small, wiry man who had avoided the tendency toward obesity so common in the tribes these days, the result of a change of diet that, Martin admitted to himself, was the white man's doing. Fast food, grease, sugar, and pop had triggered something latent in the Indian physiology, and now, just when the dominant society with its health-food fetish was buying traditional blue corn from the pueblos to make chic munchies, the Indians themselves still gorged on junk food at the nearby trading posts and had the highest incidence of diabetes in the nation. The National Institutes of Health were doing studies, but so far not at Santo Esteban. Martin's attention refocused on the oppositionist who stood implacably before him, shod in moccasins, traditional red band around his head, a turquoise necklace hanging on his plaid shirt.

"You have spoken well," Martin said, adding a term of respect and switching to English. "I'm sure that you recall my father's thoughts about these things, the need for jobs here in the pueblo, the money to match the funds from the Indian Health Service so that we can have our own clinic here at Amu kwa. There are so many of our fathers and mothers who would benefit from such an outpatient clinic here. And our sisters and babies."

Tupatu grew impatient. "I have heard all that. Many times we have heard that. And each new thing sounds like it would be good. But each thing, each of these *good* things, adds up to the loss of our way. Your father was seduced just as a whore seduces a man."

Martin bit the inside of his cheek at this extraordinary rudeness, and his tongue probed the small tear in his flesh.

"The decision was made," he said. "It will stand."

"The people of Amu kwa will not be desecrated."

"Antonio, the people of Amu kwa elected me lieutenant governor." He picked up the piece of paper signed by the secretary-treasurer. "And according to our constitution, I am now the governor. For at least the next year."

Tupatu shrugged. "Paper. What authority resides in paper? You have spent so much time away from here, in the city, in the university, you have forgotten that real authority resides in the consensus of the people, the invocation of the old way. Not paper. Not the white man's ballots. The ceremonies still must be done. And they shall not be." Tupatu turned, and the three men filed out of the office.

Martin stood up, crossed the room, and closed the door. He caught himself wishing his father were still here, and apologized, thinking of the mountains to the east and the well-earned realms beyond.

He looked at the black plastic appointment book that lay on the desk. He opened it up, found the pages that told what his father had officially planned for the rest of his life. In ten minutes the lawyer named Beck would arrive. So it begins, Martin thought: the treadmill. No, it was simply continuing at its previous pace. The only difference was that he was now standing alone on it.

When Connie Barnes called in to the production office that morning, they told her to come over to a large warehouse a few blocks off St. Francis Drive. An assistant director wanted to meet with all the extras who had been selected, get all the papers signed, hand out schedules, go over their roles. Connie had hung up, a bit miffed. As the wife of Po'pay, the ringleader of the entire rebellion—even if she would have nothing to say—she did not think of herself as an "extra."

"Nnmph," she grunted.

"Uh-oh," Mo said, stepping lightly through the door into the living room. "What's the matter?"

"Nothing."

"You sound miffed."

Sometimes Connie wished that Mo was not blind. Had he not lost his vision in that mining accident years ago, he would not have developed his other senses so finely. If he could see, he'd just be a normal slob, like other men, and he wouldn't be able to read her like an open book. He could sometimes even tell her mood from her body temperature, sensed across the room.

"Something's up," he said.

"It was going to my head," Connie said. "My role. Po'pay's wife. But they called me an extra." She laughed. "It's real dangerous out here in the white world with all its pride."

"Humble pie ain't on the menu. It went out with the

THE KNOTTED STRINGS 67

Renaissance. Anyway, don't let 'em rile you. I get the sense they're pretty self-absorbed. Like a lot of artists, I know. Are you going down there today? I'll go with you."

So Mo Bowdre found himself standing against the wall in a warehouse where he could hear a small army of carpenters and craftsmen building sets. Mo could smell the newly sawed two-by-fours and the acrid odor of latex and acrylics. Someone named Arnold was trying to establish order among a large group of Indian people, loudly mispronouncing their names as he read from a list and shunted them to one or another destination.

"José Marteens?"

"Martinez, sir."

"Yeah, great, okay, José, you're with the warriors. Over there."

Someone approached, smelling of Dentyne gum, and stood nearby. Mo heard the gum crack in the man's mouth, felt the corrugated metal wall sag slightly as the man leaned against it.

A scratchy voice said, "You with the production?" The man, Mo reckoned, was about five-six.

"Hardly. I'm an escort of one of the extras. Talk about being a nobody. How 'bout you?"

"I wrote the screenplay."

"Did you? Well, from what I hear about these here jobs, you're about as important as me."

The man giggled nasally. It sounded to Mo something like a young pig with a sinus infection.

"Name's Joe Hill."

Mo put out his paw and felt it grasped by a thick and very powerful set of fingers. "You're—uh—"

"Mo Bowdre. And, yeah, blind as a mole on a foggy night. If that's what you were wondering. Hah—hah—hah."

"Guess you heard about the murder."

"Most exciting thing in the state since those boys in Los Alamos tried out their fat little toy."

"You from here?" Joe Hill asked.

"Born and bred. Why are you hanging around here?"

"Try and keep these guys honest. It's historical, this film. The screenplay is true to the times, seen from the Indian point of view. Every time you turn around, one of these guys is trying to make up something. It'd be more dramatic, they say. More dramatic? What the hell could be more dramatic than a bunch of Indians chucking about three thousand Spaniards out of the territory? Most successful Indian revolt in history. The *first* American revolution, is what it was. But it's *film*, they say. It's the cinematic fucking art. They already shot some of the interior stuff. In L.A. If I hadn't been hanging around, threatening these pantywaists with bodily harm, they'd of already turned this thing into a Danielle Steel romance. Gotta watch 'em."

"You've got a veto of some kind," Mo said.

"No. I been paid, patted on the ass, thanks, buddy, great screenplay. I'm on my own out here, Jiminy Cricket watching all the noses grow. All I can do is watch 'em, scream and holler if they dick around with the facts, make a scene. Pretend I'm just as crazy as all of them."

"Which you're not."

Joe Hill giggled again. Soooweee, sooooweee. "If I don't help 'em make their assholic changes, they'll hand it over to the body-and-fender boys. Talk about tin

ears. I mean, how the hell is an Indian actor supposed
to say lines that some Hollywood hack writes as if Indians were fucking street dudes from East L.A.?"

"Where are you from?" Mo asked. "East somewhere."

"I was from the Adirondacks. Now I don't know. It's
the old you-can't-go-home-again thing. I wrote a novel
about a guy like my father, now every pathological
bumpkin in my home county who can read thinks it was
about him. Two, three generations in the boondocks is
about all the gene pool can handle. I went back there
now, they'd nail my nuts to the fuckin' Lutheran church
door. Oh, there are the F-girls."

"The F-girls?"

"Yeah. Eleanor Frank and Mona Friedman. They're
doing the casting. Along with a faggot named Arnold
something. They chose that old fart Velasquez to play
Governor Otermin. God, the guy looked more like a
purser on a cruise line. The fuckin' love boat. I figure
there could only be one reason why they chose him.
One of the F-ladies must've been balling him. And you
can bet your ass it wasn't Lady Eleanor, the dark queen
of the Isle of Lesbos. Anyway, it's too bad Señor Chili
Pepper got killed, but . . ." He trailed off.

"All things being equal?" Mo said.

"I know that sounds wrong."

Mo was silent.

"Anyway, they already got a new guy. A real Spaniard."

"Who?" Mo asked.

"Some guy, I never heard of him before. An opera
singer from Barcelona. He's married to one of the

king's cousins or something. The guy from *People* magazine was talking about it."

"Cinéma vérité," Mo said. "A real Spaniard as governor and a bunch of real Indians. Whatever happened to illusion? Hah—hah—hah."

"Look, it was nice talking to you," Joe Hill said. "I'm gonna go harass the F-girls. The blonde one is kind of a piece of ass. About as friendly as an ice pick, but what the hell."

Or a broom handle maybe, Mo thought speculatively.

María Piño, who had a part-time job in the laundry—nights—at La Posada de Consuela, lived with her mother and father and older brother, Ernesto, in a three-room adobe house in Santo Esteban. The house was about a hundred yards west of those that ringed the village plaza and was located on a small rise at the end of a deeply rutted dirt track. María, who was nineteen years old, had almost finished the tenth grade in school before her life course took a three-year detour into the Thunderbird Way, down which path she had groggily veered until one morning she woke up, hung over, with the flesh on her cheek a gleaming purple, five roseate hickeys on her neck, her nether parts stinging as if sandpapered, and a nightmare sense that she had entertained an entire war party. But she had no direct memory of anything at all after leaving the bootlegger's place under the trees down by the wash. She had no idea how she had gotten home.

Panicked, she sought out the Franciscan priest and with copious tears confessed an unknown, unknowable multitude of sins and got religion. The mangled Jesus on the cross in the mission was suddenly a savior, not a white man's curiosity. The Holy Virgin gathered María up and held her to her all-giving, all-forgiving bosom as a daughter. It was a miracle.

Her conversion and subsequent piety were facilitated by the fact that she had no idea exactly what had transpired in those lost years, and within several months the nights of degradation, vague to begin with in her mind, had dissipated into a generalized cloud of remembered guilt sufficient to keep her on the straight and narrow but not so intensely specific as to make her hopeless about achieving redemption. She had now been dry, chaste, and dutiful for three months.

With zeal that pleased and bewildered her parents, she had thrown herself into the endless round of chores expected of the women of Santo Esteban, went to the mission church at least twice a day to pray to the patron saint, the angels, and the morbid icons on the walls, asked to hear again and again the sacred stories of the Amu kwa, and eventually found night work in the hotel in Santa Fe, some twenty miles away. She had announced that she would resume her high-school education when the fall semester began.

With the right thinking that comes from conversion, she could now wonder about the propriety of her dramatic older brother's behavior, the increasing radicalism of his outbursts at home—bitter aphorisms about the venality of the white man. Her brother, Ernesto, spent many evenings with Tupatu and the other *oppositionists*, and María thought it unhealthy. He had stopped refurbishing old pickups and cars for resale, and now two of them lay around outside the house like fossils, ancient hulks with gaping mouths and misshapen body parts strewn in the dust. He would disappear for days at a time, returning without a word. Her parents, she knew, were pained. It wasn't alcohol. She knew those signs and, she assured her parents, that demon was not haunting him.

Now María was on her knees in a corner of the kitchen, grinding blue corn kernels into fine light lavender cornmeal on a black volcanic rock called a *metate*, an implement that had been rubbed smooth as a mirror by her grandmothers in a string that led back she knew not how many generations. The saint's feast day would be upon them before long, and it involved many traditional chores as well as Christian duties. She had resolved to challenge her brother about his new path when she heard an unfamiliar engine outside the house. With a grunt, she rose from her knees and was looking out through the screen door, a cold finger of panic and guilt hooking through her newly acquired piety, when she saw the police car in the littered yard.

But the car was from Santa Fe. She wondered what it was doing here. A black-haired man in a navy-blue jacket, a blue tie, and gray pants stepped out of the car—Hispanic looking—and gazed around the yard. Probably he was looking for Ernesto. What had he done?

When the policeman began to walk toward the house, María stepped back from the screen door into the shadowy interior of the kitchen. The man stopped outside the screen and tapped quietly.

"Yes?"

"Excuse me," the man said quietly. "I am sorry to bother you. I am Sergeant Ramirez."

"Yes?" María said.

"Is this the Piño residence?"

"Yes." What *had* Ernesto done?

"May I come in?" Sergeant Ramirez said. He smiled. "I would like to speak with María Piño. Is she here?"

María's lungs stopped working for a long moment. "I'm . . . her." The man smiled again and María timidly crossed the room and opened the door. Sergeant Ramirez stepped inside.

"I won't take much of your time," he said. "You're employed at La Posada de Consuela?"

"Yes. Three nights a week. In the laundry."

"Two nights ago, Tuesday. Was that one of your nights?"

"Yes."

"One of the guests, a man on the fourth floor. He was killed Tuesday night." María's hand shot to her mouth. "You heard about it, of course?" He smiled again.

"No. No, I didn't." She gestured behind her. "No TV."

The policeman's brown eyes flicked around the room like the tongue of a snake. "I just have some routine questions, Miz Piño. Checking with all the night staff. I was sorry to hear about your governor." María saw that his eyes flicked to a point behind her and came to rest. She turned to see Ernesto, standing in the doorway. His arms were crossed on his chest, and he wore a red band around his head, a black sleeveless shirt. His eyes, deep set behind the ledges of his cheekbones, burned like coals.

"Did he show you his tin?" her brother asked.

Ramirez smiled again, took out his wallet, and flipped it open accommodatingly.

"What do the Santa Fe police want here?" the young

man said as if the policeman were somehow not present.

"A man died at the hotel," María said. "Killed."

"The movie star," Ernesto said with contempt.

The policeman shifted his weight from one leg to another. "This is my brother, Ernesto," María said. Ramirez nodded.

"Your sister was on duty that night," he said.

"Was the movie star killed in the laundry?" Ernesto asked. "María works in the laundry. Like a servant. Washing dirt from the sheets and towels of the white eyes."

Ramirez looked impassively at the glowering Indian. "Chill out, kid," he said presently. "I came here to ask a few routine questions about a homicide, not to get in a discussion about ethnic destiny." He continued to stare at the Indian and the Indian stared back.

"I don't care if your brother listens in on our conversation, Miz Piño, if you don't," Ramirez said. María shrugged, and answered—negatively—all the policeman's questions. She had gone straight to the laundry and had not left until quitting time at six in the morning. She had seen nothing and nobody. Ramirez thanked her for her time and glanced at Ernesto, who hadn't moved.

"Are you the mechanic?" Ramirez said.

Ernesto said nothing. Ramirez let himself out into the sun. The screen door shut with a wheeze of the rusty old spring and a clunk.

"Ernesto, why were you so rude?" María asked, still looking through the screen door. The policeman's car started up.

"Who is courteous to a pig?"

"But the meek—"

"María, María," Ernesto Piño said. "Your man Jesus was a white eyes. The meek inherit pigshit."

Ramirez avoided the ruts left over from the rainy season when the dirt track had turned to slime, and which were now sun-dried auto killers, but he came to a place where two tracks crossed perpendicularly and he had no choices left. The bottom of his vehicle crunched and complained as first his front, then back wheels jounced into the crevices, and he assumed that the oil pan, or whatever the hell went first, was now a relic, perhaps useful one day to that two-bit Russell Means back there with all the auto parts in his yard. Ahead of him were the cottonwoods and the brown stucco tribal government building, with three men under the trees, one squatting on his heels.

He recognized the new governor, old Luis's chubby son, Martin, wearing a white shirt and a bolo tie, standing next to a gangly, sandy-haired man in a plaid sports jacket, a tie, jeans, and scuffed cowboy boots. It was the young lawyer Beck, Tom Beck from Taos, recent inheritor of his father's law practice—one devoted to lost causes. The third man, squatting, seemed familiar. He had black bushy hair and wore a faded blue windbreaker. Ramirez edged the bleeding Chrysler (he was sure he was leaving a trail of oil) along the track, avoiding the ruts, and pulled up in front of the tribal building.

The man who was squatting looked up and grinned, revealing a set of crooked teeth.

"Hey, Tony," he said.

It was Larry Collins, the crazy FBI agent who had

shown up two summers before in Santa Fe on the trail of some stolen Hopi religious artifacts. A most unusual FBI agent.

"Hey, Collins," Ramirez said, getting out of the car. "Haven't seen you around. What're you doing here?"

"You know your vehicle is leaking oil there?" the agent said in his New Yawk accent. *Mierda,* Ramirez said to himself. "What brings you here?" the agent asked.

"Routine investigation." Ramirez turned to the governor. "Did your secretary tell you?" He stuck out his hand.

Martin Rodriguez shook it gently and said, "Yes. Any problem?"

"No, not here. Just routine. Talking to all the hotel night staff."

"A shame," the governor said. Ramirez shook hands with Tom Beck and, as he rose up off his heels, the agent. "I must go," the governor said. "New job. Very demanding." He smiled and walked into the building.

"So," Ramirez said to the agent. "A heavy concentration of law and order here at Santo Esteban on this cloudless morning."

"You're on the Velasquez thing?" Larry Collins said.

"Yeah. You?"

"These guys called me," Collins said, nodding at the lawyer. "Federal property missing. Well, it's not exactly federal property. The feds gave it to 'em. Now it's gone."

"Indian givers?" Ramirez said.

"No. Not like that. Something symbolic."

Tom Beck took his hands out of his back pockets and looked at Ramirez. "Back around Civil War times, the president—Lincoln—gave the pueblos here a new set of symbols of the tribal governors' authority. The Spanish had given most of the pueblos a set centuries before. Somehow they missed these guys. Anyway, canes, silver-crowned canes. So Abe had a set handed out to let the pueblos know they had a deal with the government, a kind of reaffirmation. That's also about the time they got the idea to draw some lines on the map, establishing the tribal territories around here—land patents, what became the reservations. It's complicated, but it's something like sovereign land."

"Yeah," Ramirez said. "I heard of that." Nervously he looked at the dirt behind his car.

"I had a meeting with the governor this morning," the lawyer went on. "Turns out there's a bit of a mess here." He put his fists in his back pockets and scuffed the dirt with the toe of his boot. "You interested in hearing about it?"

"Why not?" Ramirez said, watching the young lawyer's face. Beck's mouth was screwed up into a frown, like a baby who's been pinched and doesn't yet know how to react to the pain. He stepped out of the shadow into the sun and looked up.

"Red-tail," the lawyer said. Ramirez looked up to see a large hawk disappear behind the cottonwoods.

"There's a bunch of guys here in the pueblo," the lawyer said. "A handful, and some others from other pueblos. They're called oppositionists. Of course, they call them*selves* traditionalists. They're against a lot of the programs, initiatives that old Luis put in place . . . you know, Martin's father. Right now they've got a couple of issues they're pushing. One's about a suit the tribe's got about some land south of here—Forest Service land. And they're waving their arms about the movie. A movie is high-visibility stuff. They see it as a way to get public support for their gripes."

Collins dropped back on his heels and picked up a small stone from the dust.

"They're pissed off that old Luis said they could use the pueblo here, the plaza, in the movie. They say it profanes the village." The lawyer grinned ruefully. "My firm was retained as tribal counsel here years ago when my father . . . well, it's pretty much pro bono. These oppositionists have put obstacles in the way of everything we've tried to accomplish for the tribe. They're like a bunch of ultra-right-wingers, but see, it's tribal custom to have to listen to 'em, take their views into account. Finally old Luis just decided and the oppositionists went ballistic."

"How?" Ramirez asked, watching the FBI agent toss a pebble at the dark oil spot behind his vehicle.

"Well," the lawyer said, shifting his feet in the dust. "Like this morning they confronted Martin. His first day on the job. Basically, they challenged his authority as governor. Said they'd block some traditional ceremony, not that any ceremony has legal authority over the tribal constitution. But, you know . . . Anyway Martin got nervous—he's pretty young to get thrown into this kind of buzz saw—and I guess to reassure himself, he went looking for the cane Lincoln had sent over here. Like a badge of office."

"And he didn't find it, huh?" Ramirez said.

"It's missing," the lawyer said. "Gone. And *that* got out into the rumor mill, and the oppositionists say that without the cane, Martin obviously has no authority. I told Martin he should call the FBI. It's kind of a federal thing and the county sheriff . . ." The lawyer reddened.

"Yes, my rural colleagues," Ramirez said. "They would not be . . . in a situation like this, yes, I understand." He turned to Collins again.

"I'm beginning to like it out here," the agent said. "I was back east for a little while and my old friends in the Bronx said I'd picked up an accent like one of those country music singers."

A regular Garth Brooks, Ramirez thought. He said, "So you're going to be hunting for the cane?"

"Yeah."

"Tell me, what was the cane made of?"

The agent looked up at him. "Wood," he said. "With a silver head. Lincoln's signature engraved in it. And the date, and the name Santo Esteban."

"What kind of wood?"

"Christ, I don't know. Wood. Why?"

Ramirez smiled. "I'm just curious."

The agent stood up and smiled back, his crooked front teeth gleaming. Ramirez turned to the lawyer. "Do *you* know?"

"Never thought about it."

"If you find out, let me know, would you?" Ramirez said. "Well, it's back to the salt fields for me." He got in the car. "Get this heap into the garage. Give me a call, huh, Collins? Good to see you guys."

The engine rumbled into life and he looked at the oil gauge. The car's little brain had yet to register that somewhere in its abdomen its blood was leaking out onto the ground. He could make it to the gas station on the highway near Tesuque. From beyond the cottonwoods, the red-tailed hawk screamed. An omen? These

Indians, he thought, have more omens around all the time than even his people. He waved and pointed the car down the dirt track that led eventually to the highway and Santa Fe.

"Okay, I'm done for the day," Connie said, and put her hand on the big man's arm.

"Let's have lunch," Mo said.

"Were you bored standing here all that time?"

"Hell, no. Met the author. Fellow named Hill. Nice young guy, full of good cheer, nice words for the movie business. Hah—hah—hah."

"Meaning?"

"Country boy from the Adirondacks. You know, back east in New York State. Must be something about those real old mountains they got there, all worn down and beat-up and overgrown with vines and ferns and horsetails and God knows what. Dank places." He followed Connie into the warmth of the sun. "Must affect the newborn brain some way. I mean, that boy Joe Hill is about as at home in this world as a steer in a chute. Let me tell you all the dirt I picked up about these movie people, like the F-ladies."

"Do I want to hear it?"

"Probably not."

A low-slung charcoal-green convertible sports car spun into the warehouse parking lot like an elegant beetle and stopped on the open macadam between two rows of panel trucks and rented passenger cars and pickups. An elongated man with a thatch of unruly straw-colored hair unfolded himself from the shiny green carapace of the car and looked distractedly around the lot.

"There's the director," Connie said. "Andrew Pindaric."

He had pencil-thin legs, sheathed in blue jeans with the indigo dye worn away to the vanishing point, and a pair of cowboy boots made out of the skin of some reptile—probably worth as much as Mo's pickup, Connie guessed. Pindaric abruptly squatted down and, hands on the macadam, peered under the sports car. Satisfied, he rose fluidly and looked around the lot again, spotting Connie. White teeth glowed from his leathery face, in shadow from the overhead sun, and he waved.

"Come on, Mo," Connie said. "I'll introduce you."

"Pindaric, huh? Sounds like some kind of Yugoslavian poem."

"Mo, please . . . Names are sacred." Mo's blond eyebrows rose up above his sunglasses and danced there briefly.

Pindaric stood leaning one hand on the low roof of his aerodynamic car as they approached.

"Ms. Barnes," he said. "Po'pay's wife."

Connie was impressed. She introduced Mo, and the director stuck out his hand, hesitated, glanced at the man's dark glasses, and put his hand on Mo's arm.

"Glad to meet you," he said. "You're the sculptor?"

"Just one of many lurking around Santa Fe."

"If things ever let up here, I'd like to visit your studio sometime, Mr. Bowdre. I've admired your work. Can I call you Mo?"

"If you don't, I'll wrinkle up and die of Alzheimer's before your very eyes."

Pindaric laughed mildly. "Those animals of yours. They just pulse with life."

"Well, I'm real concerned with the environment, you

know. I'd be real happy to show you my studio. Not much in there right now but a mountain sheep in the works. A ram."

"Thanks. I'd love to see it. We'll be pretty busy. Making a film is a twenty-four-hour-a-day madness. Sheer madness. And then ... well, there's this awful ..."

"The Velasquez thing? My friend Tony Ramirez," Mo said. "He's in charge of that investigation and he's as good as they come."

"I'm glad to hear that. Well, I've got to go. Makes me nervous if I don't hear cameras running." He strode toward the warehouse on his long thin legs, head in the air, like a confident stork. Some locals and tourists, milling around the warehouse, polymerized into a dense crowd and tried to accost the director, but he sailed through unscathed and disappeared into the warehouse.

"How's your heart rate?" Mo asked.

"You are jealous."

"Me? Naw. Merely a clinical curiosity."

Mo followed her to the pickup. He turned his face up to the sun. "You know? I wonder what the hell they used to keep in that warehouse before it became Sweetwater Pictures' house of mirrors. Some kind of new health food from Zaire or something? Taro root genetically crossed with hippopotamus spit. Funny smell anyway."

"I've got to come back around four," Connie said. "The makeup department wants to check me out."

"Makeup?" Mo said, settling into the passenger seat, erect as a post. "Indians didn't wear makeup, did they? War paint maybe, but makeup? I thought this was gonna be authentic. I better tell Joe Hill. Hah—hah. By the way, speaking of that, you know your husband?"

"My husband?"

"In the movie."

"Po'pay."

"Yeah. But that's not how you pronounce his name."

"That's how—" Connie began.

"Yeah, that's how Joe Hill got it, and that's how everyone else's got it. But it's really pronounced Po-pnh. A nasal sound there at the end."

"Mo . . ."

"I'm not kidding."

Connie frowned and turned the key in the ignition. The truck sputtered and roared. "Where did you hear that?" she asked.

"Couple of extras was talking about it, back in that warehouse. They're from San Juan pueblo. Same as old Po-pnh was. Thought it was a good joke on the white man, all this talk about authenticity and all. Hah—hah."

"But they didn't mind you hearing?"

"Well, you know," Mo said. "Most people seem to think a blind man is deaf, too. Say, let's go up, have lunch at the Tesuque trading post. Then I can run over and talk to those boys at the Shidoni Foundry. May want to try 'em out on that ram."

Allen Templeton stepped out of his one-story office onto one of the most attractive streets in Santa Fe. De Vargas runs for three blocks along a narrow grassy park that flanks the Santa Fe River, a well-tamed stream that flows—when it flows at all—through a deep cement-and-stone channel. Beyond the river and the park lies a thoroughfare, the Alameda, and a few blocks farther lies the plaza. At its eastern end, De Vargas comes to a T at the New Mexico Supreme Court building, and many of the elegant, low adobe buildings along its length are now offices for practitioners who for one reason or another require proximity to that temple of justice.

Listening to the pleasing rattle of a breeze in the cottonwoods lining the river, Templeton crossed De Vargas and turned to contemplate his street—what he believed to be the finest example of urban gentility in the United States. It was conceivable that some university mews somewhere equaled it, but if so, Templeton was unaware of such a place. And anyway, it would be full of academics, he thought, with their appalling arguments about meaningless abstractions, their universally menopausal politics. No, as peaceful and elegant as this street was, it was also—as far as Templeton was concerned—a nexus of reality. That is, money.

He walked two blocks upstream along the grassy edge of the channel and spotted a man sitting at a lone picnic table in the shade. Templeton strolled toward the table, noting the man's shiny black, shoulder-length hair, the hint of a mustache, skin the color of caffe latte, and a black leather vest over a lavender shirt. He was reading some sort of magazine, which he held folded over, pinned down by a thick peasant thumb, concentrating on the words with the look of someone for whom reading does not come easily. Templeton paused beside the two wayward trunks of the cottonwood tree that shaded the table, and the man with the magazine looked up.

"This afternoon," the man said. "Four o'clock. Like it was planned." He returned to the magazine, beetle-browed in concentration. Templeton nodded to himself and strolled on upstream.

four

Okay, you come in the office, you see the old guy sagging in his chair, the guy is dead, hey, you don't notice that the cabinet is empty. You don't notice that the cabinet door was jimmied, opened, the cane taken, the door closed. You don't notice because the old guy's died in his chair in the night and there's all this stuff to do, these steps prescribed or the old guy's spirit gets stuck here in the wrong world.

So nobody, not even Martin, the new governor, the old guy's son, notices the cane is missing, the cabinet door with a couple of splinters on it, until the other guys come and give you a hard time about who's boss and then you think to look. You want to hold the cane in your hands so you can feel right.

So who stole it?

Well, that's obvious, thought Special Agent Larry Collins, standing in the shade under the gnarled old cottonwoods. A breeze rattled the leaves overhead. Beyond the river, to the west, the land stretched away in a jumble of low hills and—what did they say?—arroyos, to the Jemez Mountains, blue in the distance. He stepped out into the sun and traced an arc in the dust with his shoe tip, and shrugged.

Like another planet, Collins thought, the Bronx tough guy, accustomed to brick, gray walls, garbage in the street, taunts—"Hey, honk!"— the animal shriek of the sirens and the matching snarl of what he and his few white friends had called jig music in those days, the old neighborhood his old man wouldn't leave even though it had left him—the old man who wouldn't leave until it was too late, instead got left on the floor of the shop with a black hole in his forehead above his eye, leaving him, Collins . . . leaving him that way.

Collins listened again to the hot wind in the leaves, the only sound now but for the occasional yelp of a kid in the plaza down by the river, the bark of a dog. The silent sun, empty land. He smiled. After two years he had begun to notice the landscape. At first, it had looked dumber than the moon. You'd drive miles and miles through all that colorless scrub and dirt and see maybe two houses or something, with the hills and the mesas off to the side, baking under the sun, useless. No beat, no rhythm, no action.

But he had been beguiled. He admired the unfinished look of the place—ragged, new, littered with rocks like a junked-up schoolyard. He approved of the awkward branches of the cottonwood trees, growing helter-skelter in planless anarchy. He had come to admire the quiet Indian voices with their almost musical lilt, their funny pronunciation. He rehearsed it in his mind. Like he would say "In th' *room*"—almost one word, and they would say "Inn *tha* room." Distinct. Funny.

He said it out loud: "Inn *tha* room."

Nope. That's not quite right.

"*Inn tha* room."

Closer.

Where is *tha* cane?

Two years, some of it mucking around in these old pueblos, with these dour people with their sudden bubbling up of laughter, old as the landscape, full of secrets you wouldn't want to know about, like they're just waiting, sitting on some symbol, some little diagram that has all the world's wisdom in it, waiting for us to get the hell out of here so they can study their symbol, forget about the rest of the world. But like kids, like kids with secret passwords, hiding places, scared of the dark because they still see it. . . . It all looks so simple, the land is all the same, the pueblos—all the same—but nothing here is what it looks like. There's always more to it.

He felt the sun burning the back of his neck and watched the pattern of blue shade from the cottonwood leaves shift and wiggle on the dry ground. He didn't get angry so much anymore.

He remembered the shrink's face, so open and concerned, sitting in the swivel chair, watching him lie. No, he didn't blame his old man, for chrissakes, he blamed the fucking perps. No, he didn't think they were subhuman, they were just dirtbags. No, he didn't think his job description involved understanding how they came to be dirtbags.

"That's your job," he had said. "Mine is to get 'em off the street." But of course he knew that he would be doing something else if his old man had . . . done what most of his neighbors did: get out. Yeah, and his mother would be alive maybe. So? So, the shrink had answered, give him credit for that.

Thinking this was bullshit, Collins had played along

and was sent back to work, wondering what the shrink
had meant. Credit?

Collins looked up at the cottonwoods overhead. It's
obvious who stole the cane. The guys who wanted to
screw up the symbols of authority. That's obvious.

That's why it probably didn't happen that way.

Collins walked across the dust to the tribal office
building and opened the glass door.

"One other thing," he said to the receptionist, who
looked up at him through round, sun-flecked eyeglasses.
He smiled. "Can you tell me where this fella Tupatu
lives? Antonio Tupatu? I guess I ought to go see him."

"That'll hold you till you get back."

The young man with a long greasy ponytail tied behind his neck expertly lifted the plastic bottle of motor
oil up like a practiced bartender, watching the yellow
tendril of oil grow thin as it vanished into the open
black hole. With a flourish he lowered the bottle down
the tendril, spun it in his hand, and slammed down the
hood.

"I guess you guys don't use these vee-hickles outside
o' the city much, huh?"

"No," Ramirez said. "Urban cops. We're scared of
the woods. Full of monsters."

"Tell me."

Ramirez paid up and drove into the town of Tesuque,
an old Hispanic settlement on the edge of the Tesuque
Indian Reservation. The town was little more than the
Tesuque Village Market—a restaurant—and a gallery or
two at a small crossroads in a shallow canyon. Up the
roads were dirt driveways and slightly ramshackle but
large houses, nowadays more and more the homes of

unpretentious rich Anglos looking for a more "natural" life than what is to be found in Santa Fe. The older Hispanic families lived on the north end of town. A nice place, Ramirez thought, if you don't mind living in the shadow of the surrounding hills with less of the sky.

He stopped in front of the Tesuque Village Market, a long low adobe building with a patio that held a few tables and chairs. One table was occupied by a trio of truck drivers, beefy arms crossed on the table as they leaned over their Bud Lites and smirked. They looked over at Ramirez as he stepped out of his car and watched him cross the patio to the front door.

Like a herd of three overweight gazelles, ever alert, watching a tiny cheetah amble by, Ramirez thought. People who are habitually guilty—even of breaking only the speed laws—always have to watch any predator in the vicinity, however uninterested it is at the moment. Just in case. The policeman turned and smiled. "Gentlemen," he said, and stepped inside the store.

Beyond some low open shelves containing an assortment of candy bars and chewing gum was a handful of wooden tables and chairs and a tiny bar in the corner, more like a mantelpiece, with an array of bottles. To the left was a deli counter full of bowls of leaden-looking salads made from potatoes, pastas, tuna fish. To the right was the checkout counter and, beyond it, a long room with shelves of liquor and wine and beer bottles. Beyond the handful of tables in front of him, down a couple of steps, was a back room with more tables. Ramirez heard a woman's braying laughter from the back room.

He circled around the candy counter and took a seat at one of the three empty tables. He sat with his back to the wall, which looked freshly painted with a color somewhere between turquoise and Virgin Mary blue, and looked at the blonde woman who sat with a middle-aged couple at a table some ten feet across the floor. She looked familiar. Glamorous. With a multicolored patchwork vest over a flowing silky shirt. Jeans. Lizard boots worth half his monthly salary. The elevator! It was the actress who'd been in the hotel elevator when he was going up to look at Velasquez's room. What was her name? Hispanic. Moreno. Melanie Moreno. *Belleza*. How come he had never seen her in the movies?

"See, I'm a nine," he heard the blonde *belleza* saying to her friends.

Maybe an eight, Ramirez thought.

The woman went on: "I'm in a state of completion. A life of self-service. Like, I think about people, care for people, take care of them. I'm devoted."

Self-service? Ramirez thought. Self-service was like taking care of numero uno.

"I give my *self* to others," the actress said, and Ramirez nodded to himself. Aha. "Now, what's your birthday?" the blonde woman asked.

"Seven twenty-four forty-one," the man at her table said.

"Oh, ten one! A power number. You're getting powerful."

"I hope so. At my age it's about time," the man said.

"See," the *belleza* Moreno explained, gesturing to the man's companion. "*She*'s empowering you. She's a straight ten. You could be a great team, you two"—she laughed—"if you can work out the ego problems."

"My feeling about you is . . ." the man said, and Ramirez looked away. A numerologist. Adding up arbitrary numbers for a personality profile. Like those bio-rhythms. Astrology. Looking for patterns. People always looking for patterns so they can understand each other, get along in this world maybe. Know what to expect.

A waitress appeared, put a glass of water on the table, and struck a pose with her pencil and pad.

"I'll have iced tea and a chicken-salad sandwich," Ramirez said.

"We got chicken curry and chicken tarragon," she said brightly.

"Uh . . ."

"Take the tarragon. Trust me."

Ramirez watched her sway pleasingly over to Moreno's table, where she bent down and snatched up a plate like a heron spearing a fish, and his mind went back to Santo Esteban. Who were those people? They themselves didn't know. The sign outside their little village said the pueblo had been there since about A.D. 1200. Maybe they were part of the old Anasazi, split off so long ago because of some ancient grudge now forgotten. No, probably not forgotten. These people, living up here in the high country in their little worlds, like planets in separate orbits, they never forgot anything like grudges, carried them down generation after generation—maybe the event itself forgotten—or transformed—but not the meaning. Haunted, demon-ridden by a past too intense to be anything but a vessel for grudges, everyone staring warily at the world around them, watching for omens. . . . So many omens, arguments, meanings, trying to understand each other like these people here with their birthday numbers.

Sixteen pueblos along the Rio Grande, Ramirez

thought, each isolated, a world apart, a separate history
to argue over—the same gods maybe, but with different
names, different stories. Different stories creating different worlds, but then ... How different were the old
Spanish towns up north, brooding in the mountains, isolated and xenophobic? Ramirez traced his own ancestry
back four generations to some Mexicans who had come
to the United States in the eternal quest for work, but
he—Ramirez—would never dream of going alone to
some of those melancholy old Spanish towns in the
mountains, eking out a living since the conquistadores,
watching hostilely as the rest of the world nibbled at the
vague, legendary edges of their land grants bestowed
upon their never-to-be-forgotten ancestors by the very
King of Spain by his own hand.

Further back than four generations Ramirez did not
go—emerged like Athena from the head of Zeus, or
whatever that old Greek story was—but Ramirez didn't
need any more of a past than that. It was enough. But
these old Spanish up in the mountains for four centuries
almost, they, too, were old as the hills by now....

Got abandoned once by the priests who went home to
Mexico, so they took to practicing their own rites of
memory and blood, the *penitentes* ... each year choos-
ing a Jesus from the town and ... it gave Ramirez the
willies, and he thought gloomily about what is real and
what isn't, about whether a symbol is just that or the
real thing, about wafers being the body of a man, or
the body of a townsman being made a suffering god,
and he thought how maybe numerology was as good a
way as any to reach out and say, like the man had to the
belleza Morena, "now, my feelings about you ..."

Lost in the interstices of thought, he became dimly

aware that the couple had stood up, leaving the actress at the table, that her face was turned toward him, that her hand was waving at him frantically.

"Excuse me, excuse me," she was saying with a broad and mischievous smile. "You've been staring just over my head for five minutes. Wake up."

"Oh, excuse me," Ramirez said. "I was thinking."

"Didn't I see you once?" she said.

"In an elevator."

"Oh," she said, putting her hand to her mouth. "Police. You were with the police."

"And you're with the film people. A very sad thing, Señor Velasquez and all."

"Yes. *Sí*." She smiled again, and Ramirez thought with some awe that he might just be in the process of picking up a movie star when the couple returned and sat down. Melanie Moreno turned and greeted them and a little dream aborning slipped away like a mote in the eye.

The front door darkened, opened, and Connie Barnes entered with Mo Bowdre a step behind her. Ramirez lifted his hand and Connie's white teeth flashed. Once they had settled at his table, Mo sniffed and said, "Tarragon."

"Yeah. In the chicken salad. They're pushing it today. Why are you guys following me?"

"Came to check out the foundry. What are you doing out here? This isn't the land of the SFPD."

"Routine stuff. Over at Santo Esteban."

"Ah, is the plot thickening?"

"Nope."

"No comment, huh?"

"Nope."

"Your mind just gone dead?"

"Yep."

"Hah—hah. Would your mind like some food for thought?"

Ramirez shrugged. "Sure. While I'm waiting for my sandwich." He thought about his unit, sitting in the street leaking oil onto the pavement. He looked at his watch, calculating the flow of time and fluid.

"Get this, Tony. I have been doing your work for you, listening to the voice of the people. The screenplay writer, guy named Joe Hill, he had a considerable distaste for Gregorio Velasquez. Thought he was miscast."

"So he killed the guy."

"He's a stickler for authentic detail. Or at least he thinks he is. Thought Velasquez was more suited to play a purser on a cruise line than a heroic Spaniard."

"Okay. I'll arrest him. You say his name is Hill?"

"Good. When you do, ask him about a woman named Friedman. Mona Friedman. She's one of the casting directors—who chose Velasquez in the first place. Joe Hill thinks Friedman was screwing Velasquez. She's blonde."

"Good. I'll arrest her, too. Case closed."

"Tony, I'm just trying to be helpful. Say, can you get that waitress's attention? Anyway, all is not peace and propriety on the set of *The Knotted Strings*. That's my point. I guess."

The waitress arrived and two more tarragon-chicken-salad sandwiches were ordered.

"What's that mean, anyway?" Ramirez asked. " 'The knotted strings.' "

"It's how they knew when to start the rebellion," Connie said. "Po'pay handed out—"

"Po'*pnh*," Mo said.

Connie stuck her tongue out at him and Ramirez smiled.

"The leader," Connie said. "He handed out strings with a certain number of knots tied in them, gave them to some messengers. They were supposed to run, you know, and take a string to each pueblo. You untie one knot every day, and then when the last knot is untied ..."

"*Bam,*" Ramirez said.

"But the messengers got caught by the Spaniards. They were named Catua and Omtua. They got tortured, you know? And they told the Spaniards that the knots meant something else. So some other messengers took other strings and, yeah, *bam*. All at once."

"Desert Storm," Ramirez said. "With knotted strings instead of computers."

"Same thing," Mo said. "You just got to know what you're untying."

"Tell me about it," Ramirez said.

"Are you going to tell the police?"

Eleanor Frank sat behind a desk in the makeshift office—nothing more than the back end of a trailer separated from the rest of the place by a few cartons stacked up. The place looked like a warehouse, unoccupied now except for Eleanor's "office." The desk itself was merely a piece of plywood set on similar cartons, the most temporary of arrangements in a temporary world. Her job, and Mona's, was now over. The Spanish opera singer was winging his way to Nuevo Mexico and they had chosen forty-three Indian extras. Fat little Arnold could be their shepherd. Eleanor's question hung

in the silence almost as palpably as the blue smoke
cloud to which she now added impatiently, her lower lip
jutting out to provide an upward trajectory to the column of smoke she exhaled.

"Oh, God, the police?" Mona said. "Do you
think . . . ? I mean, is that necessary?" She was sitting
on a folding chair, her elbows on Eleanor's desk, her
head bowed. It had been bugging her now for nearly
two days and finally she no longer could resist the need
to confess. Of course, confessing to Eleanor was about
the most painful thing she could imagine. She'd rather
. . . she'd rather . . . she couldn't think. Instead she had
strode in, sat down in front of Eleanor, and waited till
she got off the phone.

"What's up, hon?" Eleanor had asked. "You don't
look like someone who's about to get out of this sybaritic province and back to the angels of luxury."

And so Mona had blurted out her confession, explaining that she was—with one exception—the last
person to have seen Gregorio Velasquez alive. In fact,
he was half-dead when she'd last seen him, so drunk he
fell on his face and she . . .

"Screwing the help," Eleanor had said. "Goddamn it.
The secret in this racket is *not* to screw the help. Every
goddamn actor, every goddamn would-be actor is the
help. You put it out for anyone—*any*one—and they've
always got some claim on you in this industry. Especially men. Especially men. They get it up for you and
they think you owe 'em a favor for the rest of your life.
You can't operate—"

"I know, I know. You always say."

"Jesus," Eleanor said with acid contempt.

"Well, what should I do? Should I tell . . . ?"

"It's your conscience, Mona baby. You didn't kill him, did you?"

"Eleanor, of course not. He fell down drunk and I left."

"So? You're innocent. Tell the cops. They'll just keep you here in this adobe theme park for a few days. Ask you a lot of stupid questions, leering to themselves like boys with their old man's copy of *Playboy*."

Mona leaned back in the uncomfortable seat. "Maybe I better. Better I tell them than they find out somehow."

"Right," Eleanor said, exhaling another blue column at the ceiling. "Take the high ground, baby." She snorted. "Jesus, I really can't see it. Bad enough it's a man. But *him*? That old greaser?"

Mona Friedman stood up. "Look, we agreed to disagree about that stuff. I like men. I'm *sorry*, but I like them."

"There's no accounting for taste," Eleanor said, stubbing out her cigarette in a small glass ashtray. She grinned. "Especially bad taste. So go tell the cops. I'll see you back in L.A. And don't ever, *ever* do that again. Keep those long white legs glued tight together when there's an industry creep within a mile, you hear? Otherwise you're out on your fanny." She picked up the phone and punched out eleven numbers.

"American Airlines? Yeah, this is . . ."

Into the enzymatic congress that presided over the moods and fancies of Joseph Drew Hill's central nervous system, a ferment of dopamine, phenylethylamine, and other polysyllabic nectars flowed in excess—the brain chemicals of love at work. He surged with the giddiness of infatuation as he slipped his narrow, lined

reporter's notebook in the back pocket of his jeans. Joe
Hill was again in love. Not with the long-legged, round-
breasted script jockey Clarissa, though she was a notable piece of ass to be sure, and not even remotely with
the equally long-legged Mona Friedman, on whose confession Joe Hill had just eavesdropped from outside the
open aluminum-framed window of the trailer.

No, Joe Hill was in love with his new role, the role
he was, he realized now, absolutely destined to play
thanks to the nearly psychic insight he possessed into
human nature—insight that had once again been confirmed here in this hot, dusty parking lot.

Investigative reporter.

Joe Hill was also in love, head over heels in love,
with his next book, a book in which he would blow the
lid off the sleaze surrounding filmdom once and forever.
The classic in the field. He was certain by now that the
authenticity and sensitivity with which he had written
the screenplay for *The Knotted Strings* would be traduced by the likes of Eleanor Frank and that overrated
geek, Andrew Pindaric, and his phalanx of Macedonian
faggots, all of them devoted to the banality of the box
office. Something good had to arise from this travesty,
and it would be his book, the real story of the making
of a film that failed. Failed to be true, honest. The pa-
thology of the movie industry—the creeping mendacity,
the pandering of the Big Song-and-Dance Act. The Celluloid Lie.

Joe Hill, feverish with a chemical energy akin to lust,
saw himself in the book, a kind of Ishmael—the ubiquitous observer, yes, but also participant, just like in
Moby Dick. Truth itself would be the elusive white
whale; Pindaric and his slime-bucket minions the cap-

tain and crew of the *Pequod*, looking for the truth that would kill them in the end if they ever allowed themselves to countenance it. Joe Hill's mind careened on through what he recalled of an American-lit course he had audited at a backwater upstate New York community college—a college too remote to see the politically correct handwriting on the wall. Thus, at the time, it still offered those classics written by the dead, white, English-speaking males discredited elsewhere as unwitting tools of industry and imperialism, racism, sexism, ageism . . . sins that Joseph Drew Hill had since been alerted to and, with the exception of Indian rights, considered to be as important as the regulations governing the ingredients of Girl Scout cookies.

Joseph Drew Hill saw his new role emerging: the Hemingway of Hollywood Horseshit.

Joe Hill, Observer, looked on as with a third eye while Joe Hill, Participant, took out his narrow reporter's notebook and flipped the pages to his notes on the Friedman revelation and he read them over and they were good. He put his notebook back in his jeans and leaned his head back against the aluminum siding, and the sun warmed his face and it was good. He smiled when he recognized the ancient itch of the male on a hero quest for the Grail, for the final confrontation with the great bull, and he reached down and scratched his balls and it was good. . . . Oh yes.

Oh shit.

He looked the other way as Mona Friedman walked past, fortunately too distracted to notice the slab-shouldered Hemingway of Hollywood standing where he had no business, holding his crotch.

* * *

At twenty minutes to four, Allen Templeton again stepped out on his beautiful urban street and felt the breeze lift the white hair with which he had been graced at a relatively early age, conferring on him what he took to be a patina of wisdom that complemented his smooth, tanned face and piercing dark blue eyes. A lawyer's lawyer.

He strolled across the narrow park, headed for St. Francis Drive and the warehouse where the movie people had set up part of their bewilderingly complex production. A few minutes later he took up a position against a wall facing the large parking lot outside the huge, prefab warehouse, now filled with cars, pickups, and people standing around. Beyond, above the warehouse, the mountains were cloaked in dark green.

Occasionally, someone would exit the warehouse and arrow off self-importantly toward one of the Sweetwater trailers parked in the lot like great cows. So many people doing so little, he thought, all these incremental missions, adding up to what? A film, an entertainment, three weeks, a month in the theatres and then consigned to the shelves of rental stores with names like Bonanza Flicks like so many boxes of cereal. What had he heard? It would cost between forty and fifty million dollars? A lot of money. He had also heard that the movie studios had developed a creative accounting system by which they made no taxable profit regardless of income.

Now, *that* suggested intelligence, he thought, and looked at his watch. It was two minutes before four. Nearby, leaning against a disreputable-looking red pickup, a man in a lavender shirt and a black vest glanced over at him. Templeton raised a white eyebrow and the man pushed away from the pickup, looked around aimlessly, and crossed over to Templeton's wall, where he stood without a word a few feet away.

Templeton noted a magazine rolled up in the man's back pocket. Part of a black-and-white photograph showed a bikini-clad woman with a mountain of dark hair leaning on what appeared to be an automobile, staring coquettishly at the camera over her moonlike buttocks.

Templeton looked away and watched the small crowd of gawkers, who in turn watched the comings and goings of the production personnel. Another pickup entered the lot and nosed into a space near the gate. He saw a black-haired woman emerge from the driver's side—a familiar-looking woman, Indian—and followed her with his eyes as she entered the warehouse. He looked back at the pickup and saw a muscular forearm jutting out of the window on the passenger side, a bulky silhouette in the passenger seat. It was that sculptor, Bowdre. He guessed that his half-breed Hopi girlfriend had landed a part as an extra. Glancing again at the crowd, he saw a thin woman in blue jeans with mouse-colored hair pull a reporter's notebook from her purse. Noting that it was now five minutes past four o'clock, he looked over at the black-haired man near him and raised his eyebrows. The man shrugged, then gestured with his head toward the lot entrance.

Yet another pickup paused inside the gate and parked beside the sculptor's. Antonio Tupatu and three other Indians climbed out, one a white-haired man, the other two maybe in their twenties. All wore red headbands, turquoise necklaces, and moccasins. The two younger ones fetched some cardboard signs tacked to laths out of the back of the truck and the four men began walking toward the warehouse door, staring implacably ahead.

Reaching the door through the small, parting sea of gawkers, the two young Indians turned to face the people and raised their signs while Antonio Tupatu knocked imperiously on the door. The old man stood to the side motionlessly, his old shoulders bent. One sign said SWEETWATER POLLUTES OUR RELIGION and the other said, simply and mysteriously, PROTEST. Templeton smiled. A white panel truck sprayed dust as it stopped in the parking lot and a cameraman leaped out, face fixed to his camera like a lamprey to a fish.

The warehouse door opened, a man stuck his head out, looked quizzically at the Indians, listened as Tupatu said something, smiled, and shut the door. Tupatu turned and frowned at the crowd.

"We are here to protect our sacred heritage," he said in a loud voice. "Our religious rights, our basic human rights. These movie people want to put their cameras in our holy places, our shrines, our plaza. We speak for the traditional elders of the pueblo of Santo Esteban, for people like this man here, Popova."

The old man looked up at the crowd, then down. Tupatu scowled.

"It tears the hearts out of our old people," Tupatu went on, "to see our religion profaned. We are here to demand that the Sweetwater people stop their plans to use the sacred ground of Santo Esteban to make this . . . movie. This is our outcry, that we be recognized as equal to any other five-fingered people. We will not leave here, we will not let anyone in or out, until we have spoken to the man Pindaric and explained why he must stop." Tupatu crossed his arms over his chest and fell silent, while the gawkers, utterly stunned, looked nervously at each other. Presently, a few Instamatics clicked and buzzed and Tupatu glowered at the sound.

"We are not a tourist attraction," he declared. "We are not here for your amusement. We are here to protest another"—he paused—"another invasion of our rights as human bein's."

Allen Templeton noted a few people jumping out of the movie trailers. They stared at the Indians, and one climbed back in. A moment later the warehouse door opened and Andrew Pindaric stepped out, blinking in the sun and towering on long thin legs over the four Indians. He smiled boyishly and bent his head down as Tupatu turned to face him.

Templeton edged away from the wall to a point nearer the backs of the gawkers where he could hear.

"Mister . . . ? Mr. Tupatu, I'm Andy Pindaric. What can I . . . ?" The tall, angular director bent down farther and listened, his head cocked to the side. "Perhaps you'd like to come inside and discuss . . . no? Okay." He smiled ingratiatingly and Tupatu said something else.

"Well, look, we—uh—Mr. Tupatu, we did talk with the governor of Santo Esteban, we were all terribly sad to hear that he had passed away, yes, but we did sign an agreement with . . ."

Pindaric listened again.

"Yes, of course, we will do a little building, but we guaranteed that we would restore—"

"How?" Tupatu said in a loud voice, turning his face to the gawkers. "How can you restore something that is profaned? What ceremonies do you people do for that?"

The gawkers murmured in evident sympathy and the two younger Indians moved closer to their leader.

"Look, Mr. Tupatu," the director said. Templeton could see annoyance replacing the man's diplomatic aplomb. "We signed a paper with your governor. There's a copy of it in the governor's office. You can go read it. We are bending over backward here to make a truthful, authentic film about a great moment in *your* history. We are using your people in the film along with other native Americans, and we . . ."

Tupatu spat on the ground and stepped back. At the same time the two young Indians moved a step closer, jostling Pindaric.

"Hey, listen," he barked, and a compact figure, something like a stump in clothes, suddenly hurtled out of the building's shadow and past the crowd, slamming into one of the young Indians, knocking him sprawling against the other in a tangled pile on the ground.

"What the . . . ?" Pindaric said. A woman shrieked. The stumplike figure arose from the pile, grinning. The gawkers lurched backward, Tupatu stood frozen, and the old man shuffled his feet in the dust.

"Goddamn it," Pindaric yelled. "You crazy bastard. What the hell are you . . . ?"

The two Indians began to disentangle themselves.

"It looked like trouble," Joe Hill said, and giggled nasally. "Best to nip it in the bud."

"Get out of here, you lunatic! Get out! Go home to the Adirondacks, anywhere, just get lost!" Joe Hill stood grinning at the director, who turned to Tupatu. "I'm terribly sorry, Mister . . . this man has nothing to do with . . ."

"Hey, Andy, I wrote the screenplay. Have you given

it to these guys? So they can see at least *I'm* on their side?"

Pindaric put his arms out to the side, his hands cutting the air like hatchets. "Out! Get out! Get! *Out!*" he seethed, and Joe Hill shrugged his slabby upper torso and went off grinning. The director put an apologetic hand on Tupatu's shoulder and said, "Please come inside." The Indian stood still, looking at the hand on his shoulder, and then nodded. As the two men disappeared through the door into the warehouse, a police cruiser edged into the lot and stopped.

Allen Templeton watched two officers get out of the police car and begin pushing their way through the crowd, with the mousy-haired reporter as well as two TV people letting them run interference. Templeton looked over at the black-haired man in the lavender shirt, who was leaning against the wall with a bored expression on his dark face. They nodded tersely and the lawyer, smiling inwardly, turned and bumped into a large man. It was the sculptor, Bowdre. The blind man.

"I beg your pardon," Templeton said.

"Pray don't mention it," the sculptor said, and Templeton set out at a dignified pace for his office.

"Sergeant? There's a person here to see you. A Ms. Friedman." The officer slipped a sheet of fax paper on Ramirez's desk. "And this just came in from UNM."

Ramirez glanced down at the sheet, but before the few words scribbled on it registered on his brain, he glanced up and saw a tall, angular blonde standing in the doorway, a handsome woman, midthirties probably, wearing what looked like very expensive black slacks and a shirt—bright red, purple, and orange. An array of gold bangle bracelets on her right wrist, a small fortune right there. He thought to stand up, remembered that not just cops don't do that—no one does anymore. Under what he guessed was a typically imperious mien, she looked nervous.

"Sergeant? They say you're in charge of the—uh—Velasquez . . ."

"Yes. The homicide. I'm Sergeant Ramirez. What can I do for you?"

The handsome woman looked down and picked at her gold bangles, which clicked—a rich sound. "I have some information to tell you. I'm not sure that it—well, it's not really relevant, but it's something I think you should know."

"Please sit down, Miz Friedman, is it?" Ramirez gestured toward one of the two uncomfortable chairs that were crammed close to his desk in the small cubicle that was his office.

"Miss," the woman said. She sat down, crossed her long legs, and looked up at Ramirez with blue eyes the color of the winter sky. Then, in measured tones, she talked and Ramirez said nothing until she finished.

". . . so I got dressed and left. I went to my room on the third floor, tossed and turned for a while, and went to sleep. I know I should have come—uh—forward right away. I hope . . ." She trailed off uncertainly.

Ramirez leaned back in his chair and tapped his desk with a pencil. "So you were the last person to see—"

"I was the *second*-to-last person to see Greg alive," she interrupted.

Ramirez shrugged. "As you say, Miss Friedman."

"You believe me, don't you?"

"About what? That you were there?" Ramirez said

with the practiced cruelty of the cop. Someone, he reflected, had said that wealthy people were different, and
he knew they were, but not in the police station. "We
can confirm that, of course. Whoever *was* there left
some hairs in the bed"—the woman reddened—"blonde
ones on the pillow and a black pubic hair on the sheet.
We can take samples of yours and see if they match.
But perhaps that isn't necessary, since you have confessed. Of course, we will have to take down this confession formally, but later . . ."

"I'm trying to be helpful, Sergeant," she said, and her
voice cracked slightly.

"Yes. Well, tell me this, Miss Friedman. What makes
you so certain he was alive when you left?"

"What? Well, he was breathing. I thought he was
dead at first, just lying there on his stomach where he
fell. I yelled at him, told him to get up. And I heard him
snort, you know, like apnea, and then he was breathing."

"It didn't occur to you that he was dangerously
drunk? That he might . . . ?"

"No. He'd passed out on me a couple of times before. In L.A."

"I see," Ramirez said, tapping the desk. "And what
did you do as you left?"

"I got dressed and went out the door. I told you."

"What was your state of mind?"

"I was pissed off," she said, reliving the moment. "I
swore at him and left. Slammed the door."

"He had let you down before," Ramirez said.

Mona Friedman frowned. "What are you saying, Sergeant? That hell hath no fury like a woman scorned?
Look, if I murdered every impotent—well, men who

couldn't—anyway . . . I guess that sounds wrong. Am I under arrest?"

"No."

"Under suspicion?"

"Technically, yes."

"What's that mean?"

"It means, Miss Friedman, that we will have to ask you to repeat what you have told me on a tape recorder, sign various forms, and remain in Santa Fe until notified that you can go. And I think it would be a good idea for you to provide some hair samples for our forensic laboratory. Just routine, Miss Friedman, but routine is . . . very important in this kind of work." Ramirez stood up. "Stay there. I'll be right back."

The woman's shoulders drooped and she plucked at her gold bangles. Ramirez leaned around the door and crooked a finger at a female police officer. "Inez," he called. Then he turned and looked down at Mona Friedman. Her hair was an ash gold, like on the Clairol boxes he had seen in the supermarket, and it hung neatly down below her shoulders. "Do you have any idea who would have wanted Velasquez dead?"

The blonde woman looked up at him hopefully. "You didn't say 'who *else* would have' . . . ?"

"Perhaps a slip of the tongue," Ramirez said. "Do you?"

"No. No one that I can imagine. Greg didn't have a lot of friends, but he wasn't the sort to have enemies either. Do I need a lawyer?"

"They are always recommended in such situations, Miss Friedman. And you can insist on one before you go through the procedures I've outlined. It's up to you. Perhaps Sweetwater has an attorney?"

The uniformed policewoman called Inez appeared at the door. He explained to her what he wanted and Mona Friedman reddened again as she stood up. Following the policewoman out, she glanced back at Ramirez.

"It's all routine, Miss Friedman," he said. "And confidential." He smiled thinly, and the blonde woman took a deep breath and disappeared around the corner.

A bit rough on her, Ramirez thought. Probably a nice enough person. Well, probably not a very nice person. And probably she had slammed the door behind her, just as she said. So, probably not a murderer.

He glanced down at the piece of fax paper on his desk, turned it around. It was from the University of New Mexico's biology department.

Your splinter is *Fraxinus americanus* L.—common name white ash. Near relative of red ash, *Fraxinus pennsylvanica* Marsh. Report in mail.

—Jim

Ramirez shrugged. White ash. Red ash. He wondered if there was an Hispanic ash. The three cultures. He began to feel gritty, having treated that blonde woman so curtly. He looked at his watch. A few more phone calls and he would bag it for a couple of hours, get something to eat, maybe get rid of his headache. The phone rang and Ramirez glared at it, then picked it up.

"Yeah, put him on." He smiled. "Hey, man . . . Sure. You remember that place, Tiny's? . . . So I'm a creature of habit, so what? . . . Yeah, dinner, then it's back to the salt fields . . . Salt mines? They *mine* salt? No shit, I didn't know that . . . Okay, half an hour. *Bueno*."

Through his office door Ramirez saw two young In-

dian men bedecked in red headbands and turquoise
beads being led through the clutter of desks and chairs
by two uniformed officers. One of the Indians, with
black eyes deeply sunken behind a virtual shelf of
cheekbones, was familiar. It was Ernesto Piño, the onetime mechanic from Santo Esteban, the guy with the
fossil car parts in his yard. By the time Ramirez reached
the small procession, the two Indians were seated on an
uncomfortable wooden bench against the wall, and the
two cops were sitting opposite them in chairs swung
around from a couple of nearby desks. Ernesto Piño
stared defiantly into the distance; the other, a skinnier
version of Piño, had adopted a sullen pout that he
thought concealed his fear.

"What's up, Pete?" Ramirez asked. The cop briefly
described the demonstration at the warehouse. "So
what'd these guys do?" Ramirez asked.

"Resisted arrest."

"What'd you arrest them for?"

"Obstruction of a police officer in—"

"You're Ernesto Piño, huh?" Ramirez interrupted.
The Indian glanced over at Ramirez and nodded. "Can
you tell me where you were late Tuesday night, early
Wednesday, Ernesto?"

Piño stared at the sergeant. "What's that got to do
with this?" he asked.

"You tell me, brother."

The other Indian fidgeted on the bench and Ernesto
said, "We was both of us at a meeting." Ramirez folded
his arms across his chest and waited. "Making plans,"
Ernesto said. Ramirez waited. "For our demonstration.
For the rights of our people. For our religious freedom."

"How many other soldiers for freedom were there at the meeting?" Ramirez asked.

Ernesto looked down. "Three," he said.

"Wow. A real army. What time the meeting break up?"

"About two, three in the morning."

"How do I know that?"

"You can ask my parents, my sister. They know when I got in."

"What about Sergeant York here?"

The other Indian stirred. "I went straight to my job. Work in the landfill at Española. Punched in at three."

No wonder these guys are so depressive, Ramirez thought. Reporting to a frigging landfill at three in the morning.

"So how serious is this, Pete?" Ramirez asked the cop.

"They shoved us when we approached."

"Anyone hurt?"

"No."

"Fingerprint 'em, and cite 'em," Ramirez said. He turned to Ernesto. "You know, kid, you should try to learn from stuff like this. You know this movie they're making? You know what it's about? It's about when your ancestors threw the Spanish out of here. They organized everyone up and down the *río*, man, they knew what they were doing. No two-bit fracas but a real war. You want to fight for your religious rights, why don't you study? Learn some of the basics, you know? Think. This is a different world here. You already got rights, kid, like everyone else around here. Until you touch a cop. You lose a lot of rights when you touch a cop. It's like baseball. You push the umpire, you get thrown out of the game. Now, get 'em the fuck out of here, Pete. Give 'em a night in the tank while we check this thing out."

"What thing?" Ernesto asked, still defiant.

"The details," Ramirez said.

He went back in his office and noticed that his headache was gone.

Joe Hill wrapped a towel around his waist, rubbed the steam from a patch of mirror, flexed, checked his lats and pecs, thought maybe he better find a gym in this dump, and opened the door to the bedroom, where he found the world had narrowed down to a pair of incandescent black eyes surmounted by eyebrows knit tightly together in anger.

"You stupid, crazy, insane, maniacal, dumb shit," Clarissa Long intoned.

"Hey . . ." Joe Hill said.

"You moron, what the hell was that?"

"What? Oh. You mean keeping those goddamn Indians from snapping old Toothpick Legs off at the knee? Lucky I was there to break it up."

Below her thin, aristocratic nose, Clarissa Long's valentine mouth quivered with emotion.

"Asshole," she said. "Just what we need. A bunch of Indians assaulted by some madman on the set. Queer the whole production. Jesus. You've been banned from the set, you know that?"

"So what?" Joe Hill said nonchalantly, seeing his new career as investigative journalist trembling like a trailer house in an earthquake.

"That's not all you've been banned from, buster." She spun around and yanked open the door. The yellowing light of late afternoon flooded the Best Western motel room. As Clarissa Long's silhouette stepped out onto the exterior balcony that ringed the motel and led to the stairs, Joe Hill said, "So big deal. Coupla hours I'll find me someone whose ass hasn't fallen."

The door slammed, the walls shook.

"Fucking ingrates!" Joe Hill shouted, thinking she *was* a spy. He sat down on the bed, breathing deeply, seeking calm. Persona non grata, huh? Banned from the set. Shunned. Wasn't there some bunch of religious nuts that used to shun people, officially shun 'em when they upset the church fathers? Was it the Quakers? The Pilgrims? Maybe those guys with the black hats and buggies in Pennsylvania—the Mennonites, Amish. Well, it wasn't the first time in his life that he'd been shunned.

Let's just see how effective that Balkan birdbrain's ukase really is. Just let 'im try and put up some impregnable barrier against me. I can insinuate, infiltrate, penetrate. I am the unavoidable incubus of truth and I shall find my way in. . . .

Such imagery, carefully monitored by Joe Hill the Observer, led his predatory mind's eye smoothly into a review of the female cast of *The Knotted Strings*, so far as it had assembled, and he lit on the obviously dyed blonde Hispanic woman—O! broad-bosomed goddess of moist Iberian secrets! What was her name? Moreno. Melanie Moreno.

Fuckin' luscious.

He stood up and began dressing, but frowned. Moreno, no big-time star, had a little role as the wife of one of the Spanish rancheros, and he had heard rumors of a scene lately added in which she and the governor, Otermin, sneak off for a bit of colonial hanky-panky.

Not a scene written by Joseph Drew Hill, and for the very reason that there was no historical record that Otermin had a mistress. A tits-and-thighs scene just thrown in out of nowhere.

Well, he would see about all that. He rummaged through a drawer and pulled out a clean T-shirt, red with white lettering, which he pulled over his bulging chest, and admired its backward slogan in the mirror: A HARD MAN NOWADAYS IS GOOD TO FIND. He giggled out loud.

"Sooweee, sooweeee."

At the last minute she flipped the turn signal and pulled across lanes to make a right turn off Route 84 onto the dirt road. The early-evening sun burnished the empty land ahead gold and purple, and she felt like exploring a bit. After a few miles the graded road became little more than a track, and she slowed the rented Sunbird down to a crawl as it bucked across the ruts and rattled over the washboards. Rising to some high ground—a gentle hill covered with what looked like wind-stunted cedar trees—she pulled over and shut off the ignition. Far off ahead of her she saw the ragged canyons of the Jemez foothills fill with a glow, the peaks beyond a jumble of shadowed purple and gray.

She stepped out of the car into this alien world of dusty orange earth, dwarfed trees, and long shadows and stared at the clouds over the mountains, lit as if from within. She heard an engine distantly, then silence. It was windless, motionless, as if the world had stopped, taken a rest. The simple enormity filled her and she was sure that she, too, glowed from within, just like the layers of clouds on the horizon, impregnated by the last, loving touch of the sun.

The .30-caliber slug entered her left temple, plowed through the corpus callosum in a widening path, and exited the right side of her skull not quite two inches above her ear in an explosion of blood and brain cells. She was thrown sideways, arms flailing inanely. As she fell to the ground dust rose in little puffs from the body's impact, and the brutal crack of the rifle's one shot reverberated around the hills in the elegiac orange glow.

Special Agent Larry Collins licked his forefinger and reached out to touch the salty rim of the wide-mouthed goblet across the table from him. He touched his finger to his tongue.

"You know this stuff is bad for your blood pressure," he said.

"You turned into some kind of health nut?" Anthony Ramirez asked. The agent grinned, sitting opposite at the table, showing two crooked front teeth. "Anyway," Ramirez said, "I'm one twenty over eighty. Perfect. Nothing bothers me. I eat all the stuff they say you shouldn't. You listen to all the people around here, you wouldn't eat anything but rabbit food." He lifted his glass and sipped. "I hate carrots."

"How can anyone hate carrots?" Collins asked. The white-haired waitress appeared. "I'll have one of those," he said, and she drifted away across the room. "Did you really think that salt came from fields, like corn or something?"

"It's just an expression," Ramirez said, looking across the restaurant. "You find the pueblo's cane yet?"

"Hell, no. You found your killer yet?"

"Hell, no."

"Coupla supersleuths."

"Where are you working out of now? Albuquerque, didn't I hear?"

"Yeah. You hear about the little girl got off the plane? Asked her mother if this was Alba-Turkey?"

"And then," Ramirez said, "the little girl asked, 'Where's Fanta-Say?' "

"You heard it."

"Yeah, I think it was in high school that I heard it." The two men sat silently. At the next table three women were listening intently to a fourth, a busty middle-aged blonde in a black cowboy shirt and black pants, talking in a Texas accent about how she had seen Andrew Pindaric get in his green Ferrari outside the Posada de Consuela that afternoon and take off like a jet.

"It's a Jaguar," one of the others said.

"Jaguar, Ferrari, who gives a shit about cars?" the aging cowgirl said. "The man's got buns like Adonis." Her companions giggled. Emma, the white-haired waitress, put a goblet down in front of Collins, smiled, and vanished.

"There goes the neighborhood," Collins said. "Hey, you think it's anything to do with this movie?"

"What's to do with it? Some of those guys at Santo Esteban don't want it made on their land. There's always that kind of squabbling."

"No," the agent said, leaning forward. "I was wondering if the movie—you know—the *story* has got people stirred up. Old grudges."

"Like the Indians are getting ready to rise up again to

throw out the Spanish? Three hundred years later? Come on."

"Well," the agent said. "The guy who got killed was Hispanic and he was playing the Spanish governor. Very symbolic act. It's a motive for you."

"Pretty farfetched. Sounds like one of Mo Bowdre's tales."

"Yeah," the agent snorted. "Where's Bowdre when we need him?"

"Hah—hah—hah." The two men looked up. Mo Bowdre was ten feet away, carrying a bottle of Negra Modelo beer in his beefy hand and walking with measured steps toward their table. "I heard that. So it's Mack the Knife, he's back in town. How are ya, Collins?" He reached out, touched the back of a chair, pulled it out, and sat down heavily. Collins smiled and shook his head. "What brings you back to the City of Holy Faith?" the big man asked.

"Routine."

"How boring. Why is crime so boring?" Mo said. The women at the next table stopped buzzing and looked in their direction. Mo turned in his seat, facing the women with opaque sunglasses and a wide smile. "It's nothing, ladies. Not real crime. We're inventing a children's video game." The women looked away and pulled their chairs closer to their table.

Mo turned back to face the agent. "Routine?"

"The governor's cane at Santo Esteban. The one President Lincoln gave 'em? They found it was missing, so they called me. There's nothing we can do, really. It's not federal property, or anything like that." He shrugged. "So it's back to chasing pot hunters."

"Any hot new leads on your homicide?" Mo asked, turning toward Ramirez.

"What's this?" the FBI agent asked. "Show-and-tell?"

Ramirez explained briefly about his interview with Mona Friedman. "I didn't like her much, kind of a snot, you know? But I doubt she did it."

"That writer, Joe Hill, he described her as an ice pick," Mo said.

"He may be a nut, but maybe he's a good writer," Ramirez said. "That's a good description. You heard about the—uh—demonstration?"

"I was there," Mo said. "It wasn't much of a demonstration. I counted four demonstrators. Not counting Joe Hill and his middle-linebacker act. Hardly what you'd call an uprising, hah—hah. Your cops seemed to have their usual good time."

"Coupla punks from the pueblo. Pushed one of the uniforms. I read 'em the riot act and put 'em in the tank for the night. Oh, yeah. You were asking something about the wood? You know, the splinters we found?" Ramirez pulled the fax out of his coat pocket and unfolded it. "Guys at UNM say it was white ash. *Fraxi . . .*"

"Ha," Mo said and took a long pull at his Negra Modelo. "That's an eastern tree, you know. Doesn't grow west of the Mississippi."

"So?"

"In fact, it grows in the Mississippi Valley, Ohio Valley, among other places."

"So what?"

"Old Abraham Lincoln came from those parts. Maybe he'd want something from his boyhood home country as part of his gift to the Indians out here. Might've even brightened up his melancholy face for a time. 'Make those canes from the ash trees around Springfield,' is what he might have said. Country boys are like that, you know. Sentimental. So now some of these boys from the pueblo, they don't like this movie in their face, so they grabbed the cane when no one was looking and creamed that actor. He was gonna be the governor. Highly symbolic. That's how these Indians think. In symbols. Maybe those demonstrators you got in the tank are your killers. See? We got this all wrapped up."

Larry Collins grinned. "Hey, Tony, what'd I—"

"What else do they make out of ash?" Ramirez snapped.

"Aw, Tony, you're no fun. Hell, I don't know. Furniture. Tool handles. Impact tools, like hammers."

"So how many tool handles do you suppose there are around here?"

"It's just a story, Tony."

"This is real, what I'm doing. A guy's dead."

Mo shrugged. "And nothing is happening."

"Slow," Collins said, looking off in the distance. "Slow."

"You want fast, you don't come to New Mexico," Ramirez said.

Bee-e-ep, bee-e-ep.

Collins reached for his pocket, and the beeping stopped. He stood up. "Where's the phone?"

Ramirez gestured behind him with his head and Collins walked out of the room, leaving the two men sitting silently at the table. The women at the next table had ceased talking again and Mo turned to them.

"Accounting department," he confided. "Bunch of sourpusses. Party poopers. Don't understand the creative imagination." The women huddled together again.

Presently Collins returned. "So things are speeding up around here. Found a woman's body on the border of the Santo Esteban Reservation. Shot. Come on, Tony."

"That's federal. Yours. It's not my jurisdic—"

"She's one of the movie people. An actress," Collins said. "Let's go. Her name is Moreno."

Ramirez shoved his chair back and stood up. "You okay here, Mo?"

"Yeah. Fine. Connie's going to pick me up in a little while."

After the two men had left, Mo sat erect in his chair, clasping his beer bottle to his chest, aware that the women at the next table were staring at him. Two actors, two Hispanics, he thought. Now that's just as cute as a pair of porcupines making love.

five

Two young men stood silhouetted against the yellow sky, hands on hips, chests heaving. Beyond, the land stretched silently away in shadow while the sun inched its way up behind the black backbone of the mountains to the east. A tall, narrow-legged silhouette approached, then stood towering above them.

"That was great, just great," Andrew Pindaric said. "Do you think you're up to one more time?"

The two Indians nodded, looking down at their feet. Their hair was long, cut off at the shoulder and straight across their foreheads like helmets. In their late teens, both were naked except for white loincloths and deerskin moccasins. Sweat gleamed from their shoulders.

"You need a little time?"

They shook their heads.

"Okay. The sweat is perfect. The light is perfect. Back over the hill there and come when I whistle. This time . . . just the way you came last time, right past that piñon, that was perfect. Then, see, come over this way a little more. Right here, by this bush. Closer to Erik there and his magic box. Okay?"

The Indians nodded again.

"Okay, go." Pindaric slouched back to his camera-

121

man as the Indians trotted eastward and disappeared behind the tree.

"Talkative lot," the cameraman said.

"How's it look?"

"Terrific. This should be the one. Light's gonna be
perfect."

"Okay. Stuart!" the director called.

"Yo," said the sound man from behind a desert cedar.

Pindaric put his fingers in his mouth and unleashed a
piercing whistle. Presently the two runners appeared
from behind the piñon, legs churning rhythmically in an
effortless lope.

"Beautiful," Pindaric mouthed silently.

The runners drew nearer, running in perfect sync,
each holding a swaying cluster of knotted cords, their
moccasins beating a tattoo on the earth. The sky
gleamed, and as the Indians trotted toward the camera
the sun burst above the mountain ridge, rays refracting
from the prisms of sweat on their shoulders. Erik and
the camera swiveled as they went by, and in the close-in
confusion of light-shot motion, sweat, blurred silhou-
ettes, muscle, eyes glinting sharp like needles, pounding
feet, Erik said, "Jesus, beautiful!" and Andrew Pindaric
put his fist up in a gesture of triumph.

A young woman stepped in front of the camera and
clacked a strip of wood with black-and-white diagonal
stripes against a slateboard on which, upside down, she
had chalked SCENE 29, TAKE 2. "Mark!" she said.

"That's what we call a wrap," Pindaric called out to
the two youths, standing again, twenty feet away, hands
on hips. Their teeth flashed briefly as they smiled and
looked down at the ground. "Let's get something to
eat," Pindaric said.

* * *

The shooting death of Melanie Moreno had been discovered at a most unfortunate time from the standpoint of the press—which is to say, when they were out drinking and eating dinner. The print people had missed it altogether, and only a lone operative from CNN loitering in the police station later that night had gotten wind that something was up. He discovered no more than that another member of the cast of *The Knotted Strings* had been murdered, found on Indian land, and that the case was in the hands of the FBI, homicide on an Indian reservation being a federal crime. He hadn't known that and had made a bit of a scene with the night-duty officers of the SFPD until they explained it to him and told him that if he asked one more question they would carry him feetfirst into a jail cell that contained three two-hundred-and-eighty-pound homosexual weight lifters.

As a result of such policies, therefore, the story did not break on the airwaves until eight o'clock in the morning, approximately thirteen hours after the shooting had evidently taken place.

By nine o'clock Mountain Daylight Time, the homicide was common knowledge throughout the industrialized world. While the FBI and the Santa Fe police had released only the barest of detail, it had not taken much by way of journalistic brainpower to make the dark connection between two homicides in which *Hispanics* were the victims and a major film about the Pueblo Rebellion. Approximately seventy-five million Americans who, only a few weeks earlier, had never heard of this chapter of American history, had now been introduced, however fleetingly and largely owing to the lack of actual facts in the case, to the possibility that racial hatred still might run strong and deep in New Mexico, the Land of Enchantment—wherever, that is, New Mexico was. By noon, Mountain Time, the less reputable television channels had hinted that there were here "the seeds of another Wounded Knee," the mayor of Santa Fe had made five separate calls to the chief of police, each more apoplectic than the last, and the governor of the state had been flown by helicopter to the University of New Mexico hospital in Albuquerque, suffering from chest pains—a fact that soon became an important sidebar to the developing story of the eruption of ancient animosities along the Rio Grande.

Stringers for the major networks busily ginned up backgrounders, interviewing at length whichever local anthropologists and historians they could corral on short notice, none of whom would answer the reporters' hastily contrived questions with pithy sound bites, causing in turn strings of commentary about loathsome, logorrheic academics in the editing rooms in New York and Atlanta.

Never in her brief career in the movies, or even during her one-year reign as Miss Latina of San Antonio, Texas, had there been so great a demand for eight-by-ten glossies of Melanie Moreno.

Andrew Pindaric heard about it only at eight A.M. as he was wolfing down his second breakfast, a banana, prior to driving to Santo Esteban in the wake of several Sweetwater vans loaded with technicians and equipment scheduled to be set up in the plaza. On hearing the news, Pindaric slumped down in the booth in the hotel coffee shop, watched eagerly by the other diners in the room, and stared into the distance while he absently fingered his already grimy and tattered copy of the shooting script. His eyes moistened and he sat still as a piece of furniture for a full two minutes before standing up and issuing to his companions at the table a string of orders. He turned on his heel and strode out of the dining room, every eye on his hunched shoulders and grim countenance.

At a table near the cash register, Alicia Foreman of Dover, Delaware, touched her husband's arm.

"Buddy," she said. "Did you see him? Like a thundercloud. Something has happened." She shivered. "I feel like a big ball of lightning just went by."

"I got a theory about these guys," Buddy Foreman said. "Did you notice his head? It's bigger. I mean proportionate to his body. Like all these movie people have big faces when you see 'em for real. Maybe the camera shrinks faces, you know? You need a big face to be photogenic."

"Buddy, what are you talking about?"

"That's really interesting," Buddy said to himself.

In the grip of advanced Sculptor's Cramp and a generalized irritation, Mo Bowdre had sat up late the night before, barely moving at all in his large wing chair made of roots and sticks. His mind had wandered, veered from image to pointless thought stream with all of the apparent purpose of a water bug skating on the surface of a summer pond. He had gone to bed two hours later than usual and as a result had slept an hour later than usual, waking with the headache that normally attended him when he didn't get enough sleep, a remnant of the explosion in the mine, he had been told, and one that would haunt him like an idiot brother most likely for the rest of his life.

He woke up, of course, in darkness and knew at once that Connie was already out of the bed, making breakfast. He could smell coffee, bacon, and Hopi stew—mutton and hominy in a thin salty broth, warming up from the night before. He preferred Hopi stew after it had been reheated, extended, added to—the eternal stew, ever replenished, and he imagined the pot of Hopi stew extending its life forward generation after generation, always renewing itself, even as it could be imagined as having stretched back into the mists of the past, the aboriginal pot of stew from which all others arose, like a strand of genetic material marshaling an entire society around itself to accomplish its own eternal perpetuation. Like a bighorn ram, thought the onetime student of biology, his mind skittering back to his unfinished work: just a tiny coiled thread of DNA, gathering around itself a half ton of muscle and bone and glands for the single end of perpetuating the lineage of ramdom. Such single-mindedness . . .

He sighed and heaved himself out of bed, with a question hanging just out of reach. Something that had flitted by as he sat up the night before.

It would come to him.

He reached for his clothes, hung on the chair next to the big bed, changed his mind, and crossed over to the closet. He slid open the door and stood indecisively, mind straying again, fingers moving absently from one hanger to another. The next thing he knew, he was standing under a cascade of welcoming hot water in the shower, noting to himself that even if he could see, there was in fact one thing he would not be able to see, hanging down there below his protruding, if nonetheless still relatively firm, gut. He liked to think of his gut as a well-earned testimonial to a lifetime of good food happily consumed, all a part of his personal reward system, but he had to admit it was a testimonial that seemed to be growing disproportionately to the rewards. He sighed for the second time that morning and turned off the comforting flood.

A few minutes later he walked in the kitchen and, above the sizzle of bacon in the pan, heard Connie gasp.

Standing at the stove, looking over her shoulder at the apparition in the doorway, Connie said, "I forgot you had one of those." She giggled, the soprano ripple of Hopi laughter.

"Hell," Mo said. "What about three years ago at—"

"I remember now." Another giggle.

"It's still the same damn thing. It just hangs a little different now."

"A lot different," she said, eyeing the now severely strained button on the jacket of Mo's long-forgotten two-piece light tan tropical worsted suit. Below the button, and above the equally strained waist of the pants, a good bit of white belly bulged out. The blond hair of Mo's thick chest showed where he might otherwise have worn a shirt. He was also barefoot.

"Maybe it shrunk," Mo said.

"Where are you going in that? Why . . . ?" She giggled again.

Mo raised his arm to scratch his head and the jacket button was propelled into an arc, landing on the tiled floor with a click.

"Noplace," Mo said. "I don't know rightly. . . .

Maybe I was just in the doldrums, wanted to do something flamboyant." His big teeth shone through his blond beard in a wide grin. "Actually, I don't really know. Something reminded me of it. Thought I'd try it on." His grin faded and he turned to leave. "Might as well give it to Goodwill, I guess."

What Mo had called flamboyance had lifted Connie momentarily out of her own doldrums, but they soon settled again. Another day called off, out of respect for another dead cast member. The poor woman, Connie thought. She had only seen her once, across the floor of the warehouse, a vivacious, laughing woman, gracefully flirting with some crew members. Shot. And the film— was it doomed? Cursed? White man's words, Connie thought, and not taken very seriously by most white people, with their ever-so-certain categories of cause and effect. She shivered with an ingrained and ancient sense of how easily the evil that stalked the world could gain the upper hand in the lives of people.

"What?" the chief rottweiler had barked into the phone. "Another goddamned day? Do you realize what ... let me work it out ... I got insurance, equipment rental, per diems, a hundred and twenty-five a day each for all of you just to eat and sleep, for chrissakes. I got wages, the fucking unions, grips—Jesus, Andrew. You're running just under fifty grand a *day* out there. Can't you just have a moment of silent prayer? ... Yeah, I know, I know, she was a woman ... Yeah, it would look bad, a day of mourning for the old greaser and only ... But fifty grand, jeez ... Yeah, I know. She's dead. Right. What the fuck is going on out there anyway, Andrew? Some kind of vendetta? ... Whaddyou mean, the cops think they were unrelated? Two Hispanic actors in the employ of Sweetwater Pictures get killed on location in two days and it isn't related? It's related here, baby, a hundred grand on the books with nothing to show for it. That's what I call related . . . Maybe we should bag it, Andrew. Make it a documentary, or something. Use a lot of old stills, sell it to PBS, and get out of this with our ass in one piece . . . I know they didn't have cameras in those days, what do you . . . ? Look, Andrew, CNN's got this old geezer, some kind of anthropologist, says the film's opened up a whole lot of old wounds. Maybe this fucker is jinxed, Andrew. Maybe you're . . ."

Andrew Pindaric had listened for another minute as the rottweiler, his pecuniary shock wearing off, shifted further into merely petulant speculation, and then, without a word, the director hung up. He wondered who the hell he should talk to about this mess.

"Tupatu," said the stern-faced Indian. "Just Tupatu. The other is a Spaniard name."

"You renounced it, huh?" Sergeant Anthony Ramirez said as the metal door clanged shut behind them. "This way," he said, motioning down the shiny linoleum-tiled corridor that ran between the cell blocks. The Indian padded ahead of him in old moccasins. He had a red band around his head and small nuggets of turquoise hung on loops of dirty string from his fleshy earlobes. "Here," Ramirez said, and the Indian looked through the bars into the cinder-gray room. "There's your army, General."

The two young Indians sat glumly against the far wall, hands dangling over their knees. There were four

other men in the tank, sitting or lying on the cement
floor like unmade beds, having spent their obligatory
night in the can for DWI. One of them, clad in a now
badly rumpled gray suit, with a bolo tie hanging loosely
from his shirt collar, stood up and said, "Sergeant!" He
was a state senator from Albuquerque, second offense,
Ramirez had read, caught at one-thirty in the morning
doing fifty on Cerrillos Road with a thirty-year-old
blonde known to turn the occasional trick sitting next to
him. There was nothing to charge the part-time hooker
with, so the cops had let her go, cursing, her meagerly
skirted ass twitching angrily back and forth as she
stomped through the light of the street lamps, while
with great relish they hauled the state senator in and
stowed him with the other drunks. In a previous legislative session, the senator had quietly voted against closing down the state's drive-up-window liquor business,
and all the cops in New Mexico had a book on him.

"Your wife called, Senator," Ramirez said. "She's on
her way up from Albuquerque. I think the boys told her
about your, uh, daughter." The man sagged. "They're a
little short on diplomacy, huh?"

The two Indians had risen to their feet and stood a
few feet away inside the bars with the look of confused
dogs on their faces.

"The charges . . . ?" Tupatu said.

"Like I said, assaulting police officers. But we're
checking out their stories for Monday night, Tuesday
morning."

"They were with me."

"So you say," Ramirez said. Tupatu said something
in a quiet voice, and Ramirez heard the words *Amu
kwa*. The youths turned and took up their wary vigil on

the floor against the far wall. "We're investigating a homicide that took place in those hours," Ramirez said. "And another one last night."

"They were here last night," Tupatu said, his gaze still fixed on his tribesmen. He had yet to look Ramirez in the eye. Maybe, Ramirez thought as they left the cell block, he never would.

"*You* weren't here, Mr. Tupatu. Let's go. I want to talk to you."

The Indian's jaw tightened. They walked toward the metal door. "Yesterday," he said in a monotone, "after our protest, I was performing my religious responsibilities in the kiva. There were others there."

All of them reliable witnesses, Ramirez thought.

The state troopers' department had said, sure, they'd do the SFPD a favor and find the man called Tupatu and bring him in. Especially since it was also a favor for the feds. And the two potbellied troopers had confirmed that they had picked up Tupatu after he emerged from the kiva west of the plaza at Santo Esteban at seven-thirty. Ramirez's mouth felt like it was full of insect wings. He hadn't had much sleep.

The Moreno woman's body had been spotted by none other than María Piño, the redeemed one, on her way to Santa Fe for a movie with two girlfriends before reporting to work in the laundry of La Posada de Consuela. She had called, blubbering, from the pay phone outside the Tesuque Village Market and, still blubbering, had shown the state police where the body was. She had recognized Ramirez when he and Collins arrived at the scene, and he had been able to calm her down enough to conclude that she was merely unfortunate enough to have seen the body from her pickup in the vanishing sunlight, adding another terrifying unpleasantness to her life which was already on a downhill slide again, what with her brother being in jail for assaulting an officer.

Ramirez had sent the unhappy young woman on her way and he and Collins, along with a mixed bag of state and county police and the old MI, had explored the crime scene with the help of an array of portable floodlights. It had not taken long to ascertain precisely the cause of death, and its approximate time, and within a half hour they had discovered the fresh tire tracks of a pickup that had pulled off the dirt track about three hundred yards east of where the body lay. The tire tracks stood out in the sharp light and shadow from the floodlights and they looked, to Ramirez, like one of the more common treads. A few minutes later Collins had fished a .30-caliber shell casing out from under a sage bush, and it was secreted away in a transparent plastic bag. There must, Ramirez thought dispiritedly, be five hundred, a thousand old Winchester .30-30s in the county—all unregistered of course. Not much of a rifle, he thought, but an icon of mythological power that was irresistible to the would-be trail riders of the superannuated Old West.

Now as he motioned the oppositionist leader of Santo Esteban to sit down in one of the chairs before his desk, Ramirez thought of the old Remington paintings, in such great demand still, and all the other clones cranked out by the Western Artists' Association. It struck him odd that a man named Remington would paint all those pictures of cowboys shooting Indians—and Indians shooting cowboys—with Winchesters.

"You do any hunting, Mr. Tupatu?"

The man across the desk stared at Ramirez's chest.

"What kind of gun you use?"

Silence.

"You want to call an attorney?"

Tupatu's cheek twitched. It looked voluntary, contemptuous. "I am under arrest?" he said.

"I want to ask you some questions about two homicides. So does the FBI. Agent Collins will be along in a minute. You're entitled—"

"I don't need a lawyer to tell the truth. It is you people who need lawyers. To help you lie."

It was, Ramirez reflected, going to be a long day.

Alicia Foreman had left her husband, Buddy, standing on the sidewalk in the shade of the *portal* while she got in line at the Häagen-Dazs store just east of the plaza on San Francisco Street. Buddy, she knew, was content to stand around in such places, pretending that he wasn't watching young women walking by and having mini-fantasies. She also suspected that Buddy's little fantasies never took him very far: he was a most unimaginative man.

Her own fantasies included the background buzz of excitement that, at any moment, on the street or even here, she might see one of the movie people, but her chief fantasy for now was focused on one sybaritic thing: sugar. A thoroughly fulfillable fantasy it was, fueled by a swirl of such exotica on the labels over the wondrous round bins as Cappuccino Commotion, Triple Brownie Overload, and Cookie Dough Dynamo. In the course of her deliberations, Alicia found herself at the counter, and shamelessly asked for a single sugar cone of Triple Brownie Overload from the remarkably attractive young woman in a black T-shirt behind the counter. With a smile, this creature produced the cone, which Alicia took in her left hand, having fished with her right hand a five-dollar bill from her new Ecuadoran handbag—woven by mountain people out of vicuña wool—that she had bought down the street in the boutique called Origins, a place of so many admixtures of color and cloth that it would, she thought, trigger in some people a migraine.

The pretty girl quickly made change, and Alicia was holding out her right hand to receive it when she turned her head slightly and noticed a tall man behind her. Turning a bit further, she took in the shock of blond hair, the elongated, tanned face, the twinkling eyes, and realized it was none other than Andrew Pindaric, standing behind her just like another *person* in line in the ice-cream store! Her throat clogged up, and she grinned up at him.

"Are you Andrew Pindaric?"

"Yes, ma'am."

"Oh," Alicia said. "Oh!" Flustered, she turned back to the pretty girl behind the counter, who was now smirking. Alicia immediately understood from the smirk that in Santa Fe one does not ogle famous people. She was frozen in ecstatic panic, thinking how she would tell the girls in Dover, when she noticed that she was holding the change in her right hand while her left hand was empty. She looked at the girl.

"You didn't give me my cone," Alicia said. "Change but no cone."

"Yes, I did, ma'am," the girl said.

Alicia felt a tap on her shoulder, spun around, still breathless, and looked up into the director's narrow, chiseled, smiling, tanned, dreamy, godlike visage. Oh, the dazzle of it!

"Your cone," he said. "It's in there." He pointed at her capacious new vicuña handbag from Ecuador.

Whenever Andrew Pindaric felt the chasm developing within—what he identified as a need for spiritual renewal—he often sought to feed it with sweets but usually wound up filling it with speed, breathtaking, life-threatening, tire-squealing speed. Today was no different. After his encounter at the ice-cream store he had started out in the XJS Jaguar on a personal pilgrimage to the Sanctuario de Chimayo, an old mission church in the mountains north of Santa Fe where the faithful, from miles around, trekked annually at Easter time to be healed. On the walls of a room there, entered from the left of the altar through an absurdly low doorway, were hundreds of crutches cast aside by those whose legs and hips had been restored to health, and a stupefying array of icons and humble gifts filled rude shelves—gifts from the grateful living.

Most important, in the earthen floor of the room near the entrance, there was a small depression filled with sand, and it was the sand that was widely thought to be the agent of God's notable local compassion. The sand, though taken by the handful by thousands of pilgrims—possibly millions over the years—was an ever-replenishing resource, and this added to the miraculous nature of the sanctuario in spite of the fact that one of the fathers attached to the place had once confessed in print that it was he himself who, with a shovel, replenished the sand, sometimes several times a day, depending on the season.

Such prosaic matters rarely confuse the devout. The sanctuario's sand remained famous, and Andrew Pindaric, whose tastes in such matters were unexclusive, had thought to seek whatever blessing it might confer upon him. But on pulling into the parking lot that lay within and among the stucco walls that defined the sanctuary's intimate and peaceful grounds, and noting a horde of like-minded tourists all armed with cameras, Pindaric had made a tight, dusty turn and headed for the hills.

The film director had paid Mario Andretti's chief shaman and pit doctor almost twelve thousand dollars to enhance the Jaguar's German-made manual transmission and it was this miraculous concoction of metal, lubricant, and engineering wizardry that was the agent of God's protection as the Jaguar hurtled into State Route 76's mountain curves at two times the posted speed limit, emerging onto the brief straightaways at a multiple of three. A torrent of fresh mountain air thrashed Pindaric's flaxen hair, and the total concentration of mind on road cleared his head. Without really noticing, he had geared down through two ramshackle towns and now geared down again as he came up a rising curve onto a high ridge along which was strewn the town of Truchas.

Here, several years ago, Robert Redford had directed *The Milagro Beanfield War*. The credits flashed through Pindaric's mind automatically, the film itself a magical gem which, but for Dave Grusin's music, had seemed too regionally quirky for the Motion Picture Academy. Pindaric pulled up on the side of the road north of the center of town and looked out over a canyon to the mountains beyond. Without much thought, he picked out the place where the camera had stood when they filmed the astounding elegiac light of late afternoon filling the screen like a silent Greek chorus. He craned his neck and looked back at the town, its tattered yards and buildings silent in the thin air. Nothing to suggest that once film crews and beautiful people had swarmed here, nothing to recall Sonia Braga cajoling the locals to rise up against the hostile developer—nothing to recall the celluloid miracle, a story spun out of air and light. Only the town, perched on this ridge, withdrawn again into a steadfast self-absorption and xenophobia.

Pindaric was greatly relieved.

He U-turned across the two-lane road and the XJS's six cylinders hummed throatily as he cruised south. Just outside of town, on his left, he passed a cemetery—a clutter of white gravemarkers each adorned with red and purple flowers, mostly plastic bouquets, dancing gaily in the breeze. Pindaric noted that a man with caffe-latte-colored skin was standing amid the flowers, leaning on a shovel, watching the Jaguar roll past. His lavender shirt complemented the cheerful flowers. Pindaric waved—a casual upward flick of the fingers that held the steering wheel—and the man in the graveyard watched impassively as the alien sports car accelerated with a rocket thrust into the bend.

Technically, it was the sort of claim that should have been settled years ago before the United States Indian Claims Commission, which had been established by the Congress in 1949 basically to pay off the Indians once and for all for all their ancient grievances against the encroachments of the United States as it pursued its manifest destiny across the continent. These had been

mostly land claims, the law at hand at the time having
no way of thinking about such abstract ideas as the loss
of tribal identity, no way of assigning a cash value to a
mountain god.

Any Indian claim arising out of wrongs committed
after the commission's filing period of five years was to
be taken to the United States Court of Claims, the place
where citizens of any stripe (but red) had always been
able to sue their government when, in its lumbering cer-
tainty, it trampled the toes of the innocent.

So technically, this present claim by the pueblo of
Santo Esteban should have been heard (or thrown out)
years earlier by the Indian Claims Commission, since it
referred to a wrong alleged to have occurred in 1924. It
had been filed nearly a quarter of a century too late, but
there were extenuating circumstances that, in her discretion, Judge Olivia Waddell found compelling.

Judge Waddell was forty-five years old, a graduate of
the University of Virginia Law School who had eventually gone on to practice law in a large firm in Tulsa,
Oklahoma. There she had gained a nodding acquain-
tance with Indian law, but had dealt mostly with the in-
tricacies of oil and taxes. She had never married, but
was known to enjoy the company of men, with whom
she carried on brief but monogamous relationships with
a discretion sufficient to keep her name out of the
wrong parts of the newspapers.

Five years ago she had been chosen to serve out an
expired justice's term on the Oklahoma Supreme Court.
Soon thereafter, when Indian claims—mostly over water
rights—had begun to simmer in the west, she had been
given an extraordinary appointment to the U.S. Court of
Claims, specifically to get on top of all this water

trouble. The unspoken hope was that she, not known for any particular sympathies for Indians, could head off all these water claims before the Indian tribes took back America's manifest destiny and left everyone from the corporate farmers of California to the town fathers of Phoenix, Tucson, and El Paso begging tribal councils for the right to pay ten times the current price for a few acre feet of water to irrigate their lettuce fields and urban lawns.

But Olivia Waddell was no patsy. Within the constraints of the law's many corridors and labyrinths, she was fair-minded to a fault. When Santo Esteban's attorney had showed up before her in the courtroom, she sometimes borrowed from the state of New Mexico with a new reason to hear an old claim, she acceded.

The wrong—stated simply—was that the U.S. Forest Service had bought, for what was even then a trivial amount, twelve thousand acres of land to add to the Santa Fe National Forest. The Forest Service had bought the land from a Santa Fe landholder named Beatty, a small-time lawyer and wheeler-dealer who preyed on the unwitting from a small office in the state capital. Beatty evidently had managed to leverage his way rather often into backbreaking debt, in this case by grabbing off separate parcels of what had formerly been large Spanish-family land grants or equally large Indian land grants. All of these land grants dated back at least a century, in most cases several centuries, and had been vague enough to begin with without the intervening vagaries of record keeping in the territory of New Mexico.

In any event, Beatty had managed to put together enough of these parcels to create twelve thousand contiguous acres abutting the eastern bank of the Rio

Grande south of the present pueblo of Santo Esteban. These he had desperately fobbed off for a pittance on the land-hungry Forest Service. Now the pueblo had done what it apparently could not do at the time, or later when it might have made a claim to the Indian Claims Commission: it had produced what appeared to be an original, legitimate piece of documentation suggesting that the Forest Service had bought the land from someone who did not legally own it. The Indians claimed the land as theirs, and they wanted it back.

In the face of this new evidence, Judge Waddell had ruled that her court would hear the Santo Esteban claim, knowing full well that it was opening up a terrible can of legal worms. But that, she felt, was why she was now in Santa Fe in a makeshift court. It was her job to separate the writhing worms that emerged and restore fairness and order, however thankless the task.

Judge Waddell was accustomed to wearing three-piece suits and she had seen no reason to change her personal dress code when she moved to the more flamboyant realm of Santa Fe last winter. When she stood up from behind her old territorial-style desk in the room that constituted her chambers, she slipped on the gray silk jacket that matched her gray silk vest and skirt, and left.

Once out on the sidewalk across from the narrow park that ran along the Alameda, with its cottonwood trees rustling in the breeze, she felt a sudden rush of elation that she attributed to the dry, clean air and the elevation—seven thousand feet above sea level. She hoped she could prolong her stint in this salubrious place, so different from the clammy world of Tulsa.

"Judge Waddell!"

She turned to see a tall man with an elegant head of white hair striding athletically toward her. Slightly near-sighted without her glasses, she needed a few seconds to recognize Allen Templeton, who often represented clients before the state supreme court.

"Counselor," she said pleasantly as he stopped beside her.

"Which way are you going?" he asked. "May I walk with you?"

"I was going to grab a quick bite at the Inn of the Governors." She nodded at the building down the street across the narrow park. "Then back to my paper mountain."

"A quick bite? Perhaps I could introduce you to a less, ah, trammeled place? Just a block beyond the inn."

Why not? she thought to herself. She had met Templeton a time or two before at one or another gathering, and he seemed pleasant enough. Certainly a handsome man, though there was a certain . . . well, carnal look, a meatiness to his features that both attracted her and repelled her at the same time.

"Why not?" she said to the lawyer. They crossed to De Vargas and then to the pathway in the park, and she caught the faint smell of a man's cologne. A dandy, she thought, smiling to herself.

"I see that Santa Fe has reached out and touched you with its gentle tendrils," Templeton said.

Judge Waddell looked at him curiously.

"That's an exquisite pin," he said. "Navajo, of course. Nineteen twenties, I'd guess. I prefer their old work, too. So innocent. Much of what you see today lacks a certain sincerity. Have you seen what some of the Indians are selling off the sidewalk over on the plaza? Stamped silver golf-ball markers. But then, the days of innocence are over for the Indians."

They walked on, Olivia Waddell thinking that it had been years—how many? six?—since she had had so impromptu a lunch date.

"But, of course," the lawyer went on, "I don't have to tell you that, of all people."

They walked on, crossing the Alameda, passing the Inn of the Governors. "Then again," Templeton said in reconsideration, "they still seem awfully hagridden, don't they? The old spooks and spirits still run their lives. Makes you wonder if they're really ready to— ah—take up the responsibilities of citizens." He paused. "Oh, dear, I suppose that sounds awfully harsh, doesn't it? They're wonderful people."

Olivia Waddell pursed her lips into a tight line, as if to foreclose any further conversation on a topic that, however tangentially, might impinge on the cases before her.

During a brief lunch at an outdoor table within high adobe walls, Templeton amused the judge with slightly scandalous tales of the courthouse and the statehouse. Afterward they paid their separate checks, and as they parted, Templeton said, "So glad to have bumped into you. Perhaps we can do this again sometime."

Judge Waddell smiled and, on her way back to the courthouse, weighed in her ever-judicial mind the man's charm against the fact, blinking in her brain like a neon sign, that he was unmistakably a predator. She would have her clerk run a check on him, she thought, with a tinge of the old excitement.

* * *

Mona Friedman looked up from the Tony Hillerman paperback she was thinking of buying. It was about the Navajo tribal cop named Jim Chee, one that she hadn't read. She had talked to her boss, Eleanor Frank, earlier by telephone, had given her a few thoughts about a replacement for the Moreno woman, and now had nothing to do. The Hispanic police sergeant had told her when she called in that, yes, it was still advisable that she stay in Santa Fe until a few loose ends were cleared up. She was dismayed at the prospect. She had no interest in the oppressively southwestern art that was hawked all over town, all this earnest replication of someone else's symbols, and she was simply not taken by leather fringes and cowboy boots or the swirling designs of South American peasant dresses. She was now further dismayed to see the writer Joseph Drew Hill making for her through the pottery-lined shelves of the hotel gift shop.

"I hear you've been grounded," he said when he reached the array of paperbacks. "Naughty, naughty."

"And you've been banned from the set," Mona Friedman said. "So why don't you fuck off."

"Hey, I got a constitutional right to stand here in the gift shop of this hotel. Look, seriously, what's going on around here? Like there's some kind of curse on this damn movie."

Mona eyed the man.

"You've been paid," she said. "Worried you won't see your name in lights?"

"Give me a break." He smiled. "Under this urbane exterior beats the heart of a mild-mannered seeker of truth."

"That's BS," she said cheerfully.

"That's one of his best," Joe Hill said, pointing to the book in her hand.

"Maybe, but I'm kind of sick of Indians. And cops."

"But not movie people?"

"You're no movie person."

"I know," Joe Hill said with a grin. "I've got some ideas. I'd like to talk to you about them."

"I can imagine," Mona said, beckoning to the clerk behind the counter, and thinking: Hmmmm. Mona was not the sort of person to suffer deprivation gladly in her heart.

"I'll take this," she said, and put the book on the counter while she fished her wallet from her purse.

"It's one of his best," said the counterman.

"Yes. So they tell me."

"Lunch?" Joe Hill asked. Boyish charm, he thought. Fucking irresistible.

In the end they skipped lunch, and thirty minutes or so later Mona Friedman stretched her arms up over her head and felt the perspiration evaporating from her body in the silent draft of the air conditioner.

"That's some gym you go to."

"Soooweeeee."

She rolled over on her side and said, "So what was it you wanted to talk about?"

"We could talk about these," he offered. "Imagine these gentle things being placed under suspicion of murder. You didn't do it, did you?"

"Of course not," she said icily, and sat up.

"And the dumb cops probably have figured out by now that the two murders—Moreno and your boy-friend—are connected. Which should let you off the hook. Unless you were driving around last night with a rifle. So why are you still grounded?"

"Shit, I don't know." She lay down again.

"So who stands to gain the most from this movie?" Joe Hill asked.

"Sweetwater Productions."

"Naah. I mean *who*. It's Pindaric. If he can pull this off, he can get over his rep as a director of those little sensitive flicks about women and timid-ass men. You know, Alan Alda discovering his anima, his feminine self. Jesus. This movie's got balls, you know? He needs it."

What am I doing, Mona thought, lying here naked next to this lunatic?

"So," Joe Hill went on, "someone who's got it in for Pindaric is trying to fuck up the whole thing. See? It makes perfect sense. And maybe the cops think you've got some beef. So they're checking it out. That's what I figure. So I think we should team up and check it out from that angle, too. I mean, you know all these people, and with my, uh, well, intuition . . ."

Mona Friedman rolled over on her back. I am here, she thought, trapped in my hotel room by this muscle-bound megalomaniac, a neck as thick as my thigh, and on top of the neck is a hollow bone filled with spaghetti instead of normal human neurons. She had a vision of her boss, Eleanor Frank, approaching through clouds of blue smoke. The black woman was laughing.

Mo Bowdre patted his big clay ram on the ass and heard the footsteps on the lawn outside the old mill-house studio.

Connie had gone off on some errand or another,

Ramirez and Collins were shut in with their sullen and intransigent suspects, there was no one else Mo could think of to pester, no point in rehashing in his mind what little he knew about the two homicides, even less point in trying to imagine something about them— nothing to do but try to gin up some enthusiasm for what was, after all, his damned job: completing the ram for the Fish and Wildlife people before the month was out. So he had stood in his cool studio, hands playing over the unfinished beast, willing his mind to see it again, and was relieved when the cellular phone on the tool bench emitted its horrible shriek. With a lightning lunge surprising in so large a man, Mo had reached the phone before it could shriek again.

It was Andrew Pindaric, asking if he could visit the studio, this unfortunately being a day of mourning, and Mo, delighted at the prospect of an interruption, had given the director instructions into his place on Canyon Road, telling him just to come through the sagging wooden gate he hadn't gotten around to fixing, and cross the lawn to the old stone mill house. And so here he was now, tapping on the frame of the door that faced north, allowing an enviable glow of perfect light into the room, where it didn't make any difference at all.

"Come in, come in," Mo said in a loud voice. "Just in time to rescue me from the curse of mankind. Hah-hah. Work, I mean."

"Wow!" said the director. "That's—"

"The current cross I bear. Glad you could come."

Pindaric stepped back and forth in front of the unfinished sculpture. "I don't see how you do it. I mean . . ."

"Being blind? Well, you just see other ways, is all. I don't see how you do what you do either, making films out of all that sea of humanity, those little short screen-plays. I read one once, long ago. Didn't look much like a movie to me."

"So you don't talk about your work? You let others explain it?"

"Hell, yes. Let 'em imagine what they want. I just make these things. Old Frazier down at the gallery, he names 'em. Has a tendency to pretentiousness, I've noticed. If I was to name this here ram, I'd call him *Old Cojones*, but you can bet your ass Frazier'd get all puffed up like a bladder and wheeze something about market expectations or some damn thing. I'd be willing to bet he winds up calling it *Mountain Sentinel*."

"I like *Old Cojones*." Pindaric chuckled. "You're going to cast this?"

"Yep. Bronze. Edition of ten is what Frazier says he can unload. First one goes to the Fish and Wildlife people."

"He's only got eight to sell."

"Well," Mo said, "I'll be damned. Now, that was easy."

"And I'll call mine the right name, *Old Cojones*."

Mo stood erect against the cool stone wall in the silence that followed. Pindaric, he sensed, was looking at the few pieces—mostly small—on the raw wooden shelves at the south end of the room.

"Amazing," Pindaric said. "This eagle bust."

"Made the original for Connie. Out of marble. Big damned thing. She's Eagle clan, you know, out at Hopi. Then I made a little version, cast a bunch of 'em. Take it. It's yours."

"Really?"

"Sure. Now there's two of you movie directors got

one. Redford got one because it reminded him of a Hopi friend, another Eagle clan guy named Abbott. You know, he put ol' Abbott in that film he made up here, the beanfield wars thing. Plucked Abbott out of a group of friends who were visitin' the set and put him on a porch, I heard. The poor man had to stand there and shake his head, say no at Sonia Braga. I'm told that shakin' your head no to Sonia Braga runs exactly opposite to fifty thousand years of human male evolution."

"So he had an Indian playing a Hispanic? That's original."

"Hah—hah."

"That's sort of why I'm here," Pindaric said. "I need to talk about all this to, well, someone who knows. . . . See, I've heard about you."

"Uh-oh. You want to go over to the house, have a beer?"

six

In the grip of high-altitude windstreams, a regular array of clouds quicksilvered across the blue-black sky, and a colorless sun blinked with each passing, alternately shading and lighting the dusty ground that sloped away from the Piño home in Santo Esteban. Two detectives from the state police, enlisted the night before to assist the FBI, exited the Piño house, and the tattered screen door squeaked and thumped behind them.

"Nothin'."

"What'd you expect?"

"Nothin'."

"Let's go."

"Lookit all that junk, will you?" The two men surveyed the yard, cluttered with the metallic innards of an ancient Dodge pickup, now an empty and doorless hulk, its open engine compartment and raised hood seeming poised to take a dinosaurian bite from the piñon tree before it. The pickup had once been green, but the sun had baked it into a mottled olive—matte finish—and its innards were scattered on the ground, mingling at some unplanned frontier with those of an old, once blue Camaro, its wheels now resting immodestly on cinder blocks twenty feet from the hungry pickup. A shadow slipped across the yard and the air was suddenly cool.

"Not a trace of rust on them fuckers," said the larger, meatier of the two men.

"Indyinn landscaping," snorted the other.

"Watch your language. Them people're just inside the door. We best check it out. The warrant says premises."

Weight thrown backward, their heels digging into the dusty ground, the two men made their straight-legged descent into the field of junk, stopping to peer through mirrored sunglasses at each sandblasted metallic organ.

"This stuff is all gone to hell."

"Sell it for scrap is all you could do with it now."

The meatier man approached the driver's side of the old Camaro, his paunch thrust out as if he had caught the vehicle speeding and intended to ask the driver to step out. He bent over and peered in the open window.

"Phew! Somethin' died in here."

He tried the handle, rough and crackly with its chrome veneer peeling away, and the door opened with a metallic shriek. Bending over again, he stuck his head in, pulled it out, and again said, "Phew!" After a deep breath he leaned in, pulled the driver's seat forward, and rummaged around on the floor with a gloved hand.

"Fuckin' mice or something. Had a nest in here. Hey! Look at this." He stood up, holding a shiny, rounded object in his palm.

The smaller man walked up to him and looked at the object.

"Son of a bitch," he said.

"It was under the nest." The larger man pulled a clear

plastic bag out of his pocket, opened it, and put the shiny object inside, pulling his fingers across the top to seal the zip lock. With heavy, unhurried steps, he walked up the dusty slope to the house and tapped on the screen door. In the shadowed interior, he saw the young woman, María Piño, standing a few feet back from the door. He held up the bag.

"You seen this before?"

"We ... uh ... we've all seen it. What's it ... ?"

"What's it doing here on these here premises? That's a damn good question. We're gonna have to ask you to come with us down to the police station in Santa Fe. They's some fellers there'll want to talk to you about what this is doing here. You want to step out here ... ?"

The Jaguar hurtled downhill. Pindaric smoothly downshifted and accelerated with a genteel roar into a curve, and Mo Bowdre pressed his right leg on the side of the leather-bound cockpit against the g-force, cool air buffeting his hair and dark glasses.

"This thing sure does hug the ground, don't it?" he said.

"Too fast for you?" Pindaric asked with what seemed genuine concern.

"How the hell would I know?"

They were headed north to Taos, Pindaric opening her up on the narrow two-lane road that snaked along the eastern bank of the Rio Grande. An hour earlier, sitting in Mo's living room with a bottle of Negra Modelo, Pindaric had explained that the idea of talking to Mo about his film's travails had occurred to him because Mo knew about Indians, knew the cops involved, and was rumored to have engaged in some imaginative brainwork in the past couple of years, working with law enforcement people. Pindaric confessed that he had known he was stepping onto a minefield, just trying to make this film. But he hadn't expected anything like these explosions. He needed to get an insider's opinion, he needed a better feel for all of the crosscurrents. It was like a curse had been placed on the film, and he didn't believe in such things really, but maybe, if Mo could give him a better picture, he would know—*intuit*—how to proceed.

He had always operated on his intuition, but this was like swimming in a murky sea. You could only see the nearby sharks: what else lay out there, out of vision . . . Pindaric said he would be perfectly frank. His last two films had not, well, been successes, either with the critics or with the public. Certainly, in the course of a twenty-year career as a director, he had offended a number of people in the industry, "but not mortally, for God's sake. I mean, I'm not inclined to paranoia, but it's as if someone had it in for this film—for me. This is, well, make or break for me, this film."

The big sculptor had sat erect and motionless in his enormous and bizarre chair made out of driftwood for what seemed more than a minute. Then he smiled broadly and said, "*That's* why I put on that old suit this morning."

"Huh?" Pindaric said, beginning to regret his decision to open up to this strange, hulking man.

Mo explained. "Suit," he ended. "Suit. Lawyers wear suits. Lawyers do lawsuits. I was thinking last night, couldn't remember this morning. Brain's going, turning to damn oatmeal. I hate oatmeal. Anyway, what I was thinking last night was about the lawsuit, the one Santo

Esteban has going. It's got people over there in a snit, the way they get, you know? Factions and all. It's about some old land they say is theirs. Part of the National Forest over there."

"I'm not sure I understand," Pindaric said warily.

"I don't see why you should. Trackin' a thought process through oatmeal. I can hardly do it myself and it was me had the thought. Anyway, they've got themselves a lawyer, young fellow named Beck, up in Taos. Earnest guy, poor as a church mouse and you don't find that much among lawyers, do you? Beck's always takin' on the problems of the downtrodden. Thing about the downtrodden is that they're not only gettin' screwed all the time, they haven't got any money. Most lawyers hate the downtrodden, is my experience. Anyhow, Beck oughta know what the hell is going on with those people. Maybe he can tell us what's lurking out there beyond the current shark attack." Mo reached out a big paw and lifted the telephone receiver from a side table next to his chair.

"To finish up your metaphor there," he added.

Within a few minutes the two men had set out for Taos, two blond heads rising an inch or two above the little windshield, Mo holding his black cowboy hat in his lap and maintaining a brave front of silence as the lunatic director, piloting his seventy-five-thousand-dollar hornet of a sports car, treated Mo's soul to a foretaste of the journey it would one day make unsheathed and alone into the unknown and improbable hereafter.

In archaic script, etched and oxidized black in the shining silver bulb, were the words

SANTO ESTEBAN
1863
A. LINCOLN

"Looks like someone just polished it up," Larry Collins said. "Bet you there's not a print on it."

"No bet, but we'll try," Anthony Ramirez said. He stuck his head out the door of his little office and crooked a finger, handing the transparent plastic bag to the uniformed woman who approached. "Forensics," he said, and she nodded. "And get me that kid, the Indian. You know, Piño."

Ramirez slipped around behind the desk and sat down. "So there's your cane."

"Part of it. But why keep the head? Obviously he tossed the wood off somewhere in the fucking desert out there. Somewhere."

Ramirez stared at the FBI agent. "It's silver," he said. "You just don't throw away silver."

"I would."

"Not if it was also something that was practically sacred. I mean, this thing came from Abraham Lincoln. It's a badge of sovereignty."

Collins sighed. "So this kid, Piño, Ernesto Piño? He swipes this sacred cane from the old governor's office and trots on down to the hotel and bashes the brains out of a drunken actor. Then he trots on home, chucking the broken wood parts into the bushes somewhere, and hides the head under some shit in an old Camaro junker in his yard."

"It looks that way."

"For what?"

"A symbolic act. Like you said. With the cane miss-

ing, the new governor's claim to office may be screwed
up. These guys don't like the movie. So, they make
enough of a mess, maybe the movie goes away. I don't
know. But the kid did have the head of the cane in his
car. So probably all these guys, these oppositionists,
are . . . I guess we'd better get 'em all in here, huh?"

"You know who they all are?" Collins asked.

"Martin, the governor, he'll know."

A beefy uniformed cop appeared at the door, and
Ramirez nodded. The cop pushed Ernesto Piño into the
office. He stood, hands balled up in his back pockets,
staring at Ramirez's chest from behind the ledges of his
cheekbones.

"What now?" he said.

"You're under arrest, kid. For homicide. In the death
of Gregorio Velasquez in La Posada de Consuela, Room
403." Ramirez rattled off the date and a two-hour time
span.

"And," added Collins, "suspicion of conspiracy to
commit homicide in the death of Melanie Moreno. On
the Santo Esteban Reservation. That's a federal crime,
kid. You want me to tell you the dates, times, or do you
want to go ahead and call a lawyer?"

Ernesto sagged. "What . . . ?"

"You don't want to say anything, kid," Collins said.
"Not till you got a lawyer with you. But me and the sergeant here, we're going to have a lot of questions.
You're gonna tell us who all your friends are, these 'oppositionists.' "

"I don't—"

"Look, kid," Ramirez said. "We found the head of
the Lincoln cane in that old rattletrap of yours, the
Camaro. And the actor was hit with something like a

cane, something made out of the same wood as the cane. So, do you know a lawyer, or do you want to call the public defender's office?"

The Indian stared at the floor. "I didn't ... I don't ..." He took a deep breath. "Maybe that guy, you know, Beck."

"Forget it," Collins said. "He's the tribe's counsel. He represents the governor's office. He can't help you. It'd be a conflict of interest. Call the PD for him, Tony. How come you kept the head of the cane, huh? I mean that's real stupid, you know, kid?"

Piño glanced at the agent, opened his mouth as if to speak, and clamped it shut.

"Smart," the agent said. "First smart thing you've done in three days." He turned to Ramirez. "Okay, you gonna book the others? I'll go talk to the governor. Martin Rodriguez. Get the names of the oppositionists."

Ernesto Piño turned as the uniformed cop stepped in the office. "You'll have to arrest the whole tribe," he said.

"Hey," Collins said, flapping his hand as if it had been burned on a stove. "Spunk. Real spunk. I like that in a murderer, don't you, Sergeant?"

They watched Piño disappear around the door, and Collins said, "How did the old governor die?"

"Heart attack."

"Yeah," Collins said. "Maybe he had a heart attack when that kid started waving the goddamn cane around the office. Or maybe it was something else. Maybe we should disinter him."

Ramirez leaned back and looked at the wall. He cleared his throat and leaned forward, resting his elbows on the desk. "It's your jurisdiction over there. But I'd let that dog lie asleep."

Collins winced. "Why?"

"We got 'im for one homicide, suspicion of another. How many do we need?"

"But, shit . . ."

"Look. Collins. The old man, his family, they didn't do anything. It's a real problem for these people, you know, digging them up, fooling around with them after they've died. All that. It's a religious thing."

"Yeah, but . . ."

"We—you know, us, our society—we've already dug up a hell of a lot of Indians. Maybe we don't need to this time. What difference will it make? Really." Ramirez looked down at the desktop and Collins stared at him.

"I've heard of hookers with a heart of gold," Collins said, his crooked teeth showing through a sly grin. "Never heard of a cop like that. Okay, so for now, anyway, we let the lying-down dog sleep." He stood up. "Did I get that right?"

They drove across the bridge over the river, now a languid trickle of reddish-brown, flat calm within low, cottonwood-lined banks. A little gang of Indian kids was throwing rocks into the muddy water, and Joseph Drew Hill slowed down, eyeing them. He wore jeans, sneakers, and a black T-shirt that said:

> TIME FLIES
> LIKE AN ARROW
> FRUIT FLIES
> LIKE A BANANA

"I used to do that," he said. "When I was a kid. North branch of the Saranac River. Hours at a time, pegging rocks."

Mona Friedman was slumped down in the passenger seat of the rented sedan, one black-sheathed knee propped on the dashboard, looking at the unfamiliar world through sunglasses that tinted everything a warm orange. She was thinking that probably every boy who ever lived on the planet threw rocks into water, and then, when grown up, remembered it as some sort of compelling, even defining moment in their lives. As a little girl she had thrown a few rocks into a stream and had not found it especially fulfilling, certainly not enough to slow down on a narrow bridge decades later to watch some other kids do it. She wondered what she had missed.

"Where'd you grow up?" Joe Hill asked.

"L.A.," she said. "Where are we going?"

"A cool place I want to show you."

"Great," Mona said. "We've seen the crime scene back there. And that scruffy little Indian village. What could top that?"

They had driven past the place where Melanie Moreno's brains were blown out, a bit off the wash-boardy dirt road, with the yellow police ribbons swinging gaily from their stakes in the breeze. But for that, and the bored-looking cop standing smoking by the police car parked nearby, the crime scene looked like any other piece of high desert around here, just part of the endless, pointless scrub of pale green-gray bushes and dwarfed trees. Mona could not imagine living in such a place. What she had seen of the pueblo of Santo

Esteban as they drove by said nothing more to her than rural poverty adobe-style: a sad, run-down little dump.

The car rose through denser woodland with taller and what she thought more proper trees, the road curving, rising and dipping below red and gray outcrops of rock, and Mona saw a sign pointing to Los Alamos.

"The atomic bomb place? We're going there?"

"Nah. A cool place. I'll show you." He took a left.

They passed a few areas enclosed by chain-link fence and nestled among the trees, places with ugly low buildings that looked like warehouses, each labeled TECH AREA with an accompanying number. A few trucks were parked outside each one, but otherwise there was no sign of humanity and they seemed ominous to the woman, Strangelovian, no doubt harboring shiny machines with glowing innards, tended by quiet-spoken wonks with neither chins nor morals, arrays of pens and pencils in their short-sleeved shirts, fine-tuning their doom boxes with all the banality of retirees playing a game of bridge.

At what looked like a 1950s shopping center paralleling the road, Joe Hill swung off to the left, slid past a busy gas station, and entered an improbable realm of tightly packed, small and unattractive homes, which, in spite of obvious attempts to keep them trim, still managed to look a bit seedy in the shadow of the surrounding high forest.

"Is this it?" Mona said.

"It's the town of White Rock. It's like a suburb of Los Alamos."

"Christ," she muttered. "Probably everyone here is radioactive. They don't have streetlights, see? Probably the whole place glows in the dark."

Joe Hill giggled and the car wound through more of the suburban jumble and came to a stop in a dirt parking lot. There was another car parked in the lot, but no sign of anyone. They got out and walked, Mona stepping languidly over the rough ground a few paces behind Joe Hill, who strode erect as a stump with his arms bulging out slightly to the sides, barely swinging at all. They walked among big clumps of ragged gray rocks that Mona guessed were old lava, sharp and unwelcoming. Crushed beer cans lay here and there, glinting in the light of the high sun.

"What's this, the town dump?" she asked. "Where all the gnomes throw away their used Geiger counters?"

"Magnificent," Joe Hill said, and stopped. She eyed him curiously as she stepped up beside him and the earth fell away, leaving her reeling with dizziness. They were on the edge of a cliff of rugged gray rock that fell almost vertically down to a thin brick-colored ribbon— the river, now trivially small, like a drawing. Beyond, a gray escarpment rose against the pale sky, every shadow, every rock visible in existential detail, as if there were no air at all over the chasm intervening between her and the far-off cliff. It all was vast and miniature at the same time, two-dimensional. Mona caught her breath, looked down again at the shiny ribbon, and spotted a tiny canoe with a few Day-Glo orange ants in it moving slowly around a curve.

"Jesus! It's gorgeous."

"Gorgeous gorge," Joe Hill quipped.

"How far up are we?"

"I guess it's about six hundred feet to the river. Maybe more. Can you imagine what the fucking Indians thought when they first saw this place?" Joe Hill breathed deeply and flexed his arms, triceps twitching like knots on trees. "That's White Rock Canyon. Over there, on the other side, above where the river enters the gorge—that's the Santo Esteban Reservation." He pointed. "I think this is just . . . cool." He stooped down, picked up a rock, and squatting like a baseball catcher, flipped it over the side. Mona watched it fall— how far? two hundred feet?—before it glanced off a ragged boulder, bounced up, and bounced again out of sight. Only then did she hear the distant click of rock on rock arising from the chasm.

Mona took off her sunglasses, blinked, and the world was blue. She was close enough to the edge that nothing but space showed in the periphery of her vision. She was suspended in space. A thought, no, an urge, passed over her like a shadow. Jump. Go ahead, jump. She shuddered as the urge skittered away and took a step backward from the edge and felt Joe Hill's hands grasp her upper arms from behind.

How did he get behind me? What was he doing? Oh, Christ, he's a serial killer, this maniac, killed Greg, Moreno . . . now me. Oh, God, oh . . .

The fingers were like a vise on her arms, pushing her outward, leaning her over the precipice. She glanced down in terror at the little ribbon, the tiny canoe piloted by orange ants, so microscopic, so silent, and she tried to scream, there had to be someone nearby, tried to scream *help*, but her throat was paralyzed, oh shit, oh *shit*!

"Beautiful, huh?" Joe Hill said. He giggled nasally. "Almost like flying. Gives you an urge to jump, doesn't it?"

Again, the nasal giggle.

* * *

Bent Street runs east and west above the plaza of Taos, a narrow and usually crowded thoroughfare lined with old historic buildings that have been converted mostly to shops, galleries, and restaurants. Miraculously, a parking space on the street beckoned a few dozen feet from the entrance of one of the restaurants, and Andrew Pindaric's Jaguar swept into it fluidly, humming with the rich sound of precision-honed pistons.

"A restaurant?" Pindaric said. "That's where we're going?"

Mo Bowdre nodded. "Yep."

"A law office in a restaurant."

"In Taos, wonders never cease," Bowdre said as the two men stepped out of the car onto the sidewalk, the big sculptor walking to one side of the director and a pace back. "You heard about the Taos Hum? See, a lot of people here have been complaining about some awful low sound, messes up their sleep, even messed up a marriage or two. Only one spouse could hear it. Constant hum. Some geologist set out some equipment and picked it up—infrasound. You know, too low for most human ears."

They entered a hall leading to the restaurant, hearing the clatter of tables being bused and reset, and Mo said, "Up the stairs. A lot of people figure it's the military up to something, maybe some kind of Star Wars communication system." The old wooden stairs squeaked pleasingly. "Other folks say it's just got to be those physicists at Los Alamos, cooking up some damn doom machine on the sly. Still others, of course, think it's Mother Earth trembling with wrath at all the developers nosing around up here with ideas about golf courses and condos for the parasitical and materialistic rich. Well, nobody knows what the hell it is. I myself have never heard it. Here we are."

"Rare and Out-of-Print Books?" Pindaric said.

"Naw, that's Art Bachrach's place. He's got a real bookstore across the street. He's an expert on underwater archaeology from back east, so naturally he winds up here in Taos, selling books about the desert. Beck said his new office was next door to Art's place."

"That makes sense," Pindaric said, and tapped on a door bearing a small brass plate: THOMAS BECK. ATTORNEY-AT-LAW.

They were welcomed in by the tall, baby-faced lawyer, who immediately began to apologize. "After Dad died," he explained, "we didn't need so much space, so I moved up here for a while. It's a little cramped but ... well, sit down. Here." He pushed at two chairs that sat before his cluttered desk. "So it's kind of a mess."

The men sat down, and after a pleasantry or two, Mo said, "Mr. Beck, this—"

"Tom, please."

"Good. I'm Mo. This here is Andrew I was telling you about on the phone. He was wondering how to get a better feel of things at Santo Esteban and I thought of you."

"What can I tell you, Mister—Andrew?"

Pindaric suddenly had doubts. The lawyer's office was severely cramped by the presence of his old territorial-style desk, the two chairs, a table with a PC set up on it, and three battered filing cabinets. The lawyer's desk had several small but messy piles of papers on it, some of which looked like unopened envelopes, and there was a color photograph in an imitation leather frame of a young woman smiling bravely, holding a little boy who was smiling crookedly and leaning disjointedly against his mother. Here and there, among the clutter, were a few pots, brick-colored and decorated in black with the fanciful geometry of what Pindaric took to be several Pueblo tribes. Nothing here suggested the calm wisdom of the Law, especially the lanky young lawyer sitting behind the desk with his casual dress and a pinched look on his boyish features.

"I'd like to get a better idea about this fellow Tupatu," Pindaric said. "The one who was in charge of that demonstration the other day. Where does he fit in? What authority does he have? Things like that."

Tom Beck picked up a pencil from which he had previously chewed off the eraser, and tapped it a few times on the desk.

"Antonio Tupatu," he said, "is a Vietnam vet, and I believe he's a member of a veterans' group called the Walk of the Warriors. That's a group of what you might call radical traditionalists. These guys fought in that war, fought for the United States, and they came home to find the same old thing going on in their reservations. Poverty. Alcoholism. Drugs, more and more. A cash economy coming in more and more, and that means big-time material wants—TVs, VCRs, all that—but not much cash. There's a lot of unemployment. So there's a lot of debt. So these vets, these patriots, come back and find their people deeper in hock than ever to the white man's economy on top of everything else. So they get radical. They want to go back to basics."

The lawyer paused and put the pencil down, carefully aligning it along the edge of a blank yellow legal pad. "You guys want some coffee or something? One advantage of an office over a restaurant." The two men shook their heads and the lawyer resumed.

"They like to say that Native Americans are the nation's landlords, and the rent is due. They want their religious rights, and that means their land and water rights. They want everything they once had. They see every intrusion, every influence of the white man's culture as planned genocide. It's an extreme view, but of course it's arguable. But it's hooked to a utopian idea of what's possible. It's like the Earth First!ers, remember them? The radical enviros, saw any development as forest-cide. They were arguably right, but their goal was to return to the Pleistocene."

Pindaric leaned forward. "Is that Warrior Whatever behind this? Trying to scuttle the film?"

"I doubt it," Beck said. He picked up the pencil and tapped it idly on the desk. "My guess is that this is purely local action. Tupatu's basically pissed off at his own tribal government. Too accepting of white ways. Handouts. He's got sympathy from a few guys from other pueblos, but mostly this is real parochial stuff."

"How far would they go?" Pindaric asked.

Tom Beck's face clouded over, his normally pinched look becoming a pout.

"You mean the homicides, of course."

"Yeah."

Beck leaned back in his chair, blew air from his mouth, and said, "Well, it'll soon be public knowledge." He hesitated, then went on. "The feds have arrested Tupatu and two kids—well, guys in their twenties—who are followers. They've stuck 'em with that actor's murder. Suspicion in the woman's. Martin, the new governor, just called me. They found the head of the Lincoln in one of those kids' vehicles. You know about the canes?"

Beck explained about the Lincoln cane, found missing the day after Gregorio Velasquez was killed, the matching wood type. The lawyer noticed that Mo Bowdre was smiling, and trailed off.

"What?" Beck asked.

"Nothin'. Just thinkin'."

"Frankly," Beck said, "I can see Tupatu stealing the cane, or having someone steal it. It would throw some more confusion into the pot, you know, weaken the tribal government's authority in the eyes of the people. A lot of power goes with symbols in these tribes. Well, everywhere I guess. I can see him doing that to turn his people against the movie. But, two things. My guess is that the movie is a convenient excuse. And I just can't see Tupatu killing anyone, much less strangers. Which he denies, by the way."

"What'd he do in Vietnam?" Mo asked.

"Special Forces, I think."

"Then he already has," Mo said. "Killed strangers, I mean."

Beck folded his hands before him. "Is there anything else I can tell you, Andrew?"

"What's his agenda, you know, overall? I mean, if the film is just a convenient excuse, as you say ..."

"It's really hard to say. These fanatics, any political, religious fanatic, they can make a lot of sense if you accept their original premise. But they're crazy, paranoid. Tupatu's focused on the tribal government as the source of all evil in the tribe. The white man's patsy. So he wants to discredit it. Like in this land matter that's coming up."

"Tell us about that," Mo said, nodding.

Briefly, Beck explained the history of the disputed land, and the appearance recently of an old archival document that tended to prove that the land had been sold by an illegitimate "owner" to the Forest Service. The land in question, the lawyer explained, contained a number of places holy to the tribe.

"Ancient shrines," he said. "They've been trying to get the land back ever since the Taos pueblo got Blue Lake back, in Nixon's time. The problem is, they aren't about to tell where exactly the shrines are. They're scared of vandalism. So it's always a tough problem legally. Certain rules of evidence have to be suspended, and the courts don't like that much, as you can imagine. But this document . . ."

"And Tupatu is against *this*?"

Beck smiled. "It sounds ridiculous. Here's the tribe with a chance of recovering title and control of some ancestral land, *traditional* land, and these self-styled traditionalists are against it. But here's their beef. They say that the land we're talking about is only *part* of their ancestral lands. We're not asking for it all, so they'll never have a chance to get it all back. They're right about that, too. This is like a one-shot deal in the Court of Claims. No court'll ever hear another claim of this kind from this tribe."

"So Tupatu is against that, too?"

"The claim is being brought by the tribal government," the lawyer said. "That's really why Tupatu is against it. He hates the government and thinks any of its works are illegitimate and evil. So he'll do anything to discredit it."

"Anything?" Pindaric asked.

"As I said, I don't see Tupatu or anyone in the tribe killing those actors. That's just not their . . . I know, I know, the Indians killed a lot of Spaniards three hundred years ago, and Tupatu was trained as an army ranger. But, well, look. Think about warriors. Indian warriors. They might have been pretty sneaky tactically, but they never made any bones about what they were doing strategically. They never denied they were on the warpath. Tupatu says he's out to do the movie in, and the land case, but he says he didn't kill anybody."

"What about those young guys?"

"Tupatu says they do only what he tells 'em to do."

"And you believe him," Pindaric said.

The lawyer shrugged. "I guess that's up to the judicial system now," he said.

Mo Bowdre moved in his chair. "Well, now, let's see. You got this case you're bringing to get some land back for the tribe, right? And these dissidents are running around raising hell. What's that do to your case?"

Beck's mouth pulled together into a thoughtful O. He fiddled with the pencil. "That's hard to say, of course. The pueblo's claim rests on law, legal precedent, all that. Of course, I think it should be decided in their favor, simply on the basis of law. And of course on the basis of how other suits like this have been handled. Whatever confusion the dissidents are causing . . ." He paused, drummed the pencil on his desk a few times. "Judge Waddell has a reputation for being fair-minded, and she seems that way to me. So far. But she *is* something of a cipher. All in all, I don't think that all this trouble should prejudice our case. It's not really relevant. It's politics. This is a matter of law."

Pindaric sat hunched over like a heron, his elbows on

his knees. "Well, let me ask you this. What about the Hispanic thing?"

"I'm sorry?" Beck said.

"There's a lot of speculation, you know, in the media, about the old grudges, between the Indians and the Hispanics, that sort of thing."

Beck picked up his chewed pencil and tapped absently on the desk. "What can I say about the media?" He smiled ingratiatingly. "Bless their palpitating little hearts. But to answer you, yes, there are some old bones still being picked, some old resentments between Indians and Hispanics. But this simply isn't colonial times or the wild Old West anymore. People take their disputes to court these days. It's not as exciting for the press but . . ." He shrugged.

The Jaguar hurtled around a tight bend, rose out of the great valley, and descended again, following the road that snakes between the steep foothills that flank the Rio Grande.

"Is there something wrong with Beck's kid?" Pindaric asked.

"Some kind of degenerative disease, I heard. Muscular dystrophy, something like that." They lapsed again into silence. Presently, Mo Bowdre felt the late-afternoon sun on his face, a pleasing warmth spreading over him under the thrashing of the wind and the thoughts of mortality induced with each alternation of sideways g-forces. To distract himself further, he said, "I suppose it's natural enough that lawyers place a whole lot of faith in the judicial system."

"You don't?"

"I never did win anything in court that I deserved,"

Mo said. Pindaric was silent. "After my accident, when
I lost my vision, a union lawyer got the mining company to pay all my medical expenses, all that. Seemed
reasonable enough. He also got me a bunch of money
for what you might call general distress. Since then I've
decided that everyone is in general distress and they
don't get paid for it. And I knew the risks, working in
some underground tunnel like a mole with a bunch of
lunatics. Sometimes I think we got us a system where
we pay people extra for being stupid. In any event,
whether I deserved it or not, I blew my general-distress
fund pretty damn quick."

"You mind if I ask on what?"

"Self-pity, mostly. Hah—hah—hah. Anyway, I've
come to think that the judicial system is the last resort
for scoundrels."

"And Beck? Is he a scoundrel?" Pindaric asked. "Oh,
hey, am I going too fast for you?"

"No, no," Mo said. "Life here on the edge has zest."
Pindaric eased up slightly. "And no, I reckon Tom Beck
told us pretty much the truth of things as he sees it. I
can see those boys swiping the cane. But I can't see
'em using it as a club, even though that's what Tony
Ramirez surely thinks they did right now. It seems log-
ical enough, but a lot of Indians have a different kind of
logic. You Roman Catholic?"

"I was once."

"Well, you know them wafers and wine? Just junk
stuff you buy in a store. But they are the real thing, too,
the blood and flesh and all that, if you're a believer.
They aren't some symbol to remind you, they're the
real thing. Same with those canes. They *are* the office.
I don't see a man like Tupatu using that cane for some-

thing it wasn't designed for, any more than he'd use a kachina mask at a Halloween party."

"So you think Beck was right?"

"As far as he went. Lawyers don't ever tell you everything they know. And they don't always know everything either, though God knows they act as if they do. Part of the training, I'd guess. Dissembling 101. Prerequisite in every law school even though you don't find it in the catalog."

"So the killer . . . ? Still at large."

"Maybe there's two of 'em," Mo said.

The Jaguar sped on, swerving through the turns, in and out of the warmth of the sun. "I think I'm out of my league," Pindaric said.

"That makes two of us."

Sergeant Anthony Ramirez knew it was hopeless, but he tried anyway.

He knew how easy it would be for someone in the press, not to mention the quick-to-be-offended watchdogs of Indian rights, to see the arrests as yet another racially motivated vendetta against Indians in general by a white society bent on genocide. The department had postponed making a statement to the voracious journalists and paparazzi until well past the deadline for the early-evening news programs, and even then, all it had released were a few terse sentences about three men being placed under arrest in connection with the Velasquez homicide, and there being other suspects under questioning. There had been no way to keep the pack sufficiently at bay during the comings and goings at the station to disguise the fact that the suspects, too, were all Indians, or to keep the local members of the

press from recognizing that they were all from the
pueblo of Santo Esteban. Amid the questions shrieked
from the unruly mob, Ramirez had heard the phrase
wholesale roundup and other rabid exaggerations. He
had no intention of subjecting himself to another bout
of misguided slander, so he made an attempt to slip out
of the station via a little-used freight door that opened
up into the parking lot beyond the utility wing that
housed the station's emergency generator and the
wholly inadequate engines of its quirky air-conditioning
system.

He pushed the gray metal door open and stepped out
on the cement loading dock only to be blinded by an
explosion of flashes, an eruption of shouted questions.
"You can run but you can't 'ide," he heard among the
voices, and recognized it as the Brit who slung dirt for
that supermarket tabloid.

Ramirez stopped, grinned, pulled a white handker-
chief from his pocket, and waved it. He blinked.

"No further comment," he said. "There's nothing
more to say."

"Hey, Sergeant!"

"Sergeant!"

"Hey, is it true that—"

"Did the governor's office order this roundup?"

"You doin' this to save face, keep the movie—"

Ramirez stepped lightly off the cement dock and
smiled again, holding up his hand with the white hand-
kerchief. "Wait here, you guys," he shouted. "The lieutenant may have a word for you." He ducked around
the utility wing and away from the plaintive cries of the
scavengers. It reminded him of a bunch of seagulls he
had seen once at the beach on the Gulf of California, a

swirl of ravening hunger and mutual irritation, a whole society gone mad at the thought of some crappy crust of bread.

The lieutenant, as Ramirez well knew, had left ten minutes earlier.

Later that night Mo Bowdre sat on the edge of the bed in a voluminous pair of carnelian-red briefs. Connie lay on her back, the sheet pulled trimly up to her collarbone as she watched the big man.

"I talked to Tony," he said. "Got seven of those oppositionists in the can. Like conspiracy to commit homicide along with everything else. He tried to sneak out, but the press caught him. They're all hollering about a police vendetta, racism, all that."

"What about Martin?" Connie asked.

"Martin? The governor? Well, *he's* not a suspect."

"No, how is he taking it?"

"I don't know. Didn't ask," Mo said. "How's it look to you?"

Connie put her hands behind her head and sighed.

"Bad," she said. "Everyone looks bad in something like this."

Mo sat still, waiting, and heard the old clock in the hall chime the half hour. He turned to the side, facing her with his opaque glasses, and she saw a grin creep over his face.

"Mother Earth?" he said. "Do you suppose you could be kind enough to complete your thought process there? Maybe just let me in on the next itty-bitty segment of what you're thinking?"

"I was just wondering, you know, who would want to

make the pueblo look bad. Besides those oppositionists."

Mo waited again in the silence.

"That's it?" he said.

"That's it."

"That is the sum total of your thinking at this moment?"

"Yes. Why don't you turn off the light?"

"Oh. Thought I already had." He heaved himself off
the bed and crossed over to the light switch beside the
door, thinking not for the first time that Hopis are
weird.

Nice. But weird.

seven

Pitch-black. Suffocating. Air like the hot breath of dogs. Weight—a great weight—pressing her down, hot and sticky on her stomach, chest. Where was she now?

She was in hell.

This was it, goddamn it. That old turkey of a minister had been right. There *was* a hell and she was in it now. No searing flames. Just this thick, heavy darkness. Forever. She could see the disgusting old sycophant of a preacher, wattles quivering with a nearly carnal fervor over the certitude of brimstone.

But now she saw again the little orange antlike people in the canoe, so distant, so vivid, saw them look up after she screamed, howled into the vastness of space, felt the iron fingers on her arm, saw herself falling like a rag doll, screaming, the oval black holes in the ant faces, arms waving frantically, the antic giggle above—no, behind. Him spinning her around, saying "You're in good hands with Allstate," her screaming "You fucking *bastard* son of a *bitch* Jesus *Christ*!"—shaking, sobbing, him saying, "Hey, it was just ..." Him holding her when she collapsed, sinking down on rubber knees, him saying, "I didn't, I mean, it was a fucking *joke*."

Clutching him in the hurricane of tremors, clutching him like a rock, relieved, breathing for a change, big gasps of cool air in the lungs, pulling herself to her feet, standing in the dizzy light, him rising, sooweee, sooweee, "just a joke, you know, a little thrill."

"Fuck *you*!" she had screamed, and slammed her open hands against his red ears with a single loud pop like something had died, and he fell on the rocks, howling, holding the head that writhed back and forth on his tree-stump neck.

"I'm fucking deaf!" he had moaned, over and over, and she knelt down, knees scraping on the goddamned rock, and shook him by the hair, shouting "You're crazy, you're crazy" over and over till he took his hands from his ears, opened his eyes, and said, calm as could be, "I'm not crazy, I'm fucking deaf. Can't you hear?" And she had slumped down on top of him, exhausted, drained, panting, her eyes closed against the glare, and had begun to laugh.

"It *is* funny," he had said.

"No, it isn't," she had replied, but kept on laughing, and now he was a dead, sticky weight on her stomach and chest in this hot, stuffy motel room in the stygian dark somewhere in the goddamn mountains.

"Wake up," she commanded.

"I did."

"Get off me. What time is it? Where are we?"

"Near Chama. Up near the Colorado border. Don't you remember? It isn't dawn yet. We got to go to work."

"Will you get *off*? God, you're heavy for such a short little—"

"Watch it, Mona baby." He slid off. "See, I've been

thinking. You know who takes gas if this movie is a success? The Hispanics. I'll bet you there's some Hispanic league, filled with morbid old descendants of the conquistadores, and they're saying, 'Fuck, if these damn Indians look good in this flick, it's at the expense of our very ancestors. . . .' You know what I mean? So let's get going. Do a little research. I mean, these guys are just suffering with pride and unfulfilled macho. . . . Hell, I know what it's like to live in these fucking backwaters, generations of old grudges piling up, waiting for some nutty reason to come along, like a grain of sand in a paranoid fucking oyster. These people are crazy as hell."

"*You're* crazy," Mona said. "Certifiably crazy. A motormouth with no brain." But, she thought, remembering now, the descent into hell hadn't been all bad.

Weird as hell, but not all bad.

Samantha Burgess woke up alone as usual in her one-room apartment near the Old Pecos Trail with a sour ache in her skull, her first hangover in years. Not since college . . .

She lay on her back, mouth dry, thinking that it hadn't been worth it, bar-hopping with those Hollywood press people. God, what gossip! Who was screwing whom, even what. Samantha was not given to having heroines, particularly among movie people, but a few women she had admired had descended from grace the night before like fallen angels who fluttered too close to the total gravity of a black hole. The simile was not original with Samantha. One of her occasional boy-friends wrote second-rate science-fiction novels for the paperback houses, and in an attempt to break the shackles of hackdom, he had tried to combine *Paradise Lost* with *Star Trek*, arriving at the notion of the bad angels being trapped in a black hole that God had slyly arranged for them when He got wise that they were acting up. Slurp! There went evil—into the warp, like flushed down the can.

Don't we all wish.

The book had been rejected, naturally enough

Samantha had to pee and raised herself with glacial slowness from the sofa bed, her fingers pinching the bridge of her nose. Slowly she opened her eyes. Outside the window the southern sky was still black.

Aspirin, she thought. Then she noticed the light blinking red on her answering machine: *1 . . . 1 . . . 1 . . .* She pressed the Messages button, and listened to the tape rewind briefly, then a hum, a beep, and a voice.

"Don't miss the fun at Santo Esteban tomorrow morning," said a scratchy male voice. "Make sure Pindaric tells the whole story. Good night, Ms. Burgess."

"What?" she said out loud. "What?" Jesus, too smashed last night to notice the damn light.

She poked at the Save button as the tape began to rewind, but missed it in the dark. The machine clicked. The message was lost. *Damn!* Her second anonymous tip since she became a reporter—the first having been a similar anonymous call but to her office, about the demonstration—and the damn message was erased. What the hell did it mean? Who the hell was it? Were they shooting at the pueblo today? How could she get in? They'd probably have it cordoned off like some kind of presidential visit. She headed for the little bathroom, thinking aspirin. Lots of aspirin.

At least the sun hadn't come up yet.

Thank God for that. And aspirin.

The old woman looked up as her husband, Popova, shuffled into the kitchen, and then she looked down at her hands, gnarled as cedars. Two old cedars, she and her husband, bent by the winds and droughts of life, arthritic and now mostly known to themselves in the daily round by their aches. Outside the little window over the sink, the final moments of the night remained.

She thrust her old hands into the soapy water and scrabbled around until she found the last spoon.

"So," she said in the language of Amu kwa, "it has come to that."

The old man paused, halfway across the kitchen, a shadowy figure in the light from a single bare lightbulb that hung from the ceiling over the sink. She looked at his bent frame, still seeing as well the frame of the young man who had long ago stood straight and assured on the rocky mesa to the south, commanding the old horizon in the glint of the setting sun. A fond picture, no less present for being from the past. The old man quivered now, like the branches of a cedar in the breeze.

"Two people gone, and now this, too," she said, mildly hectoring the old man.

"Those peoples," Popova said in English. "They are not part of this."

The old woman blew air through her lips in mild derision.

"We have our instructions," he said in the old tongue.

"There was a time when you gave the instructions," she said.

"The reins change hands," he said, "but the law we

follow remains the same." He sat down heavily at the
table with its yellow oilcloth, sparkling clean. The old
woman dried the spoon with a dish towel, put it down,
and poured a mug of weak coffee from a metal pot,
turning to set it down on the table in front of her husband.

"It will do no good," she said.

The old man shrugged. He had followed the instructions and, she knew, would have no more to say about it.

"Drink," she said. "The sun will rise soon."

Not long after the gunmetal-gray clouds over the Sangre
de Cristo Mountains had turned orange, then yellow,
and then evaporated into a crisp blue morning, Martin
Rodriguez stood under the cottonwood trees near the
tribal headquarters building and watched Tom Beck
gangle across the dirt parking lot, his usual pinched
look on his babyish face. He had left his old Toyota
parked at the far end of the lot. As usual, he looked a
bit rumpled in his checked jacket, bolo tie, and chino
pants over cowboy boots, and Martin, a conspicuously
neat dresser like so many nonwhites thrust for official
reasons into the white world, wondered fleetingly if the
tribe should be represented by a man so careless about
his appearance. He himself wore a white shirt, freshly
pressed and open at the neck, and a pair of gray trousers
with a razor crease. Of course, he knew, Beck had one
or two proper suits he wore in court appearances. With
vests.

" 'Lo, Martin," the lawyer said, smiling wryly.

"Thank you for coming. It seemed, this is the first
day . . . you know?"

"Sure. Glad to oblige." They shook hands and Martin

turned, leading the way across the dusty lot and down a hard-packed dirt path to the plaza.

"I don't expect any trouble," Martin said.

"But just in case someone—"

"Yes. I don't know who. They're all in Santa Fe now."

"How many? Seven?" the lawyer asked.

Martin nodded. He felt gritty, having yesterday given the man from the FBI—Collins—the names of those whom he knew to be Tupatu's most active supporters. Four other men from Santo Esteban. Regardless of the requirements of the FBI and the law, Martin had quickly realized the advantage to him of further weakening any possible challenge to his authority on this momentous day. There was no one left now to do so—except old Popova, now merely a figurehead, an old, old man.

They passed through a narrow, shaded alley formed by two of the oldest buildings in Santo Esteban, one-story homes of aging adobe, each brick eroded by the weather, rounded, archaic looking.

"Right here," Martin said. "They're gonna have the soldiers ride through here. They say it looks authentic." He laughed gently and reminded himself that one of his teachers had explained that a house made of adobe brick—merely dried mud and straw—was like the people who lived in it. Just like them, it would one day wear away and return to the earth of which it was made. His own house, a three-room affair just south of the plaza proper, was made of cinder block and stuccoed except for the west wall he hadn't gotten around to yet. Inauthentic, by some standards, he thought to himself.

Once in the plaza, the two men stood in the shadow of a house, watching the daily round begin. A screen door opened and a boy bolted out, loping across the dust with his upper body swaying left, right, then left. Across the way, an old woman stepped out of her house and hesitated. Then she hobbled to the next house, knocked on the door, and went in. Three dogs, sway-backed and craven with their ears laid back, trotted guiltily around the corner, paused, and trotted on. On the west side of the plaza, a woman stepped out of her house—that was Sophia, Martin thought, and her house looked pretty authentic, except maybe for the wooden window frames and the screens. She carried a metal bowl, which she set down on a ragged stone wall. She turned and said something sharply at the door, and a little girl reluctantly came out, frowning, and submitted to having her hair washed. From inside, somewhere, there came the sound of a tape—a drum and chanting. A pair of old men sat on a makeshift wooden bench in the shadows of the plaza's only two-story house, also adobe, sporadically exchanging muttered words. Two boys, about twelve or thirteen years old, appeared on the roof of one of the buildings on the eastern side of the plaza, looking out at the low hills and the mountains beyond.

A cloud of dust appeared on the hills and resolved it-self into a white van, followed by another, and another. They gleamed in the morning sun, and as they de-scended the dirt track toward the plaza, Martin could see the dark green flash of a sports car. He wondered why the director would drive in the dust of the others. The caravan approached slowly and disappeared behind the buildings. On the rooftop, the two boys turned and shouted into the plaza, and screen doors opened and slammed as the people of Amu kwa began to assemble in understated curiosity.

"Should I go out and greet them?" Martin asked.

"Let them come to you," Tom Beck said. "That's the crew that just arrived. Here come some of the actors." The two men watched two more vans appear in the dust over the hill, followed by a pickup.

"It's like an army," Martin said.

"Yeah." They watched one of the approaching vans on the hill pull off the track and stop. A small group of men got out and stood in the cloud of dust. Sun glinted silver from them as they turned this way and that. "There's your army," Beck said. "The Spanish soldiers. I wonder where the horses are."

"This is going to be weird," Martin said. "Isn't it?"

"Like nothing either of us have ever seen," Beck said.

The next half hour reminded Martin Rodriguez, the new governor of the ancient pueblo of Amu kwa, of nothing so much as one of those unsettling PBS shows documenting at intimate range the lives of insects. The dusty plaza, with its squat adobe buildings brooding around it like silent old men, was soon abuzz with alien people with alien machines, going about their alien business with the single-mindedness of giant bees. People with headsets, others with clipboards, floodlights, large metallic-looking panels, long cables like snakes, oversized cameras—all bustled in and out, following some pattern held in their collective mind—good-natured, terse-spoken, transforming the eastern end of the plaza into an eerie space-shot version of itself.

The director, Andrew Pindaric, had loped across the

plaza toward Martin when the colony of human bees entered, and asked if Martin might take on the task of explaining that the people of the village were welcome, of course, to watch the entire thing and would he ask them to remain behind the line of tape being strung up and try to be silent whenever the cameras were running? Martin gladly accepted the task and now watched as a man in a T-shirt and jeans squinted into an enormous eyepiece on a large black camera on wheels pointed down the shaded alleyway between the two oldest houses. The man pulled back, looked around, and said, "Have a look, Andy."

The lanky director leaned over and peered through the eyepiece like a large bird. Then he stood up, smiling.

"Chiaroscuro," he said. "I love it. Remember, you'll want to stay in tight on these guys when they come through. Like a documentary."

"Roger."

"Maybe we should reflect a little more light in there, do you think?"

"Nah, it's good."

"Okay," Pindaric said. "We want 'em bursting out of the shadow into the light. Like shattering a mirror. Right?"

"Roger."

The western half of the plaza was crowded with the people of Santo Esteban—old ladies in shawls sitting in folding aluminum chairs with plastic webbing, as if they were waiting for a plaza dance to begin. Teenagers stood on the flat roofs, poking each other. Little kids darted among the crowd. Dogs slunk in and out of the little knots of people. Pindaric was bent over on his long-shanked legs, talking to a group of Indian women and children, along with two old men—the extras. A few were residents, others Martin recognized as being from neighboring Tesuque, as well as Pojoaque and San Juan. They were dressed in moccasins and traditional garb, the old men in white bloomer-type pants Martin had never seen except in the old black-and-white photographs in the museums in Santa Fe. Pindaric gestured broadly with his arms and the women giggled, looking down at the ground.

A spavined dog of many colors and more lineages trotted under the tape, among the tangle of cables and equipment, and into the shadow at the eastern end of the plaza. Pindaric watched it with a smile and crossed over through the dust to where Martin was standing with the lawyer.

"The dog," he said excitedly.

"Sorry about that," Martin said. "We'll chase 'em all out of here."

"No, no, it's great. If some dogs run by, that'll be great. You guys had dogs back then, right?"

"Oh sure."

"You just want to get the collars off 'em," Pindaric said.

"They don't have no collars," Martin said. "They aren't that kind of dog."

"Oh." Pindaric smiled again. "Yeah. Well, great. We'll play it by ear. If they get in the picture, fine." He went off, looking distracted. Standing beside a camera in the middle of the plaza, he took a headset from a subaltern and spoke into the tiny microphone. The cameraman turned aside and Martin saw that his black T-shirt bore a red silhouette of North America and said

INDIAN COUNTRY. A little dance ensued, in which the director and the cameraman alternately peered through the viewfinder, gesturing, fiddling with the controls. Martin noticed that the extras had taken up positions at the east end of the plaza, self-consciously watching the director. One woman knelt poised before a stone *metate*, ready to grind corn—he recognized her as a Tesuque woman but couldn't recall her name. Another sat on a low wall, an unfinished basket of yucca strands in her lap. The two old men in white pants sat in the shade.

Martin looked back at the people, watching expectantly, squinting into the sun. Leaning against the wall of a house, beefy arms crossed over his chest, was the sculptor from Santa Fe, Mo Bowdre, his black hat tilted down, almost touching his sunglasses. He was talking to Tom Beck. Martin looked around the audience for the sculptor's Hopi-Anglo girlfriend and spotted her sitting with some of the Santo Esteban women. He glanced back at Bowdre, standing like an immense statue, inches taller even than the gangly Tom Beck. Martin reminded himself that the sculptor's girlfriend had some sort of role in the movie, explaining the big man's presence, but he wondered what a blind man would get out of such a vigil.

As if by some unseen signal, the human bees were now still. The Tesuque woman began to grind corn on her *metate*, the other one plucking a strand of yucca from the pile at her feet, weaving it dexterously into the basket on her lap. A voice boomed, "Quiet! Quiet on the set!" A young woman stepped forward and clacked the slate board in front of the camera and said, "Mark!" Martin held up both hands to signal his people to be quiet, a baby cried in the crowd, and Pindaric, standing behind the cameraman, turned and smiled benignly, nodding his head. Beyond the pueblo, a group of horsemen started down the hill, dust churning up around them, sunlight glinting. As they dropped out of sight beyond the buildings, a boy in a loincloth ran past the women at work, followed by another.

Pindaric, walking gingerly, crossed over to the camera pointed in the alleyway and, to Martin's surprise, tossed something in the dust in front of it. Two mangy dogs approached hesitantly, tails between their legs, confronted the object, and snarled at each other, hackles up, as horses' hooves clattered beyond the alleyway. One of the dogs lunged at the object and bolted, the other slinking off in the other direction, as two armored horsemen, riding abreast, burst out of the shadows into the plaza, horses spraying sweat and dust, bearded and helmeted riders holding their antique and clumsy-looking rifles erect, their faces implacable. The Tesuque woman leaped up off her knees and ran off camera, screaming, as two more horsemen erupted into the light, and the basket maker also leaped to her feet, yucca strands spraying, and raced after the first one, her face ashen. A third brace of horsemen thundered past the camera as Pindaric yelled, "Cut, cut! Oh, Jesus, beautiful!" and Martin, watching the two women extras running into the crowd at the other end of the plaza, still screaming, mouthed the Amu kwa equivalent of the English word *shit* as the blood in his veins turned to ice.

Pandemonium broke out among the crowd, old women leaping to their feet, teens ducking down off the roofs, small knots of people jabbering. The two extras disappeared around a building, followed by some of the crowd.

"That was great!" Pindaric exclaimed, turning to the crowd. "Hey, what the . . . ?"

Martin waved at Beck. "Come," he shouted, just as more screams pierced the hubbub of voices in the plaza and two women in skirts and blouses ran out of the dust and shadow of the alleyway, followed by several men. Martin spun around. It was his staff, the government of Santo Esteban. The horses, bunched up in a circle, began to heave and wheel, the helmeted actors sawing at the reins. "What the fuck is *this*?" one of them said. The crowd of watchers began to thin, melting away. The office staff crowded around Martin, all talking at once, as Beck approached. Over the heads of the staff, the lawyer said, "What the hell was that, Martin?"

"We've been witched," the governor said.

They found the first one—ominous in its crudity—a few minutes later, fixed to the adobe wall of the house near the spot where the basket-making extra had sat weaving yucca fibers. It consisted of nothing more than a few long strands of black human hair held together at the top by what was either glue or a piece of scalp. Some two feet long, the hairs hung from a crack between the adobe bricks. Three more hanks of long black hair were soon located in the tribal office building, one taped behind an office door, one in a supply closet, and the third inside the leg space of one of the metal desks in the office of the tribal secretary-treasurer.

Martin, feeling dizzy, had supervised the search, hanging back as Tom Beck explored the walls in the plaza and the offices. He took each one down, put it in a paper sack, and gave them to the bent old medicine man who had been summoned. The solemn old man, saying prayer in a loud singsong voice and sprinkling cornmeal from a leather pouch in a half circle around each site, took them away, returning fifteen minutes later. But for the old man's continuing song, a suffocating silence had fallen over the pueblo.

The plaza was empty except for the film crew, which had been ordered to pack up when Martin explained what had actually happened while the cameras were rolling. The horsemen had led their spooked horses out of the plaza and back up the hill to the awaiting horse vans.

Andrew Pindaric stood with Tom Beck and Mo Bowdre under the cottonwood trees near the tribal office building. A breeze set the leaves to rattling softly and innocently.

"Well, that tears it," the director said. "That just tears it. Back to boards and budgets, see if we can salvage this thing. We're jinxed, hexed, cursed."

"That's what someone wants you to think," Mo said. "Along with all these people here."

"What do they do now? I mean about all this ... witchcraft?"

Tom Beck shuffled his boots in the dust. "That old man? He'll be busy through the day and the night, exorcising it. Then another one will try to figure out who did it, who the witch is. Probably use a crystal. Quartz. They call it *makah-yohoh*. It gives second sight."

"Then what?"

"In the old days, once they figured it out, the witch was executed."

"My God," Pindaric said. "Like Salem. What do they do now? You know, these days?"

Beck shrugged. "They don't tell people like me about

that stuff. It's real private. But these people along the
river here, they've always been terrified of witches.
That's why they're so polite to each other. You never
can tell who's a witch. Could be someone in your own
family."

"So what happens?"

"Someone usually dies," the lawyer said. "After a
while."

"Jesus Christ," Pindaric said. "What century *is* this?"

"Here," Mo mumbled as if to himself, "in this kind
of thing, it doesn't make any difference what century it
is." He stood upright as a tree.

"We need to shoot more in the plaza," the director
said. "Think we can?"

"Not for a day or two," the lawyer said. "Maybe
more. It's up to Martin. How persuasive he is. This kind
of thing . . . everyone here will be shook for days. A lot
depends on that old medicine man, too. And whether
they identify the witch. The world has to be put back in
order."

"That would be nice," Pindaric said. "I guess I better
talk to Martin."

Samantha Burgess slowed down nearly to a stop, and as
she turned onto the dirt road that led to Santo Esteban,
she saw an Indian in what looked like a park ranger's
uniform hold up his hand. He stood beside a dusty
Chevrolet bearing a seal: SANTO ESTEBAN TRIBAL PO-
LICE. She braked and leaned out the window, thrusting
her press credential out as the man approached. He
looked about twenty years old, if that.

"I'm with *The New Mexican*," she said, smiling.

"Can I see your driver's license, registration, please?"

"What for? This has all the information. . . ."

He pointed behind her with pursed lips and a lift of his chin. "Stop sign back there."

"Back where?"

"At the turn, ma'am."

"And I stopped, right?"

"Well, see, ma'am," he said, trying to make his youthful countenance appear stern. "Here in New Mexico, a stop sign means that all four wheels have got to stop."

"Oh. They didn't? I mean, I never thought of it that way exactly. Do I get a ticket, officer?"

"Just a warning. This time."

Samantha smiled at him. "Thanks very much. I'm with the press and—"

"The village is closed to nonresidents today, ma'am."

"Because of the movie? See, that's what I'm here for."

The young cop looked uncomfortable. He looked down the road toward Santo Esteban, and Samantha followed his gaze. A column of vans appeared over the rise, dust rising around them in a golden cloud.

"I guess you're too late," he said. Samantha looked at her watch. Eight-thirty.

"How come they're leaving so early? They couldn't have been here very long."

The cop shrugged. "About an hour and a half, maybe two." He shrugged again. She searched his face for some sign of an expression, but the smooth features were as empty as the cloudless sky.

"Trouble?" Samantha asked, knowing it was pointless.

He shrugged again.

It's like talking to a goddamned wall, Samantha fumed to herself while she smiled again: "Well, thanks, officer."

"There's a stop sign on the way out," he said.

"Yeah. All four wheels. I got it, officer."

Jesus, she thought as she put the car in reverse. Whatever happened to the world I was living in yesterday? The vans were approaching, and she rolled up the window to avoid eating their dust. Four vans lumbered past, heaving bovinely over the ruts, rear wheels lifting plumes of fine earth into the air. Behind them, a pickup lurched into view, driven by a familiar face framed in jet-black hair. Through the dust, she glimpsed the blond beard and dark glasses of Mo Bowdre, the sculptor, in the passenger seat. Oh, right, Samantha remembered, his girlfriend Connie's an extra.

Ha!

She rolled down her window and stuck her face into an eddy of dust from the vans.

"Hey!" she shouted into the grit. "Hey!" But the pickup rolled past. Swearing to herself, she backed into the scrub and spun the wheels back onto the dirt track in pursuit, ignoring the stop sign that was largely concealed by the branches of a desert juniper.

Samantha kept the pickup's sunlit plume in sight as she rattled along the washboard road, thinking her old Toyota was going to tear apart and fall away around her piece by piece, wondering if she could put the bill for reappointing the interior—the falling plastic panels, loose nuts—on the expense account. Five minutes later, with the most profound sense of mental and physical relief, she turned right on the blessedly smooth blacktop of Route 25 and saw the pickup halfway up the rise before her. Ten minutes later and utterly puzzled, she watched as the pickup turned onto Frontage Road that led to the Downs, Santa Fe's racetrack. Even more puzzled, she watched it pull into the parking lot outside the local Channel 2 television station north of the Downs and saw Bowdre and his Indian woman enter through the glass doors.

What the hell was a blind man doing in a TV station? she asked herself. She decided to wait, approach the strange pair when they came out. There was more to this, she thought, than the Hopi woman having a role in the film. The big blind sculptor was a pal of the cop, Ramirez. They had worked together a couple of years ago on some stolen Indian artifacts—the Hopi gods. And she had heard he'd had something to do with some smugglers down near the border last summer. Now he's hanging around this film—yeah, his girlfriend is in it, but why him unless he's . . . ? Well, she'd done him a couple of favors. She reminded herself that they had, in fact, traded favors. Even steven. She opened both doors to let whatever there was of a breeze flow through the Toyota, baking in the sun.

Mo Bowdre stepped through the doorway and onto the hot pavement, a videocassette tucked under his arm. He waited while Connie emerged and stood beside him.

"Well, that was mighty accommodating of those folks," he said.

"Do you mind telling me what's up with that tape?" Connie asked.

"Now that's what you're going to tell *me*."

He heard the footsteps before the voice, which introduced itself as Samantha Burgess.

"Sure I remember you," Mo said. "What, did you switch media?"

Samantha explained that she was still an inky scribe for *The New Mexican*, covering the film, and wondered what had gone down on the set today.

"More confusion," he said, remembering that the phrase *going down* meant something altogether different now than when he had first heard it.

"I sort of figured that. I wondered what kind of confusion."

"Let me explain to you about that—"

"Mo," Connie said sharply.

"It's okay, Connie. This here is a friend. See, the place got witched."

"Witched?"

He explained briefly and reminded her that he reserved the right to ask her a favor in exchange. "Remember," he said. "My name is Informed Source."

"Much obliged, Mr. Source."

Mo heard her footsteps moving off, a car door open, and a six-cylinder Japanese engine roar.

"She's gonna need a valve job," Mo said. "Now let's go home, get something to eat, get your VCR cranked up."

The Indian kid looked as tired as Ramirez felt.

José Vigil, aged twenty-two, a jeweler from San Juan pueblo working four shifts a week as a chef in room service at La Posada de Consuela, had driven the night through from the Indian craft fair in Sedona to arrive an hour late for his new four-day stint on the day shift. The hotel manager, a kinsman from the pueblo, had chosen not to reprimand him for being late. It was punishment enough that young José had returned from what had turned out to be a notably unsuccessful fair only to find out that the police wanted to talk to him.

"Report to your station," the manager had said, "and I will let Sergeant Ramirez know you're here." The manager then relented, telling the young man that the police only wanted to ask if he had seen anything unusual the night of the murder in the hotel. The murder? José had asked. Didn't they have TV in Sedona? the manager asked in turn, explaining that José had to be the only person on the planet who had not by now heard about the murder of Gregorio Velasquez, the movie actor, by repeated blows to the head in Room 403. José, his mind reeling back to that night, replied that he hadn't been watching no TV set in Sedona, the pretty potter from Santa Clara still smiling in a niche in his thoughts.

When the manager's call got through to Sergeant Ramirez, the policeman had been fretting in his office, seeing his case against the Indians—seven of them now cooling their asses in jail—unraveling in the face of further checking. Sixteen men from Santo Esteban, many of them outspoken supporters of the tribal government, swore that the oppositionist Tupatu had been present in the kiva at the time the Moreno woman had been shot with a Winchester .30-30 on the reservation. Political differences, they told Ramirez, were not permitted to interfere with the serenity required for ceremonies. Ernesto Piño and his young cohort had, of course, been in the lockup at the time. Piño swore he had not taken the cane, that someone had put it in his old junker. A frame-up, he had said with believable passion. Meanwhile, for what it was worth, Tupatu's wife had sworn that her husband and the two young men had been in the Tupatu house—along with two others—from nine till two in the morning the night Velasquez was clubbed to death, except for brief visits to the outhouse. Had she not kept the coffee brewing while they planned the demonstration? She had named two of the other men— now in jail as well—who had said they were present during the entire night of discussions. Meanwhile the representatives of an Indian rights group, with offices in San Francisco and Washington, D.C., a collection of Indians in business suits and white women in moccasins, was milling around in front of the station, making their case to the cameras. Ramirez was about to talk to his boss, Lieutenant Ortiz, about calling the district attorney to see if there were any point in keeping any of the Indians in custody—except perhaps for the Piño kid (the cane head still needed explaining, after all)—when the manager of La Posada de Consuela called him.

Fifteen minutes later he was sitting in the hotel manager's office with the skinny young man from San Juan pueblo, José Vigil, reassuring him that he only had some routine questions.

And useless probably, Ramirez thought, but he welcomed the quiet tedium of routine. Patient, plodding, painstaking, boring routine, the bane of the cop's existence, but also—more often than not—the key to most solutions of criminal events. Go by the indispensable book.

The Vigil kid, as tired as he looked, also seemed excited, the way surprisingly many honest people do when they think they may be of help to the police in solving a crime. At about one-thirty, José Vigil said, the waiter on duty ("You talked to him, officer?") had just come back from taking an order to the third floor—maybe it was Room 307, he couldn't remember, but it would be on record—ham and eggs, breakfast in the middle of the night, and the waiter had then gone to take a leak. Before that, the waiter had bet it wouldn't be the last call, and Vigil had wagered two bucks it would, and began cleaning up the kitchen. When the waiter came back, Vigil had gone out into the back alley, well, more like a yard ("You been there? Yeah, like a cement yard.") to dump some bags in the Dumpster. Across the street ("Yeah, Rosario. I can show you.") he saw an old pickup, maybe an old Ford, red, beat-up, with its hood up and a guy bending over screwing around with the engine. There was no one else around on the street, and Vigil had called out, asking the guy if he needed help. He was black-haired, maybe medium height—about five-six, seven—Hispanic probably. No, not Indian. ("He didn't—well, you can tell, you know. We can, anyway. They don't—uh—stand the way . . .") He hadn't seen the guy's face. He had just kept screwing around with the engine for a few seconds, then got in, started it up, and drove off. He hadn't really noticed the license plate, but he seemed to remember it was New Mexico. Jeans. He was wearing jeans, and something dark, like maybe a vest. Long hair, like almost down to his shoulders.

Vigil took Ramirez back to the kitchen area where the room-service crew held forth, took him down the hall, through the metal door, out into the yard where the Dumpster sat, and pointed out where the red pickup had been parked on Rosario. Every spot on the street was now filled with cars, a teal-blue Pontiac Grand Am where Vigil said the pickup had been. The nearest street lamp was thirty feet away. Ramirez walked slowly back the way they had come, noting that the metal door to the yard could be opened from the outside.

"You keep this unlocked?"

"When we're on duty," Vigil said.

"And," Ramirez said in the hallway, "a guy could walk right down this hall and you might not see him from the kitchen."

"Yeah. I guess so. If we were busy, we wouldn't notice."

"What year would you say that pickup was, the red one?"

"I don't know. It was dark. Maybe late seventies. It looked like my father's does. His is a seventy-eight. Two fifty."

"Did you win?" Ramirez asked.

"What?"

"The two bucks. Your bet."

"Oh, yeah." Vigil grinned. "No more calls the rest of the shift. I polished some of my jewelry for the fair. Alonzo, the waiter? He studied. Going to be an accountant or something."

So, Ramirez thought, having thanked the Vigil kid and started back to the station, there was a Hispanic guy (maybe Hispanic) out back of the hotel at the right time of night who could have been in the hotel, could have waited till the waiter went across the hall to take a leak, and then walked past the kitchen while Vigil was busy screwing around with the trash, gone outside, and found his truck wouldn't start, so he was fixing it when Vigil comes out to the Dumpster. Then again, he could have been a Hispanic guy (maybe Hispanic) who returned from someplace, a girlfriend's place or something, found his truck wouldn't start, maybe something wrong with the spark plugs, hell, Ramirez knew shit about engines, and the guy didn't want any help. Maybe his girlfriend had thrown him out and he was pissed off.

When he got back to the station, he would call the hotel manager, see if they'd had anyone registered who fit the description. Probably Hispanic, about five-six, long hair, vest, drives a beat-up old red pickup that doesn't start without outpatient surgery, maybe a Ford, maybe New Mexico. Sure sounds like a patron of La Posada de Consuela, doesn't it—guy willing to pop for $125 a night for a single?

Maybe a deliveryman.

Maybe some kind of stud, what do they call 'em? Gigolo, banging one of the Hollywood ladies. He'd have to check the hotel suppliers and the city's companion agencies. He'd have to check the whole night staff again, see if they could remember seeing such a guy— now, their memory refreshed by a hint or two.

More time-consuming routine.

Grasping at hay, but what else could you do?

That evening, Buddy Foreman from Dover, Delaware, sat in his room in the Best Western motel after an early dinner, watching *Entertainment Tonight*. John Tesh solemnly explained that production of Andrew Pindaric's epic film on the Pueblo Rebellion of 1680 had been halted yet again. Already, he reminded the viewers as clips of Indian rights activists filled the screen, two deaths among the cast, called homicides by the Santa Fe police, had brought production to a halt and seven Native Americans had been jailed. Now, just this morning, an altercation of some sort had brought filming to a halt in "the ancient pueblo of San Estobel." There were, Tesh went on smoothly, rumors of witchcraft arising from ancient animosities between the Native Americans and people of Spanish descent. Old racial tensions had evidently been unleashed in the Land of Enchantment.

"Sweetwater Pictures," Tesh said, "when asked for comment, said only that they had the utmost confidence in director Pindaric and that this remarkable film about a little-known chapter in American history will be completed on schedule. Mary?"

"Alicia," Buddy said. "Did you hear that? They got witches flying around here. Halloween in summer, for chri—for heaven's sake. God, I'm glad we're leaving tomorrow. This whole place gives me the creeps. Skeletons in carts. Indians. Witches. Weirdos in the streets, with crystals. I mean, this place is sick."

"Buddy," Alicia said from the bathroom, where she was studying her face in the mirror, remembering happily that it had been her right profile—her best—that she had turned to Andrew Pindaric in the ice-cream store. "You don't have any imagination anymore."

"What's that got to do with it?" Buddy Foreman asked.

eight

"Well, let me explain to you about that," Mo Bowdre said.

He sat back in the director's chair on his patio, clutching a half-full bottle of beer. Overhead, and beyond the stucco wall that enclosed his yard, the sky was turning a deep gold. A few birds nattered and bleeped in the branches that hung over the yard, expressing their intentions to make a day of it. Three other men sat in director's chairs around an open pit in the flagstone patio, now filled with the ashes of earlier fires. A breeze rustled the leaves overhead and the temperature had begun its daily plunge, there being too little moisture in the arid air to retain the sun's daily offering. Connie Barnes lay, largely out of sight only a few feet away, enveloped in the cotton mesh of a luxurious hammock hanging from the *portal* that ran the length of the low adobe house. They had dined on copious bowls of Hopi stew—mostly mutton and hominy—a doughy blue corn "bread," and, however untraditionally, cold Mexican beer.

Andrew Pindaric had regaled them with delicious insider stories of filmdom during most of the meal, but inevitably, with Tony Ramirez and Larry Collins pres-

ent, the topic had in due course turned to the sorry
events surrounding the filming of *The Knotted Strings*.
Ramirez had explained the unraveling of the case
against the oppositionist Indians, complaining that he—
and Collins, of course—were left with no detectable
pattern to events. Events that had seemed connected,
explicable at least in outline, no longer were. Pindaric,
hunched over in his chair, his chin in his hands, elbows
on his knees, listened with the silent intensity of a heron
peering at the opaque surface of a shallow pond, hoping
to spot the familiar movement of fish.

"It's like that ram in there," Mo said, nodding in the
direction of the old stone mill house across the lawn,
now in shadow. "Or like any live animal. If its head is
in one position, then you can tell right off how its ass
is supposed to be. Or vice versa. Change the head and
the ass has to move. There's order to it, see?"

Larry Collins fidgeted in his chair. "Is this science
class, or art class? What lecture hall we in this time?"
He grinned, showing his crooked front teeth.

"The world according to Bowdre," Ramirez said.

"Now be patient, class," Mo said. "There's poetry in
anatomy. Even the anatomy of events, once you've got
'em figured out. There's rhythm, pace, meaning, some
form of symmetry . . ."

"It's art class," Collins said.

"Yeah, definitely."

Mo grinned broadly. "A good story has a beginning
and an end," he went on, and swallowed some beer.
"And these here events that have got you boys so confused are more like a case of hiccups. Spasmodic."

"Maybe it's science class after all," Collins said.

"First," Mo said, "you got the cane stolen. The old

man dies, maybe because of that. Then the actor dies. Murdered, and violently with a whole lot of malice aforethought. Then you get yourself a little demonstration that's outright against the film. Invasion of religious rights and all that. Then that woman Moreno is shot. And then the whole damn pueblo is witched—the plaza and the government. Whoever designed those events is no poet. Got 'em all out of order."

Mo leaned forward. "See?"

"No," Collins said.

"There's two kinds of events. Three of 'em are designed to create and magnify tribal dissension about the film. The cane throws doubt on the legitimacy of the government who invited you guys in." Mo nodded toward Pindaric. "The demonstration brings public attention to the dissension. And the witchcraft is supposed to scare the shit out of the tribe, make it impossible maybe for Andy here to keep working. There's a kind of nice logic to those events.

"But then you throw in a couple of murders in between. Now, those are just different kinds of acts altogether. I know, I know, people are supposed to get sick, maybe even die, if they're witched, but this witchcraft wasn't aimed at any one particular person, the way it usually is. It was a kind of general curse. See, it's like taking the cane was the ass, and witching the tribe was the head. Kind of a beginning and an end.

"But those murders in there. They're direct attacks on people from outside the tribe."

"Right," Ramirez said. "Two actors. Both Hispanic. That does make a pretty strong statement, doesn't it?"

"It's two statements we got here," Mo said. "Two voices."

"I don't see why it couldn't be a two-pronged attack," Collins said. "Fuck up the tribe to scotch the movie, and while you're at it, fuck up the movie, too."

"Inartistic," Mo said.

"What the hell has art got to do with it?"

"A lot of Indian people don't distinguish life from what we call art. They call it harmony. They think poetically, see. The cane-demonstration-witchcraft events tell a story, a psychologically coherent story. The murders tell a different story. In fact, they tell a backward story."

"What do you mean?"

"There's a nice buildup to a crescendo from the cane to the witching. But the murders are clunkers. Thud, thud. And they're in the wrong direction."

Collins sat back in his chair. "Man, I don't know what you're talking about."

"If you got someone thinking in symbolic crescendos," Mo said, "why kill a big-shot actor first, a major figure like Velasquez? He was going to play the governor, the major *major* Spaniard in the whole goddamn territory north of El Paso. You kill him right in the very hotel where all the glamorous people are staying. And *then* you go out and shoot down a bit-part actress nobody's ever heard of. And where? Standing in the boondocks on the reservation. In terms of a story, that's kind of an anticlimax."

"Opportunity?" Ramirez said.

"Oh, just random unplanned events? Hah—hah. I agree. Different minds at work there. Two stories by two different storytellers."

"This is awful abstract," Collins said.

"What else you got to go on besides what I like to

think of as forensic mythmaking?" Mo sniffed. The sky overhead was now a deepening lavender. "Think we ought to build a fire?" He stood up, walked back under the *portal*, and returned with three piñon logs. "It's the light we need, not heat, of course," he said. He put the logs in the pit, reached around behind his chair, and held a can of charcoal lighter fluid over the logs. "A long time ago," he said, "I was a Boy Scout. But since then I went high-tech. This is the end of the twentieth century, after all."

"You could've fooled me," Pindaric said. "After this morning."

Mo sprayed a stream of fluid on the logs, fetched a kitchen match from his vest pocket, and ignited it with a thumbnail.

"Now, Jesus, Mo," Ramirez said. "Watch it!"

The big man flipped the match and the logs exploded in flame. The three men lurched backward into their chairs, emitting expletives.

"Things are under control, friends," Mo said. "Don't fret yourselves none. See, I got to thinking all about this because of what Connie said."

Connie stirred in the hammock.

"What *I* said? When?"

"The other night. You said you wondered who it was who'd want to make the tribe look bad. That got me to thinking. Those oppositionists, they'd want the tribe to get so shook that the people would reject the movie. Taking the cane and all the rest, ending up with witching the place. That'd be enough. At least, that's what they would think. That's good old standard fractious Pueblo style, right, Connie?"

Connie remained silent.

"But if people think the tribe is actually killing people outright, that's a different kind of looking bad. See what I mean? Two voices. Two plans. Someone else has got it in for Santo Esteban as a whole and they're running their own number. Like they're piggy-backing their story on the true internal dissension, magnifying it. Except they got a tin ear for events."

The fire in the pit had calmed down to a gentle flame licking at the logs, and the pungent smell of piñon smoke filled the yard.

"That's real nice, Mo," Ramirez said. "But when you try to bring it down to the concrete—you know, like what really happened? Then I got a problem with it. These two separate plans."

Mo's dark glasses fixed on the policeman as if with an astonished stare.

"Your way," Ramirez said, "taking the cane was done by the Indians, probably sometime Monday night by Tupatu or one of his guys. Probably that Piño kid— thinks of himself as another Dennis Banks. Braining Velasquez was done early Tuesday morning, like an hour or so after midnight, by this mysterious outside force you've invented. How did it get a hold of the cane? Because then the head of the cane winds up in Ernesto Piño's junked car in his yard. Is this cane something like those sticks the relay racers use, passing it from guy to guy? How do you explain that?"

"Hah—hah—hah."

"What's so funny?"

"Maybe I misled you. With one of my imaginative little tales. The one about old Abe Lincoln, the sentimental country boy."

"How so?"

"Do we know for a fact, an absolute and incontrovertible fact, that it was the cane that was used to beat old Velasquez over the head? After all, it *could*'ve been the handle of a hammer. There's a lot of stuff made out of ash wood." He paused. "As you pointed out yourself, Tony. Anyway, stealing the cane was a pretty serious thing, you know. God knows what kind of retribution there is over there for screwing around with what are nearly sacred objects. Suppose that Piño kid was the one appointed to grab the cane. He wouldn't want to get caught. So he'd get rid of it . . . except maybe he just couldn't bring himself to throw away the silver head. So he hides that in his wreck."

"Why would he keep it if he knew we thought he had used the cane to kill Velasquez?" Collins asked. "He'd know we were going to hunt around his place. He's not stupid, this guy. I mean, with that about to go down, he'd get rid of the thing. It tied him directly to the killing."

"Let me ask you," Mo said, leaning forward, his glasses pointed at the fire. "When did he find out that you thought the cane was the murder weapon?"

Ramirez sighed. "When he was already in the can."

Mo crossed his beefy arms over his chest. "Q.E.D.," he said. "*Quod erat demonstrandum.* Thus it was demonstrated. Oh, the geometry of life."

Collins grinned. "Math class."

"Well," Ramirez said. "That does work out, I guess."

"And," Mo said, "all your Indian suspects do have alibis, if you want to believe 'em. So someone else is up to no good. How's that? Concrete enough for you, Collins?" Mo stood up. "See, these things were all tangled up, like a big old knot. Now we've untied the sucker. Chances are, there's someone out there who took advantage of the fact that Tupatu was making a fuss about Andy's movie and stuck his own knife in there to make the tribe look bad. Like Connie says. And now it's time for more beer."

Andrew Pindaric stirred and stood up, unfolding himself from the chair like a fluid piece of machinery. "I'll come with you, give you a hand. I'm not sure how to feel about all this. If this other guy, group, whatever, doesn't have it in for the movie itself, then he's using it for some other purpose. In a way, I'm relieved. Like it's nothing personal. But at the same time, it seems even worse. Who is it? What's the beef?"

"That's another knot we got to untie," Mo said. "And thanks, by the way, for the metaphor. Is Tecate okay with you guys? I'm out of the dark stuff."

"This place is a ghost town," said Joseph Drew Hill, craning his neck as he backed the rental car into a narrow passageway. "I mean a fucking ghost town. Tierra Amarillo, the center of the great rebellion back in the 1960s. Some visionary Hispanic nut, a guy named Tijerina, got the locals all stirred up about getting their land grants back. Wanted to start a new kingdom right here in New Mexico. Then, at some meeting or demonstration, they shot up a couple of deputies and the governor sent in the National Guard. Fucking tanks, can you believe it?"

Mona Friedman yawned. "Can we get something to eat?"

"Not in this dump." Joe Hill turned the car around, issued forth from a narrow street lined with run-down houses into the dead, open plaza where the Río Arriba courthouse stood, looking naked. It was embarrassing almost, like staring at an old man with no clothes on. "That's where the deputies got shot," he said. "Jeez, the place is deserted. I would've thought it was still the seat of power, you know? Some old *patrón* sitting on the courthouse steps, having an evening drink with his *compadres*, dispensing favors, assigning hit men, all that stuff."

"Maybe everyone is eating dinner," Mona said, slumped down in the passenger seat, both elegant knees on the dashboard.

"Okay, let's go. There was a place back on the highway." They drove out of the town, now evidently sinking under its own morbid weight, and past the valley where a few ramshackle buildings and junked cars and trucks bespoke abandoned farms. In five minutes they were seated at a table under a window in a roadside restaurant that apparently was owned and operated by Ellen Griego, whose taste in colors ran to dark brown. Everything in the place was dark brown, the tables, chairs, walls, the carpets. A few wall lights weakly fought the gloom. There was another room beyond, through a narrow doorway, and sounds of human beings issued forth from it, but the homely waitress with a plastic name tag that said DOROTHY had shown them to a table in this otherwise empty room and then vanished. The window above the table had a small round hole in it.

"A bullet hole?" Mona asked.

"Maybe a rock," Joe said.

"Great."

Dorothy approached, looking crestfallen. She held out two battered menus. "We're out of green chili stew," she said. Over her pink cotton dress, she wore an apron that proclaimed ELLEN'S—THE BEST IN MEXICAN-AMERICAN! Mona took her menu, slumped down and studied it.

"So, you're Dorothy, huh?" Joe said, a big smile on his face. "I'm Joe. This is Mona. We're from Sweetwater Pictures." Mona's head jerked up. "Yeah," Joe went on, "we're scouting the area for a major movie. Say, what do you recommend here, Dorothy, if there's no green chili stew?"

Dorothy shrugged. "It's all good."

"Maybe you could help us," Joe said. "We'd like to talk to the boss."

"She's not here."

"No, I meant the *boss*. The big guy around here. The *patrón*. You know, get his cooperation for this major motion picture we want to do. The life story of Reies Tijerina." Mona slumped down in her chair again, her face buried in the menu. "What's the *patrón*'s name? I keep forgetting." Joe smiled ingratiatingly.

"I'll be right back," Dorothy said, and walked across the room, vanishing through a dark brown door.

"What the *fuck* was that?" Mona hissed.

Joe Hill fingered a small brochure stuck in a round chromium clip attached to the salt-and-pepper-shaker holder. "Research," he said.

"You're out of your mind. We're in a restaurant with a bullet hole in the window and you're asking questions like that? Jesus, we're in another world here. You don't just—"

The outside door opened and two preposterously overweight young women encased in slacks entered, giggled, and took seats at a table across the room. They began talking in Spanish.

"Trust me," Joe Hill said.

"Great. Great." She studied the menu unenthusiasti-
cally. "I guess they can't do too much to chicken fried
steak. I'd eat anything."

"That's my girl," Joe Hill said.

Mona stared at him as if he had suddenly turned into
a frog, and what was evidently the kitchen door opened.
Dorothy emerged, followed by a man with long, nearly
shoulder-length black hair, and a chest and shoulders
like a tank. His face, behind a scraggly black mustache,
was totally without expression. He was wearing a blue
work shirt and a black leather vest.

"You the one askin' questions?" he murmured.

"Yeah, we're with—"

"You want to eat?"

"Yes, and I'd also like to—hey, you're not the
patrón, are you?"

"You want to eat, you shut up and order."

Joe Hill reddened, the heat creeping up his thick neck
to his temples. He stood up. "Look, pal, I just asked a
polite—" He broke off, staring at the point of a large
and often-honed hunting knife poised just a few inches
beyond his nose.

"Fuck off, mon. We don't serve food to you people."

Mona stood up, glaring at the two men, and stomped
toward the door. She turned to see Joe Hill, the slab-
shouldered little maniac, clenching his fists and flexing
his triceps in a silent fury as he stared cross-eyed at the
knife blade, now an inch closer to his nose. "Come
on, for Christ sake!" she said, and went through the
door. She crossed the dirt parking lot and climbed in the
car, where she sat staring icily through the windshield,

thinking maybe Eleanor Frank was right. The world would be better off without these assholes.

Joe Hill opened the door on the driver's side, saying, "Fucking hoodlum. Jesus Christ." He sat behind the wheel. "All I said was—"

"Take me to Santa Fe," Mona said quietly.

"What about dinner?"

"I said take me to Santa Fe."

"Well, shit . . ."

"You goddamned moron."

"The boys down at Channel Two were kind enough to give me this," Mo said, holding out a videocassette. They had moved inside into the living room, where Pindaric and Ramirez sat on the red sofa they had swung around to face a huge console that looked like a recording studio. Among the dials, gauges, and buttons in the gleaming machinery given over to sound production was a television screen. Collins sat on the floor near the kiva fireplace, eyeing a carved wooden saint mounted on the chimney. It held a fish in one arm and a wooden staff in the other, with a gourd of some sort on top.

"Who's that?" Collins asked.

"San Rafael," Ramirez said. "See, he's in the clothes of a pilgrim. He's a guide, a patron of travelers."

"Through this land of travail and woe," Mo said. "Hah—hah—hah. He also protects people against eye trouble. Around here, we take all the help we can get. Now take a squint at this tape."

Connie took the cassette from Mo and inserted it in the slot of the VCR. Mo sat down in his vast wing chair and said, "We took a chance that something might show up here. Studied it this afternoon. Well, Connie did."

The screen filled with the backs of people and the camera veered dizzyingly around, finally coming to rest on the faces of two angry-looking Indians. Ramirez recognized Ernesto Piño and his cohort. They were holding signs up.

"The demonstration," he said. "So what?"

"Watch," Mo said.

The camera panned around to the right, pausing on some of the faces in the crowd, then moving on.

"That's you," Ramirez said.

"None other." '

Abruptly the camera veered back to the Indians, zooming in on Tupatu. The door behind him opened and the famous face of Andrew Pindaric flashed on the screen.

"There's Andy," Ramirez said.

"Okay, that's enough," Mo said. "Let's rewind it."

"Gee, that was terrific," Collins said, smirking. " 'My day at the big Indian demonstration.' Like home movies."

The machine whirred briefly and Connie pressed a button. The tape fast-forwarded through the long shot of the Indians with the signs, panned across the crowd, and she pressed another button, stopping the video just as the camera slid past Mo, standing erect with the sunlight glinting off his dark glasses.

"You got it?" Mo asked.

"I'll be damned," Ramirez said with a sudden intake of breath.

"See the fellow in the suit? Standing next to me? Does anyone know who that is?"

Ramirez glanced at the figure on the screen. "It's that lawyer, the big shot. Templeton. Allen Templeton."

"Looks out of place there, doesn't he?" Mo said. "Smelled out of place, too."

"Huh?"

"I was standing there, listening, and I smelled this cologne. Expensive cologne. I wondered who it would be, a guy with expensive men's cologne, watching a spontaneous demonstration on a movie set. Santa Fe is pretty chichi, but men's cologne isn't the big thing here. So what was that lawyer Templeton doing there? I heard him say something, too, something that didn't seem to fit the circumstances. He said, 'charming,' kind of under his breath."

"Talking to himself?" Collins asked.

Ramirez stood up and approached the screen. "Maybe talking to this guy," he said, pointing to a man next to the lawyer, staring off to the right. "See this guy? See him?"

"Yeah," Collins said. "What about 'im? He looks like he's not paying a lot of attention."

"See?" Ramirez's voice rose. "He's got black hair almost down to his shoulders. He's Hispanic. He's got a black vest on. And see? Behind him? That looks like a red vehicle."

"So what?"

"One of the night staff at the hotel. He came back this morning and says he saw a guy out on the street about one-thirty the night Velasquez's brains were beaten in. He was out in the street, this guy he saw, wearing jeans and something dark like a vest, the witness said. He was fixing something in a red pickup parked across Rosario Street from the hotel. The guy, works in room service, saw him when he went out to dump some trash. Called out to him, and he just got in the truck and left."

"So can we find out who the Hispanic guy is?" Collins asked.

"Like finding a needle in a hay field."

"Stack," Mo said.

"Yeah, haystack, whatever. We're already running a check through DMV, looking for a red late-Seventies pickup, probably a Ford two-fifty. But you know how that is. The guy from room service thought it was a New Mexico plate, but he didn't really look at it. Guy could be from anywhere. We got his description out to all the cops in the region. What the hell, someone may know him if he's local. There aren't that many people around here anyway."

"Not such a big hay field after all, huh?" Mo said. "Maybe, you could find him through the lawyer. Templeton."

"There's not a whole lot here that says they knew each other," Collins said, standing up. "Could be just two guys happened to be in the same crowd. So the lawyer says something to himself. What was it? 'Charming.' The kinda comment some snot-nose might make looking at a rinky-dink demonstration like this."

"On the other hand," Mo said, grinning widely, "this could be the next knot on our string. We've established that someone else is out to make the whole pueblo of Santo Esteban look bad. Maybe we're looking at them right here, courtesy of Channel Two local news. How can you find out who Templeton's clients are?"

"Clients usually pay retainers," Collins said. "I can get a run on his bank account."

Pindaric looked alarmed. "You can? Just like that? Don't you need a warrant?"

"We do it all the time."

"Isn't that unconstitutional?"

Collins shrugged. "When we find we need a warrant, we get one. Nobody gets hurt but the bad guys."

Pindaric shook his head. "Well, I don't want to— uh—you know, come on like some Hollywood chapter of the civil liberties union, but it sounds illegal."

"Not as illegal as killing people."

Divorce, Olivia Waddell thought, sipping the last of a snifter of Courvoisier and unfurling her legs from beneath her to reach for the TV selector. She pressed the green button and a local car dealer's grinning face imploded and disappeared with a click. She leaned back into the cushions on the sofa, cluttered with legal briefs and documents, and sighed. The living room of the rented house was classic Santa Fe style, the old log beams—what were they called, *vigas*?—overhead, the voluptuous belly of the kiva fireplace, the curved archways, tiled floors bearing Oriental rugs, the happy miscegenation of Spanish and Indian motifs in the wall hangings, the unisex rawhide-and-bronze shaman with a triangular head standing in a corner staring blankly into its soul with cutout eyes. The sculpture had been made by a man named Kelly, who had also made the humpbacked flute player named Kokopelli, fashioned after the ubiquitous petroglyph figure of fertility, that stood in a recessed and arched niche near the chimney, cleverly lit by an overhead spotlight.

Like a foreign country, she thought, exotic but comforting, and all hers for now thanks to a divorce. It had

been one of those noticeable but unusually tidy Hollywood divorces, and part of the settlement had been this
house, sold to a local real-estate company that had decided that since the market was a bit viscous, they
would rent it. It was not the first time that Olivia
Waddell had benefited from divorce one way or the
other, however temporarily.

The unencumbered life, she thought—free of posses-
sions, and possessors. It had its disadvantages, of
course, but they were far outweighed by the lightness of
freedom, the airy sense of dancing into and through this
world, living out her personal bargain with gravity, particularly the staggering weight of marital and other economic responsibilities that drove so many to such
desperate acts. Olivia, on the other hand, was free to
bolt at any time and without a moment's notice or regret. So buoyantly free was she that she hadn't so much
as glanced at a paycheck for more than a decade, and
had not felt the need even to balance her checkbook for
years. Every now and then, she merely cleared out the
excess and told the bank to invest in an IRA. Since she
had more than enough of it, money simply bored her,
though she knew the power it had over most people,
even and perhaps especially the rich. Olivia Waddell
was anchored to the world only so long as her lagoon in
the ocean of the Law remained interesting.

And now her particular lagoon was challenging indeed, especially in the matter of *The Pueblo of Santo
Esteban v. the United States* scheduled for a hearing on
the merits next week. She had ruled, in the preliminary
hearing, that the newly found land-grant document
would be admissible, over the vehement protests of the
U.S. attorney representing the government, who had

raised a series of razor-sharp objections based on various judicial rulings in other courts on other matters, about the sudden appearance of the document. The young lawyer, Beck, representing the pueblo, had told the court how the document had been found serendipitously in and among some obscure records concerning a different pueblo in the state archives and how its validity as an historic document had been attested to by a variety of experts. After hearing all of the U.S. attorney's objections, Olivia had explained her ruling on the technical matters raised and then took off her gold-rimmed glasses and stared down at the man pleasantly.

"In addition," she said in a firm but conversational tone, "it simply does not seem reasonable to penalize the plaintiff for the historic incompetence of the government's system for filing important documents. Retaining such material in an accessible manner would seem to me to be one of the first duties of stewardship. And I have noticed that, in their long history, the territory and the state of New Mexico and the federal government have often taken a rather whimsical approach to this duty. So this court will hear the claim."

Deciding the matter would, of course, be an entirely different bit of reasoning. She was well aware of what the main lines of arguments would be. If the government were ordered to return public lands to a tribe, lands that in this case the United States Forest Service had bought nearly a century ago in perfectly good faith and according to then-current principles and law, then a Pandora's box of such claims would open, putting the entire legal underpinnings of the structure of the public land system at risk. In other words, it was a political case, pure and simple, though an amplitude of law would be cited. On the other hand, citing other law, the plaintiff would stand implacably before the bench, waving its newfound document and insisting on simple and innocent fairness. And neither of the two bodies of law that would be cited would, in fact, have much to say to the fundamental issue, which was that two irreconcilable visions of the world were confronting each other—one tribal and religious, the other national and economic—and the Law simply had nothing to say as these two trains hooted in the night.

And now there was yet another complexity, another claim covering some of the same land—raised by that lawyer Templeton in behalf of some Hispanic family: Torres. She would have to look at it more closely in the morning. Maybe the hearing would have to be postponed.

Judge Waddell was known to do more than the required homework, reading widely in any area of concern that came before her. She had read up on the minimal historical record of these Pueblo people, and the local television newscast had sent her mind back into some old events. There were, he had said, rumors of witchcraft at Santo Esteban and a local "expert" had opined on how this fit into the turmoil at the pueblo that had already apparently led to two homicides connected with the movie that was under way. Olivia recalled reading about a case in the nineteenth century when four men from one of the pueblos had been arrested for homicide. They had explained that they had merely acted in accordance with the laws of the tribe. A witch had been identified among them, and they, as enforcers, were asked by the village chief to accord the witch the customary punishment: execution. Upon hearing such a straightforward and utterly outlandish admission, the judge had simply stopped the trial and sent everyone home.

She wished it could be so simple nowadays.

The more Joe Hill thought about it, the more focused he grew.

I'm like a laser, he thought, ever unable to be completely unaware of himself as actor, participant. I am a rod through which rays of light become coherent, focused, a force like lightning. Well, lightning is electricity, he thought, not light ... screw physics, bunch of nerds, these physicists, with their pockets lined with ballpoint pens.

A distraction.

The source of Joe Hill's clarifying anger pulsed again, there being nothing like humiliation to pump the engine of rage. Thoughts flitted through his mind— Mona Friedman's long slender legs, the pure, irritable lust that had driven her, the production wonks wanting history rewritten, turning his story—his truth—into dog meat for the masses, his banishment from the set ... his mind was ripped, jerked back and forth, spinning, spiraling.

He had dropped the kinky Mona off at her hotel after an hour of absolute fucking ice-cold glacial goddamn silence, sitting there in the car with her head turned, looking out the side window as they plummeted through northern New Mexico. He had watched her hips sway under those black slacks as she crossed the sidewalk and went through the door of the hotel. Not a word. Not a glance. Not even much of a sway.

He had started with beer. Somewhere he had parked

the goddamn car and walked, wandering into this cock-roach pit of a bar frequented by a handful of suspicious-looking Hispanics, and he'd ordered a beer and another as his mind began to seek order out of the seething bubble of lava boiling up from below. The bar consisted of one large, low-ceilinged room with a pool table at one end and a bar that somehow looked fortified at the other. There were a couple of flea-market tables with chairs to match scattered around the cement floor under naked lightbulbs. It was a gloomy dump, depressive, hopeless.

Later he had switched to tequila—straight, over ice—and made it clear by what he imagined to be a whole-body glower that he didn't want to be disturbed. The others in the bar, carrying on sporadic conversations in near whispers, regarded this slab-shouldered intruder as one might a black widow spider—something potentially dangerous but amusing to stomp on whenever the time came.

Joe Hill was too preoccupied, however, to read the force fields playing around him like distant sheet light-ning on a summer night in upstate New York. Instead the tequila loosened the connections between the neu-rons in his brain, rehooking them into an ever more simple and direct explanation of his troubles—an emerging target for all his gathering fury.

"Hey, amigo," he said to the bartender with a wolfish grin and a plan forming in his brain, a plan of Heming-wayesque simplicity.

"Yeah?" the man said without interest. "Another?"

Hunched over, elbows on the bar and his head sunk down between his thick wrists, Joe Hill said, "Yeah, and I want to talk to you."

The man approached with a half-empty bottle of José Cuervo and Joe grinned up at him, seeing him for the first time. A middle-aged guy with a sorrowful mustache and a big belly. Eyes like brown glass that has been made dull by too much time in the desert sun. "I need some help, need to find out about a guy. One of your people." Joe Hill went on to describe his target, not seeing the bartender's gesture. Abruptly, he was lifted off the bar stool by many hands and, after an incomprehensible squall of violence, found himself lying on the sidewalk, his head over the curb, his cheek touching the street.

For the life of him, he couldn't figure out what had happened. It occurred to him momentarily to get up, walk back in the shitcan of a bar, and break every fucking Hispanic skull in the goddamn room, pow, one after the other. Instead he shut his angry eyes, gathered his strength and his newly focused resolve, and got up off the cement with blood in his eyes. Without even a glance over his shoulder at the bar entrance, he stalked off into the night.

Sergeant Ramirez closed the creaky wooden gate behind him, and Mo Bowdre leaned his beefy forearms on it. The night had cooled off considerably—down to about sixty. There was plenty to think about, plenty to do first thing in the morning.

"Good night," the big man said. "Drive safely and all that." He turned and disappeared into the shadows. The two other men, Larry Collins and Andrew Pindaric, stood a few yards away on the sidewalk under the thin light of a street lamp. Except for a barely perceptible breeze, Canyon Road was silent. Across the narrow road the houses were dark and, downhill, several cars were parked a bit haphazardly along the road, outside wheels in the road itself.

"Where you parked?" Ramirez said. "We're up there." He gestured uphill with his head.

"Down there," the director said.

"You got to take a left at the intersection. It's one-way after that," Ramirez said. "Well, good night. We'll talk tomorrow."

They heard a wheezing rumble and peered down the hill. A truck, wide as it was old, was coming toward them in the gloom. It slowed down about fifty yards away and crept through a narrow part of the road. Ramirez could make out that it was loaded some six feet higher than the cab with something—a rickety pile of junk, box springs, God knew what.

"Maybe some guy getting an early start to the flea market," Ramirez said, watching as the truck, now crawling, leaned ludicrously far over to its left. "The crap people buy ..."

"God, that's right where my ..." Pindaric said, and the three men watched as the load in the truck shifted and what seemed to be a metal box spring slid off as the truck lurched forward.

There was a clank as the box spring hit a parked car. Pindaric said, "Shit!" and took two steps down the road when the yellow flare went off, then orange, and the thunder slammed into them.

Collins bolted downhill, and Ramirez leaped into the middle of the road, holding up his hand to the truck. "Stop! Police! *Policía!*" It was unnecessary. The truck had already stopped, most of its load thrown across the road, smashing the large picture window of a house

across the street. Ramirez approached the truck in the
wan glare of its one headlight, and a man stepped out
of the cab, gibbering in Spanish. Ramirez grabbed him
by the shirt and pulled him uphill, away from the truck
and the fire he could see behind it. Collins raced past
them, up the hill.

"Get down, for chrissakes!" the agent shouted, plow-
ing into the spindle-shanked director, as a far more intense flare fired the night and Andrew Pindaric's dark
green aerodynamic XJS Jaguar with the specially engi-
neered transmission courtesy of Mario Andretti's pit
doctor was blown into fragments that sprayed like
shrapnel into the old adobe walls of the homes that
lined the quaint and narrow lane called Canyon Road.

nine

At least, Sergeant Anthony Ramirez comforted himself, he was racking up a lot of leave time. It was seven-thirty in the morning, Saturday. He bit off a crescent of nail from his little finger and spat it across his desk and wished that circumstances had allowed him to pursue his degree in archaeology. Dead people, sure, but long dead. Nobody gave a shit why they died except in the most abstract sense. Patterns of mortality among the pre-Mimbres settlements of southern Arizona, or some such crap. He wondered momentarily how many ways the pre-Mimbres people had invented to wipe out their fellow man—probably a pretty simple arsenal. Club 'em over the head, stick 'em with a spear, drown 'em in some perennial stream—not too many options. Let 'em croak from some disease and claim it. Hey, I'm a witch. Keep your ass away from *me*, man, I'm dangerous. That was supposed to be a time when things were pretty peaceful, all the little guys growing corn and praying and all, but chances were the archaeologists one day would find that about two percent of the population was homicidal and kept everyone else in the pueblo in a state of perpetual fear.

Just like now.

Methods didn't make any difference, Ramirez thought glumly, but God knew there were a hell of a lot more ways of chopping down people now than then.

Progress. Blow up a man's car. First you got to invent the wheel. Then the engine. Then the bomb. There it is, he thought, the history of technology in a nutshell.

He held the telephone receiver cradled in his hand, on hold. On hold.

Come *on*! Goddamn it!

I got to get some sleep, he thought, real sleep. Like maybe six big ones in a row.

The guy who had arrived from Albuquerque an hour after the explosion, the bomb guy, had said there wasn't enough of anything left for him to tell much. He got all puzzled and interested about how it had gone off when the box spring hit the car. Instead of when the ignition got turned on, which was standard among your run-of-the-mill professional car bombers. It had to be some mechanical device that tilted when the weight of a man—or a falling box spring—was supplied. An amateur, the bomb man had said. Primitive, he had said, what with electronics being what they were these days. And stupid, too, since any drunk staggering around Canyon Road that night could have stopped and sat on the low-slung little Jaguar and blown his ass into the next county.

Damn lucky it was only a box spring and a truckful of junk. Well, they'd probably never figure it—hell of a blast, dynamite most likely, hell, anyone with access to a construction site can get dynamite, it's a wonder more people don't use it, you know, for homicides—you can get rid of a hell of a lot of evidence with dynamite—

like here. Virtually nothing left of the bomb or the trigger.

They'd know more in the morning, maybe. But they don't get a lot of this kind of thing. Street gangs in Albuquerque aren't into blowing stuff up yet.

God help us, the bomb man said, when they find out how much fun dynamite is.

Ramirez waited on the phone, knowing it was too early to get any further report about the bomb, but he was not about to let his counterparts in Albuquerque imagine that the Santa Fe cops were anything but, as he put it, eager beagles.

"Sergeant Ramirez?" said a woman's voice. "They say there's nothing to report. To call back maybe about ten."

"Bueno," he said, and hung up.

Breakfast came to mind, and Ramirez slipped out the back way to see if he could avoid the press. A small pack accosted him in the parking lot and he explained smoothly that he didn't know much about any car bombing. He was homicide and evidently no one had been killed. Across Cerrillos Road, he bought a copy of *The New Mexican* from a red metal box and went into the doughnut shop. A few moments later, seated at a plastic table with a large Coke and a pair of glazed, holeless doughnuts sprinkled with powdered sugar, he glanced at the horoscope: Pisces. He didn't put much faith in such things, none at all in fact, but it was harmless enough to see what the fruit loops had cranked out. The horoscope writer, who typically had it in for Pisces, told him that if he buckled down and finished up some ugly chores, he would finally feel better about himself.

Six days, he thought to himself. Six days earlier and

I'd've been an Aquarius. They're always telling the Aquarius people how their creative genius is going to flower even more brightly today, once they answer the phone and gracefully accept the eighteen million dollars they won in the lottery, or some crap like that.

There was, of course, nothing in the paper about the car bomb. Only more non-news that the PD had fed the wolves yesterday.

Ramirez was having trouble focusing his mind. Within minutes of the blast, Mo Bowdre had reappeared, standing behind the gate, sniffing the air and saying dynamite.

"Listen, Tony," he had said, "if there's one damn odor in the world that I know, it's dynamite."

And then he had left, disappearing into the dark behind the adobe wall around his place, saying he'd check in tomorrow. Usually, Mo Bowdre hung around any situation that was out of the ordinary, like some busybody *chismoso*. Of course! It was dynamite, in the mine, that had ... Ramirez smiled sadly. Some things were too much even for a brave man in the small hours of the night.

He stood up, thinking that he had to stop eating this kind of food, and returned to his office, where he found Larry Collins slouched down in one of the little chairs in front of his desk, his feet crossed over the arm of the other one.

"You eat yet?" Ramirez asked.

"The FBI never eats, never sleeps, never even takes a leak. We just spend every hour of every day rooting out evil."

"Yeah, like the post office in rain, sleet, snow."

"We get snow days," Collins said brightly. "Here,

look at this." He tossed a few sheets of paper on Ramirez's desk. "It's a list of everyone who's paid that lawyer Templeton more than a thousand dollars in the last year. I figured he wouldn't make out his mother's will for a retainer smaller than that."

"So what's there?"

"Templeton's a busy man, lot of big-time clients."

"Doesn't he have that little place over on De Vargas? Just him. No partners. How does he handle it?"

"He pays a few local firms to do a lot of the scut work. Cuts 'em in on fees, sometimes just pays 'em outright. He's almost like a high-priced legal consultant. An arranger. Like a lot of Washington lawyers."

Ramirez lifted up the sheaf of papers. "You got all this from Washington overnight?"

"Came in on your fax twenty minutes ago. Big Brother knows all."

Ramirez looked down the list, recognizing several chichi galleries in town and the names of several prominent Santa Feans. Sprinkled among them were about twelve corporations with out-of-state addresses. A few insurance companies from the midwest that he recognized, a couple of what were evidently Texas oil-drilling consortiums and a couple of mining companies, and the outfit with a name that sounded like something out of *Star Trek*, a wholly owned division of Martin-Marietta. Then his eyes rested on the name, Montezuma Automotive, Inc. from Los Angeles, California.

"What do you suppose Montezuma Automotive in L.A. does?" Ramirez asked.

"It's a big auto-parts operation. Sells in California and three other states, including this one. Specializes in parts for antiques, classics. Machine tools a lot of special-order stuff. Real big in the low-rider market. Makes those hydraulic things that lifts 'em up, lowers 'em."

"How do *you* know that?"

"Big Brother. I told you."

Ramirez shook his head and pondered the list. "So this automotive-parts company paid Templeton five thou in February this year. Not one of Templeton's best clients, it looks like."

He looked through the papers. "What's this? On the bottom?"

"It's a printout of the officers for each of the corporations on the list. The guy who runs Montezuma is named Torres, Manuel Torres. Ring a bell?"

Ramirez glanced up, frowning. "No. Why should it?"

"He was from here, New Mexico."

"You think all us Hispanics know each other or something?"

Collins shook his hand up and down. "Whew! The boy is grumpy this morning. Take it easy. I looked him up while you were eating breakfast. His old man was Geraldo Torres."

"Holy shit! The *patrón*."

"Died two years ago, according to your files in there," Collins said.

"So the old man's son started a business in L.A., hires Templeton to represent him. So where does that leave us?"

"On your own, Tony. On your own."

Ramirez looked at the agent, who was examining something on his own shirtfront.

"Meaning?" Ramirez said.

"I got another little message, along with that stuff. They want to transfer me."

"When, where?"

"Monday they want me to report to the field office in Miami. Miami, Florida. You ever been there?"

Ramirez shook his head. "I hear it's real muggy there."

"So I heard." The agent shifted in his chair, crossed one ankle over his knee, and stared at his running shoe. "I faxed 'em back, told 'em to shove it."

"Huh?"

"I resigned. I'm a private citizen. Well, it'll take a day or two to process the paperwork."

"You quit? Just like that?"

"Yeah. I like it here. I don't want to go chase illegal Haitians around the fucking Everglades." He stood up.

"So what are you going to do?" Ramirez said.

"Now? Get one of those ugly doughnuts across the street. I'm allowed to eat now."

"No, man, what are you going to *do*?"

"I was thinking," Collins said, showing his crooked front teeth in a grin, "maybe open a dance studio. I'll be back in a few minutes. I'm still officially on this thing." He disappeared through the door, then poked his head back in. "There's one more thing in there that'll interest you. On the last sheet."

Joe Hill had arisen from the tangle of sheets on his bed in his room in the Best Western motel after two hours of purposeful marching in the streets of Santa Fe in search of his car and three more of sleep. The remnants of José Cuervo Gold still heated his metabolism and oiled the single-mindedness of his goal. Fumbling into his clothes and cursing, he stomped down the outside staircase and found his car, fuming about the absolute anonymity of the typical goddamn American car, all of 'em designed by some machine with one stupid idea. . . .

An hour and a half later, at approximately eight o'clock A.M., as the police report would later state, Joe Hill pulled up outside Ellen Griego's restaurant, featuring the finest Mexican-American cuisine, and pounded on the glass door next to the window that had a bullet hole in it. Receiving no immediate satisfaction, he kicked the door in and plunged into the deserted brown dining room of the restaurant, shouting more or less unintelligibly about shitheads and knives. At that point, Ellen Griego herself peered out of the door between the kitchen and the deserted dining room, shouting something about not being open for breakfast, then shrieked, "Ramón! Ramón!"

Before her spindly, gray-faced husband, Ramón, could take two terrified steps, Joe Hill seized Ellen by the folds of her neck and demanded to know the whereabouts of the shithead with the knife. Ellen shrieked yet again and all two hundred and forty pounds of her fell to the floor, dragging her assailant down with her.

As they thrashed in the doorway, Ellen's husband, Ramón, grabbed the phone, punched out a familiar number, picked up a large iron skillet, and spoke into the phone. Then he proceeded to the doorway and, on his second attempt, brought the skillet down on the head of the insane killer who was lying on top of his wife, saying "Wait, wait, wait. . . ."

With nothing better to do that she could imagine, Samantha Burgess sat in her car on the street near the police station, watching squad cars come and go and eyeing the little crowd of her fellows from the fourth estate who were looking bored on the sidewalk. Her mind idled in a reverie, and she shook her head into alertness when she saw Mo Bowdre, the sculptor, emerge from a compact yellow taxi, a laborious process something like a bear leaving its den for the first time since hibernating. Within seconds she was walking beside him.

"Mr. Bowdre, it's me, Samantha Burgess."

The big man stopped and turned to face her. He grinned broadly. "You're following me," he said. "I'm honored."

"No, no. But I figure you're involved in this—"

"The murders?" Bowdre beamed. Several members of the press pack began moving closer. "Yes. I am. I can no longer bear the guilt. I'm turning myself in. Voluntarily, you'll notice." He began to shuffle. "Perhaps you could lead me to the door, Ms. Burgess."

"This is bullshit," Samantha said, but the other reporters were beginning to buzz. A flash flared. She took him by the elbow. "What are you doing?" she asked in a vehement whisper, but the sculptor merely walked on by her side, smiling. She looked behind her. "You jerks," she said in a loud voice. "He's kidding!" She left him at the big bronze doors, turned to laugh in scorn at her colleagues who were still behind her, and realized that she still didn't know what the hell was going on.

A bit preoccupied, Mo Bowdre stood in the reception area of the Santa Fe Police Department rather like an ice floe without an ocean current to propel it, listening to people walking back and forth and the confusion of voices.

"Yes?" A familiar voice to his left.

"Officer . . ."

"It's Inez, Mo."

"Inez. You smell sweet as roses today."

"Harassment," Inez called out sotto voce. "I'm being sexually harassed."

"Hah—hah—hah."

"You're here to see Sergeant Ramirez?"

Mo nodded, and the young officer propelled him through the comings and goings in the reception area and through a door where he could hear a lot of telephones and cursing and knew his way.

"Maybe it's hyacinth," he said, and in measured steps walked along the wall until he stood in the doorway of Tony Ramirez's office. He heard the policeman say, "Look, you can put this Hill guy in the can, yeah, whatever you want, but bring the other guy, Gallegos. Can you find him? You get him, bring him in here, okay? *Bueno.*"

Mo reached out and found a chair. He eased his bulk into it and smiled as Tony Ramirez replaced the receiver.

"Hill? Did you say Hill? That couldn't be our writer, could it? Joseph Drew Hill, the steward of truth in fiction?"

"What are you talking about?" Ramirez said. "Yeah. Hill, the screenwriter. Sheriff from Río Arriba called, they picked up this guy Hill, busted into a restaurant like some kind of maniac, grabbed the owner, an old woman, turns out he was looking for our guy."

"You're ahead of me," Mo said.

"We know who he is, a guy named Gallegos."

"You're ahead of me still," Mo said. "What guy?"

"The guy, the guy with the vest, the guy the kid saw outside the hotel the night that actor Velasquez got killed. Same description. The sheriff called, said this nut Hill broke into a restaurant up near Tierra Amarillo, on the highway, screaming about this guy. Apparently this guy chased him off with a knife yesterday, last night, and so the nut Hill goes back this morning on some kind of revenge trip. Anyway, he describes the guy, and the sheriff says it fits the description we've got out, so he calls. Those guys up there, that's unusual they'd call. But they owe me a couple, and the sheriff says he likes to see justice done, and all that, and can he have the Californian, the Hollywood guy."

"He's from upstate New York."

"Same thing. Not from Río Arriba County. Anyway, this guy Gallegos that Hill was after. Drives a red eighty-two Ford two-fifty. They know where he lives, well, where his people live. Hangs out with an uncle in Truchas. They're gonna go pick him up."

"So," Mo said, "in the most wildly circumstantial manner, you've solved all those crimes we were talkin' about last night?" He had heard the rare, metallic excitement in his friend's voice. "There's more," he said. "Right?"

"Yeah, a bit."

Mo wished he didn't have these conversations like this, not being able to see expressions—oh, yes, he could hear the change in his friend's voice, he could imagine . . . What could he imagine? Goddamn it, he was sick of imagining. Suddenly he was depressed. It came upon him from time to time, and he knew it was nothing but the rankest self-pity, and he *snarled* at himself. . . . Jerk! You've got life anyway.

Like a mantra.

You've got life anyway. What did Tony Ramirez look like? Maybe five-ten, presumably dark-haired, probably black-haired—damn! You didn't just go up and run your hands around a guy like that, find out what his features are like. A voice. A voice. More than that.

You've got life, you've got life. The man's excited. You can be part of it. You *are* part of it.

He wished Connie were with him. It would be better. Once, last year, in a tight spot, she had said, like God speaking, "I am his eyes."

God should speak for all of us, Mo thought. Well, maybe He was She. Maybe whatever the hell it was that we think about at the oddest goddamned times doesn't have a gender. And what does God have to do with it? This man here, Tony, thinks he's found the perp, the second part of the story, the non-Indian tin-eared poet of mayhem, the second part of my story. I should be pleased.

Right. I am pleased. My friend is succeeding, the saints look down upon him and smile, oh, yes. Let's knit up the raveled sleeve of . . . What?

I wish Connie were here. I like it when she's here. I really and actually and down deep somewhere south of my brain and north of whatever else I got working for me know, *know* goddamn it, that this woman's absence makes me blind. Not some damned explosion in the mine, not some dynamite, not any of that, that's just Godwork, deciding how things are goin' to be overall.

Well, I could say that better. Her *presence* lets me live in a colorful world again. That's it.

Goddamn it, I got me a whole lot of leeway here, still.

"What's that again?" Mo asked.

"You asleep?"

"No, I was thinking. Now what the hell were you saying?"

The phone rang on Sergeant Ramirez's desk.

"Yeah. Yeah? You got him. *Bueno, bueno.* So you'll bring him down. And what? Read it to me. Yeah, out loud. A bill of sale. No charge. Montezuma Automotive, Inc. From L.A. Well, see, you got a big shot there. A real big shot. Hey, *compadre,* thanks."

Ramirez hung up the phone and said, "We got him."

"Who?"

"The guy, the guy. He's a nephew of Manuel Torres. And Manuel Torres is the nephew of the guy who used to *run* Río Arriba County."

"I remain in the dark," Mo said.

"And Manuel Torres's aunt has filed a suit through Manuel's family corporation in L.A., in the court of claims. You know, that new judge—Waddell. They want to recover the land her family lost—an old land grant from Spain. They say it was illegally taken from them and then transferred to the National Forest."

"Where have I heard this before?" Mo said.

"The land overlaps the land Santo Esteban is claiming. It's like a counterclaim. See? And her dead husband's great-nephew, Rafael Gallegos, fits the description of the guy we're looking for, the one in the TV news film. See how that works?"

"Hah—hah. Maybe you better slow down."

"Yeah, this could be hard for a gringo. Gallegos, the guy who we're looking for, is the nephew

of Manuel Torres of L.A., but used to be from here.
Manuel Torres's aunt is the sister of the old *patrón*. And
the corporation hired a lawyer named Templeton."

"Our . . . ?"

"The same."

"I presume that our rocket of an FBI man scooped
this all up with his electronic Hoover vacuum cleaner?"

"Most of it," Ramirez said. "He quit, you know."

"Quit? Quit what?"

"The FBI. Didn't want to go to Miami."

"Well, I'd say that's good thinking. What's he going
to do with himself? He don't have a whole array of talents, as I see it."

"Says he's going to open a dance studio."

With yet another strange notion impinging on his life,
Mo's mind strayed yet again. Dance studio. Well, of
course, he's kidding around. But dance . . . it was not an
art form Mo could any longer appreciate, not that he
ever had. He wondered, and not for the first time, why
cooking was not considered one of the fine arts—
something that appealed to the sense of smell and taste.
Why did what everyone thought of as fine arts refer
only to the eyes and ears? Sensory imperialism. Now
that would make a hell of a lawsuit, wouldn't it?

He wrenched his mind back to the stuffy little office
of his friend Ramirez.

"Collins quit?" he said. "Well, under the circumstances, maybe he'll be more use as a civilian, or whatever the hell you call it."

"How so? What circumstances?"

"The need to bend the law?" Mo suggested.

Mo heard Ramirez lean back in his chair. "Listen,
amigo. This is police business now. You were real help-

ful the other night—clarifying some things, finding that tape, all that. But now the Santa Fe Police Department is going to be interrogating this guy Gallegos, who probably did those killings. So we'll wrap this thing up—with any luck."

"You think you're gonna pin those murders on this Gallegos boy, and tie him and his uncle in Los Angeles, and *his* aunt and her land claim, and Templeton the lawyer all up in a neat little old square knot?"

"That's what we're going to try to do."

"And the car bomb?"

"That, too. Gallegos. You'll see."

"So you'd have to guess that the Torres family and the lawyer Templeton thought their claim'd do better if they got loyal young whatsisname—"

"Gallegos."

"Yeah, Gallegos—to run around, make the Indians look even more messed up than they are. That way the judge'd think the Indians weren't deserving, but the Torres family was, maybe by default, so the Torres family gets the land, and the lawyer gets a bigger fee."

"Right," Ramirez said. "Like we were thinking last night. It may take a few days, but we'll do it."

"And what you're saying to me is, basically, butt out."

"Basically."

"Well, that's good, Tony. That's just damned good. Now I can get back to my world—making art. Hobnobbing with people of wealth and ree-fined taste. Martha Wilamette—you know, she's got that big old place up off the Old Santa Fe Trail? She's having a do this very afternoon, all the swells of the Santa Fe scene. And me, of course. You know, I don't see how you put up with all this reality, day after day."

Mo made a sweeping and all-inclusive gesture with his paw and stood up.

"The rewards of doing the people's work are very great," Ramirez said.

"See you around," Mo said, and walked out of the office with measured steps and a happy grin on his face.

Again in the bustling reception area, Mo Bowdre cautiously retraced his steps toward the heavy doors of the main entrance.

"Hey, Bowdre!"

It was Collins, the new Fred Astaire.

"Collins. What's all this I hear about you—hah—hah. I didn't know white boys from New York had rhythm."

"So Tony told you?"

"Yeah. Now that's a bit of a shock."

"Life goes on."

"How long before you're officially mustered out?" Mo asked.

"A day or two."

"Are you totally disgraced or can you still get information out of the Hoover Memorial Tomb?"

"It depends."

"Well, let me try something on you for size." The big man reached out and took the agent by the elbow. "There's a saloon up on Canyon Road not far from my place. We can talk up there. Come on. You got a car, right?"

And Special Agent Larry Collins found himself in the odd position of being led by the elbow out of the halls of law enforcement by a blind man.

* * *

White-gold sunlight slanted over the adobe wall encir-
cling a meticulously tended greensward that sloped to
the southwest and lit a luxuriant array of irises, the last
of the season. It was said that Martha Wilamette—or
more accurately, the old Basque gardener she employed—had worked some special horticultural magic
to create irises that lasted so late into the summer. It
was also said that Martha Wilamette had paid a small
fortune for this feat of peasant genetic engineering, but
it never would have occurred to any of the forty-odd
people standing on the grass in the sunlight to question
Martha Wilamette's devotion to irises. The beauty of
the rice-paper-like blossoms, various shades of blue and
violet and purple, swaying above their pale green samu-
rai leaves, was deservedly a local legend in a stratum of
Santa Fe society where the value of beauty was as fundamental an assumption as the propriety of wealth.

Olivia Waddell murmured appreciatively, and her
hostess, whom she had only just met, made a comment
about addiction. "Over there," she said, "is my Moon
Garden. Later on this evening, it will be filled with
white blooms." She laughed pleasantly, and it struck
Olivia Waddell that her hostess was one of those people
of such natural aristocracy that they never felt the need
to put on airs.

"And that bear," Olivia said, looking at one of the
half-dozen large sculptures here and there around the
lawn, most of them abstract constructions that the judge
thought crude. "It's wonderful. It seems so full of . . .
vigor." The bronze bear, about twelve feet high, rose
nearly to a standing position, emerging from a tortured,

abstract base, the very contrast lending the animal its
grace and athleticism.

"It's one of my favorites. It's a Bowdre." Martha
looked around her domain. "You'll meet him. He's not
here yet, but I'm sure you'll know when he arrives."
She laughed again. "He's hard to overlook. Just like his
bear. His first words will be 'Martha, you still haven't
moved that there bear, like I told you to.' You wait and
see. He thinks the wind makes it sing off-key."

Several minutes later Olivia found herself among a
small group standing beside a linen-covered table with
a large silver bowl of shrimp and an array of brightly
colored exotic fruits cut up with Oriental precision. The
movie director Andrew Pindaric towered above the
small group, smiling boyishly as he told about how his
Jaguar had been blown to smithereens the night before.
The explosion, of course, had been on the national news
throughout the day—an odd piece of what the police
had called random violence, but what the press, who
were up to simple addition, had reported darkly as potentially another piece of sabotage of the film *The Knotted Strings*. The Santa Feans who were listening to
Pindaric's account were not about to ask the director
about such speculation, but Judge Waddell felt no such
constraint.

"It sounds," she said, "like part of the problem
you've been having all along. People here with elegant
cars usually get them scratched or dented, as I understand it. Not blown up."

"Yes, well, I've thought of that, of course," Pindaric
said, looking uncomfortable. From the gate near the
sprawling Spanish mission house, loud laughter erupted,

and looking over, Pindaric said, "There's Mo Bowdre. The sculptor."

As the small group looked toward the gate Olivia leaned toward the film director and in a quiet voice said, "Actually, I would like to talk to you about all that business. It's a matter of some concern—"

"Martha! Doggone it, you still haven't moved that there grizzly, like I said you should."

The voice boomed over the grass, followed by a staccato barking. Olivia looked toward the gate and saw a large man with a blond beard, dark glasses, and a black cowboy hat perched on his big head. Next to him was a black-haired woman, an Indian, in a brightly flowered dress.

"Connie here," the sculptor carried on in a loud voice, "says you still got it in the same place."

Martha Wilamette stepped across the grass to the big man, stood on her toes, and bussed him on the cheek, apparently saying something in his ear. He erupted again: "Hah—hah—hah." Certainly, Olivia thought, a bull in the china shop, but her hostess seemed genuinely pleased to see him. And of course, he *had* been invited.

The lanky director turned again and peered down at Judge Waddell. She herself was tall for a woman, just under five-ten, and was not accustomed to looking quite so far up at a man. "Excuse me," he said. "You want to talk about all these . . . ?"

"As a kind of background, you might say, to a matter that concerns me," she said, a bit miffed with herself for sounding so, well, judicial with this stunning man. She smiled. She had, she knew, a winning smile. "It all seems so puzzling to a newcomer. The police-department reports are not really very helpful. And the news accounts all seem as if they were hatched in Hollywood. Oh. Whoops."

Pindaric laughed. "I'd be happy to tell you what's been going on as far as I know it," the director said. "But the man who seems to see it all most clearly is over there. Bowdre."

Olivia was startled. "Him? The sculptor?" She watched the big man, with the Indian woman beside him and about a half step in front, walk across the lawn toward another small clot of people dressed in understated finery. What would a big, brash, bratty artist know? she wondered. "Good heavens," she said. "The man can't see, can he?"

"It seems to be more of a help than a hindrance for some things," Pindaric said. "I'll introduce you. He seems to have a feel for some of the undercurrents in this strange little world out here."

"That sounds interesting," she said, unconvinced.

"Hey, Mo," Pindaric called. "Got a minute?"

The sculptor turned and smiled, the lowering sun gleaming gold from his dark glasses.

"Andy," he said, "how'd you get here? Horseback?" He began moving in their direction. "One of them authentic Spanish Barb horses you brought in for the movie? Hah—hah."

"Someone I want you to meet. Judge Olivia Waddell. Mo Bowdre."

"Pleased to meet you, ma'am," Mo said, extending a big hand, which Olivia shook briefly. "Last time I met a judge, it didn't turn out all that well for me. But that was a long time ago, and I've reformed."

He loomed up over her, a grinning mountain, erect as

a post with his bearded chin jutting out. A reformed redneck, perhaps, and definitely not her type.

"Judge Waddell—" Pindaric began.

"Olivia, please," she said.

"—Olivia is interested in all the troubles I've—I mean the film has had. I told her you had a better feel for the, uh, ethnic landscape out here. You see"—he turned to face her again—"we were talking about it last night, just before the bomb went off."

The sculptor beamed. "That's just a fine idea. Now, why don't you two be my guests at dinner after this is over here? I know a real fine place, a little out of the way, you know? Quiet. Good, that's settled then. Connie? Come over here, will you? Want you to meet this lady."

Olivia glanced up at the director, who smiled and shrugged. This could be interesting in more ways than one, she thought.

ten

The figure—a man—stepped lightly into the shadows in the elegant alleyway, after three minutes of standing quietly observing the parking lot. He had seen a young man in a business suit leave through one of the back doors of the offices that fronted on De Vargas Street and drive away in a Mercedes. All of the offices in the block now seemed dark, so the figure approached one of the doors feeling relatively secure.

It took him three more minutes of contemplation and gentle probing to deactivate the security system and only a matter of seconds more to enter the back room of the offices of Allen Templeton, Attorney-at-Law. Passing through a low doorway into a hall lined with bookshelves and wooden cabinets that gleamed with furniture polish under the low light from his pocket flashlight, he entered the main office and shone the beam around the walls. He noted the carved *santos* standing prayerfully on the mantelpiece, the alert kachina dolls in the niche in the adobe wall, the fine old territorial-style desk, as neat as a pin, bearing nothing except an expensive leather desk set. Below the niche with the kachina dolls was a gleaming cabinet made out of some reddish, fine-grained wood—probably cherry.

He crossed the room silently and crouched down before the cabinet. The two doors swung open easily, revealing two drawers, both locked. He peered at the drawers, shining the fine beam of his flashlight back and forth in their seams and, in another two minutes, replaced a metal tool in his back pocket and opened the drawer on top.

He riffled through the tabs on top of some twelve thick file folders, and the smell of old dust enveloped him. He came to one marked in hand-written, calligraphic script with the words RECORDS: THOS. CATRON, and lifted it out.

With a smile that revealed two crooked front teeth in the faint glow of the flashlight's narrow beam, he put the file on the floor and, kneeling over it, began to flip through the batches of old papers, neatly pinned together, dry and fragile documents and letters written in faded archaic script.

Five minutes later, carrying a brand-new manila file folder, the kind with a little string that wraps around a paper button, which he had liberated from Allen Templeton's well-stocked supply closet, the figure slipped out the back door, leaned over for a moment to fiddle with a wire, and then walked past the parking lot and two blocks down Gallisteo Street to his car. Along the way, he whistled a tune so off-key that had anyone passed him on the sidewalk, it could not have been recognized as the title song from the old Fred Astaire movie *Top Hat*.

Mo Bowdre put his meaty forearms on the linen tablecloth, interlaced his fingers, and leaned forward into the candlelight. The restaurant was a place of a mere half-

dozen tables, only one other of which was in use, and
that by an elderly couple who, Pindaric had pointed out,
both wore hearing aids and nonetheless kept saying
"What?" to each other. It was late—nearly ten-thirty,
closing time—and a waiter in a purple silk shirt and a
pair of tight black pants periodically poked his head in
the room hopefully.

". . . So that's how it might have been," Mo said.
"And now they've caught this boy Gallegos—well,
that's a matter of speakin', I don't know how old he
is—and my friend Ramirez is probably grilling him this
very minute. If Gallegos did all that mayhem, then the
chances are he did it 'cause his uncle told him to, and
his uncle's old aunt is the one who would rightfully get
that old land back if things went their way in your
court."

Olivia Waddell wiped her mouth with a linen napkin
as she stared into the man's opaque dark glasses and
frowned.

"If this is true . . ." she said.

"Well, see, that's what no one knows. Right now it's
just a story some of us made up to fit the facts. Me and
Ramirez, and Andy here, and an FBI agent named Collins." He turned to Connie, who was leaning back in her
chair expressionlessly. "Collins quit, did you hear that
yet? Starting next week he's unemployed."

Connie's eyes widened, but she said nothing.

"I've never heard anything so reprehensible," Olivia
said, as if to herself. She looked up. "If it's even near
the truth. An officer of the court . . ."

"I guess," Pindaric said, "there's a lot of money involved. It's like a drug for some people."

Mo leaned back in his chair. "Olivia, can you tell me what's at stake here? I mean with these land claims?"

"Well, I can hardly talk about the details of a case before me—to anyone. But I can tell you a few things in general. These kind of claims are not unusual. Many of them have been made and resolved in the courts. Most of the old Spanish land-grant claims were resolved around the turn of the century by a special board. In the 1920s, there was another board that heard a few Hispanic claims that their lands had been given to the Pueblo Indians. And most of the other Indian tribes' land claims have also been resolved in various courts and commissions, more recently, for the most part."

"With what results?"

Olivia smiled. "Very few tribes get the land back."

"So they're wasting their time?"

"No, no. In one case here in this region, the Taos Pueblo had Blue Lake and the surrounding basin returned to them. It was a sacred place, where their souls come from, I believe. But it had been in the National Forest for years, supposedly maintained for their use, but people were camping up there, that sort of thing. A judicial commission established what they call aboriginal title, and finally Congress and President Nixon decided to give it back to them. It was more a question of freedom of religion than just a land claim. But that's rare."

"What about these old Spanish claims?"

"As I said, they were all resolved years ago. Anything since the turn of the century has been pretty flimsy when it gets to court. Most of them don't get that far. That's what puzzles me."

"How so?" Mo said. "If I can ask that."

Olivia picked up her napkin and put it down again. "An attorney representing such a claim knows it's high risk. Any claim is, but especially one of these. Attorneys usually work on such claims just like accident cases—on a contingency basis. Baldly, that means they get a piece of the action. Like a third. But if they win a land-claim case, they don't get a third of the land. I don't see why an attorney like Templeton would bother with something like this. It's flimsy to begin with—historically speaking—so what's in it for me? He doesn't seem the type to take on something like this just for a straight fee. Even with the hourly meter running, it's pretty small potatoes."

"A puzzle indeed," Mo said. "Maybe we should go. I hear that waiter breathing heavily back there." He put his hand out and took the check, which had been on the table for nearly ten minutes, and stood up. "One other thing. What happens in most of the Indian claims? The ones who aren't as lucky as Taos."

"If they can make the case that they really did use the land in the old days before the Europeans came along, and if they can show that it was taken wrongfully—like a reservation boundary was mis-surveyed or an old land grant treated illegally—the courts sometimes agree to a settlement."

"A money settlement but no land?"

"Generally speaking," she said.

"How confusing," Mo said, grinning broadly. "Well, Olivia, I hope all this has been useful to you. This is a pretty good place, huh? How was that lime mousse?"

* * *

Seated on the bed, Connie brushed her long ebony hair in languorous strokes, waiting for Mo to emerge from the bathroom.

"Well, now," he said over the sound of the faucet through the half-open door. "That judge lady sure is a walkin' talkin' Frigidaire."

The water stopped running with a clunk.

"Damn pipes," Mo muttered, and stepped into the bedroom. "What was that message on the answering machine?"

Connie continued pulling the brush through her hair.

"From the production office. They want me there tomorrow."

"Tomorrow's Sunday."

"They work every day."

Mo sat on the bed. "You're doing that smiling again. I can hear it in your voice. Grinnin' ear to ear."

"Tomorrow's my day," she said. "They're shooting. Me." She laughed.

"Well, goddamn it, isn't there a better way of saying that?"

The next morning Mo Bowdre stood under his *portal*, listening to the birds in his yard wind down their territorial advertisements. He was barefoot, dressed in jeans and a vast gray T-shirt with stylized clouds silkscreened on it in the three primary colors and the legend

DON'T WORRY
BE HOPI

He heard a car stop on the street outside the wall, listened to the sound of a car door slamming, footsteps, the gate creaking.

"That you, Collins?"

"Yeah."

"How much longer till you turn into Tinkerbell?"

"Monday I'm just another working slob."

"Working at what? You're not really gonna be a dance instructor."

"I'll think of something. Maybe B and E."

"How'd it go? Connie left us some fresh coffee. Want some?"

In the kitchen, Collins put a manila folder on the table and fetched two mugs of coffee. "Black, right?" he said, and sat down and began untying the string on the folder. "Templeton's got a whole lot of old stuff, old records, lot of it kind of family memorabilia. Goes back to an old family patriarch, Thomas Catron."

"Ah. The leader of the Santa Fe Ring. He played some shadowy role in getting the Lincoln County War started. You know, Billy the Kid and all that. My great-uncle Charlie got killed in that fracas."

"You told me. Catron kept all kinds of little notes to himself about deals he made, copies of letters, that kind of stuff. Musty old shit." He slipped a thin batch of papers out of the folder. "But this one thing here—"

"What is it?"

"There's one of his notes, and a Xerox."

"They didn't have Xeroxes in those days."

"Hey, no shit. They didn't even have paper clips, at least not out here in the provinces. Used little pins, like sewing pins. And it looks like this note from Catron, kind of a memorandum to himself, was pinned to what someone Xeroxed and put back in the file. There are two little dots in the upper left corner of the Xerox that match the pinholes in the note."

Mo leaned back in the wooden chair, which creaked under his weight, and took a loud sip of coffee.

"Good eye," Mo said. "Maybe you should think about going into law enforcement."

Collins grinned. "Okay, the note is in that old script, like all the others—Catron's, you'd say—and it says, 'Royal land grant to Los pobla del Santo Estovan. From archives. Poss. recovr'y.' "

"And?"

"And the Xerox—it's not all that clear, a lot of Spanish stuff, faded, in weird script, looks like an old man wrote it, lots of squiggles and one of those big flourishes at the end of the name—you know, back and forth and loops and all that. But you can make out the same words here. 'Los Pobla del Santo Estovan.' There's a date, too—1689."

"Eureka," Mo said. "That's when the Spanish started issuing these babies. After the Pueblo Rebellion. Trying to suck up to all the pissed-off Indians who'd flung their asses out in 1680."

"What's Templeton doing with all this stuff?" Collins asked.

"He married into the Catron family. So he found this when he was poking around in his idol's old papers and realized he had a fortune on his hands. Some of old Tom's unfinished business, I guess." He paused. "I guess you don't have idols anymore. Just role models. Anyway . . ."

"So he gave it to the guys at the pueblo, and they have the legal basis for their claim."

"Why would he do that?" Mo asked. "How could he get anything out of it?"

"Oh, yeah."

"See, this is like a deed. A deed from the king. Probably all that gobbledygook describes the land, and probably it's signed by some member of the Spanish bureaucracy in the name of the king, whoever the hell he was back then. This is enough for the pueblo to say they were screwed, the land was theirs all along, and now it's some damned national forest. So Templeton gets diabolical.

"It works like this: If the pueblo makes a claim, waving this land grant and whatever else they got to prove the land got taken away from 'em when they weren't looking, there's a *way* outside chance they'll win. Get the land. What's more likely is they'll get bought off, get some big money settlement from Uncle Sam. Millions of dollars. And if the Indians look like stumblebums, irresponsible—worse, if they look like they can't control their own people—then it's bound to make it less likely they'll get the actual land back. The Taos people got some land back, but they came off as real humble, real sincere. It's all political. If Santo Esteban has a good legal claim, but some of 'em are raising Cain all over the place, buggering up an important film, *killing* people, for chrissakes—well, that just ain't endearing to your run-of-the-mill hypocrite in Congress. So . . ."

He paused and sipped at his mug.

"So, if the courts settle it and the Indians get a settlement," he went on, "and not the land, then there's money in it, and *that's* what lawyers like. So Templeton makes a deal for part of the settlement if he turns over this here land grant that he 'just happened to find in some wrong file in the archive.' "

"A deal with whom?"

"It's gotta be the tribe's lawyer. That fellow Beck."

"Jeez. He's a do-gooder."

"Maybe so, but he's a broke do-gooder. And he's got a lot of bills to pay for that poor kid of his. Got one of those degenerative diseases, poor little guy. My friend Art Bachrach up there, runs the bookstore, told me that Beck is borrowing office space from him. Too damn broke even to rent an office. And I checked with Martin this morning, the young governor out at Santo Esteban. They pay Beck some tiny monthly retainer, a thousand a month. That doesn't take you very far, and the tribe's about the only steady work Beck's got. What you found here confirms that."

Collins stood up and paced back and forth. "So Templeton gets the Torres family all revved up about getting the land back and suggests to them that they stir up a little trouble that looks like the Indians are out of control."

"Right."

"He has no expectation of winning for the Torres family."

"Right."

"The man is a scumbag, an all-star prick."

"Right."

"Deserves to rot in hell."

"Right. A little fire and brimstone."

"But all of this could be pretty hard to prove."

"Not if we can get that icebox of a judge to loosen up her protective robes a little," Mo said. "And we got this stuff here." He gestured toward the papers on the table. "That's evidence."

"Not the way *we* got it."

"Well, maybe Judge Waddell'd issue you a warrant."

"For what?"

"To bug Templeton's phone. Then, while you're doing that you can put this back in his file. Then, the next time someone finds it, it'll be legal."

The agent sat down again, crooked teeth showing. "What did you say you did before you started being a sculptor?"

"Hah—hah. You mean you FBI people don't know? I guess we better call Tony Ramirez and do a little choreographing."

That afternoon the wind shifted and huge cumulus clouds, their fluffy tops lit like ice cream, began sailing up the Rio Grande, making vast shadowy patches on the arid surface of the rift valley, gigantic mobile leopard spots.

Rafael Gallegos, thirty-six, unemployed and with a record in two states of sporadic pilferage, two suspended sentences, and one short hitch in a Colorado state prison for arson, was confronted with his own Winchester .30-30, extracted by a county sheriff's deputy from his uncle's shed in Truchas, along with five unused sticks of dynamite and the caps to go with them. Guaranteed that ballistics tests and other forensic magic would assure the Santa Fe police of what they already knew, Gallegos confessed to the shooting death of the actress Melanie Moreno while she stood beside the road leading into the pueblo of Santo Esteban, and the bombing of Andrew Pindaric's XJS Jaguar on Canyon Road. Pressed further, he also confessed to bludgeoning Gregorio Velasquez to death with the handle of a hammer ("He was already half-dead when I got there, mon.") and steadfastly refused to say anything else, such as how the idea for these acts had come to him. He confessed disingenuously to being an alcoholic, subject to blind rages, the details of which he could rarely remember. He was placed in solitary, awaiting Monday and the magistrate who would hasten his arraignment.

Not long afterward Sergeant Anthony Ramirez and, in one of his last official acts, Special Agent Larry Collins paid a visit to the elegant rented home of Judge Olivia Waddell and engaged her in an intense conversation that lasted two hours, during which she proved that she had forgotten nothing from her three-year stint as a prosecuting attorney in Alexandria, Virginia.

At four o'clock, a U.S. West telephone repair truck stopped outside a long dirt driveway off Bishop's Lodge Road north of downtown Santa Fe and a repairman opened the green metal box that served thirteen homes in the neighborhood, including that of Allen Templeton, Attorney-at-Law, expertly splicing new wires to the colorful spaghetti inside. North in Taos, another telephone repairman took care of the same chore on Bent Street. Half an hour later the truck in Santa Fe stopped a block from the attorney's office on De Vargas and repeated the same procedure. Simultaneously, Special Agent Collins emerged from the alleyway behind the offices strung along De Vargas minus three objects he had been carrying when he went into the alley: a one-hundred-plus-year-old memorandum in the handwriting of Thomas Catron, a Xerox copy of a nearly unintelligible land grant signed by an officer of the King of Spain in 1689, and a tiny electronic device that had cost the United States government in excess of seventeen thousand dollars. The two pieces of paper were back among the others in Templeton's cherry-wood cabinet, and the

tiny microphone and transmitter were fixed among the
feathers of a kachina doll representing Crow Mother, a
gentle and much-revered figure in the Hopi spiritual
pantheon. Out on Gallisteo Street, Agent Collins nodded pleasantly to the man in the telephone company repairman's uniform, who returned, differently dressed, an
hour later in a disreputable panel truck from an office-
cleaning establishment and parked in the lot behind De
Vargas, where the van developed—almost instanta-
neously—a flat right rear tire.

Mo Bowdre spent the afternoon puttering around in
his studio, humming off-key and working on the chest
and shoulders of his mountain sentinel, a.k.a. *Old Cojones.* That evening, amid a mild, cooling thunderstorm,
he had a quiet dinner at home with Connie Barnes, who
explained with measured enthusiasm what it was like to
be—even with a nonspeaking role—in front of the camera during the filming, refilming, and refilming again,
of a major scene of a motion picture. It was, she concluded, not unlike certain Indian ceremonies: a lot of
people milling around apparently not doing anything for
a long time before the actual ceremony begins. Then, in
minutes, it was all over.

eleven

The windowless room in the basement of the SFPD was rigged like a small-time radio broadcasting studio, with a bulbous black microphone hanging over the table at which Judge Olivia Waddell sat in her gray silk suit. Beside her was Sergeant Ramirez, watching her intently as she spoke into the fuzzy mike an inch from her mouth. Through a glass wall, a man with a headset sat before a console of countless dials and flashing lights.

"This is by no means a criticism, Mr. Beck," Judge Waddell said, winding up a conversation that had gone on for almost five minutes by the big round clock on the wall above the glass. "As I said, I have been looking over the documents submitted in this case and I wanted to be sure that the plaintiff's case was as well represented as possible, given the current climate in the courts in cases of this nature."

Through a loudspeaker, Beck could be heard clearing his throat.

"Thank you, Your Honor. I'm most grateful."

"Goodbye, Mr. Beck."

"Goodbye, Your Honor. Thank you."

There was a click, and Judge Waddell turned to Ramirez. "Well, how do you think it went?" she said.

"You would've convinced me," he said. "Now we wait." Behind the glass, the technician's hands fluttered over the console. The only sound was a nearly imperceptible hum—the ancient air-conditioning system.

"Where are your friends Bowdre and Collins?" the judge asked.

Ramirez smiled. "I don't know. Off doing something civilian, I guess."

The sound of a buzzing phone line came over the loudspeaker, and the technician spun around to face them, grinning, his finger raised. The phone buzzed three times and Ramirez said, "Come *on*! I know you're there." Then Allen Templeton answered.

"Yes?"

"Templeton. It's Beck."

"Why are you calling?"

"I just got a call from the judge, Judge Waddell, and—"

"What about?"

"The case, the case, for God's sake. Everything's falling apart. I mean, goddamn it, Templeton—"

"Will you calm down and tell me what she called about?"

"Well, she said she'd been reviewing the documents and she thought we—I—might want to put a bit more emphasis on the existence of the old Santo Esteban shrines on the land out there. She said she saw a lot of parallels with the Taos case."

"Taos?"

"*Yes*. Where they got the *land* back."

"My God. Beck . . ."

"It sounds like she's . . . I mean she obviously didn't

come right out and say it, but it sounds like she might give them the goddamn *land*!"

"Calm down, for Christ's sake."

"Nothing, nothing. We'll get nothing out of this. All those killings . . . for nothing, Jesus Christ."

"I said calm down, damn it. In the first place, there's no way they can trace those killings to us—"

"*Us!* Look, they were all your doing, not mine. You told old Torres to sabotage the thing, I didn't think it was going to come to killing people. God, those two actors . . ."

"Stop that. Stop that whining. Use your head, Beck. *I* didn't tell Torres to kill people. I just told him to rough it up a little. God knows what he told that nephew of his. That's their problem. Not mine. And it doesn't make any difference what that horse-faced judge thinks at this point. If the evidence is not presented properly in court, there's no case for giving the land back. And even if she decides to give it back in spite of the evidence, or lack of it, then the U.S. attorney is sure to appeal it. Good God, man, the government isn't just going to lie down while these peasants run off with twelve thousand acres of national forest. So calm down. We haven't lost this thing yet."

"So I throw the case?"

"Just like a boxing match. It's done all the time. Now go back to work, Beck. Nothing important has happened. I'll talk to you later."

There was the click of a phone hanging up.

Judge Waddell looked at Ramirez and smiled happily. Ramirez in turn put his thumb up, thinking that while the judge was not exactly a stunner, she could hardly be called horse-faced.

"There's about three hundred years of jail time right on that tape," the judge said. "So, Sergeant, it worked."

"Yes, ma'am. Now we just got to pick 'em up." He leaned toward the mike. "Jimmy? Call the boys in Taos, and our guys. Bag 'em. And call that Lieutenant Bendix of the LAPD."

Allen Templeton hung up the phone, raised his eyes to the ceiling, and jumped slightly when he heard something—a thump—from the back room of his offices. He stood up behind his desk and crossed the room, opening the door to the hallway lined with bookshelves, and listened. Slowly he stepped down the hall and reached for the door into the back room, but it suddenly shot open with a loud crash and a black torrent sloshed into his face, hot, searing. He screamed, covered his eyes, and more heat poured over his chest and shoulders, oozing. He fell on his knees, his mind reeling, being pummeled with—what? Pummeled with something soft, what the *hell*? A hot petrochemical odor filled the cavities of his head, made his throat gag. He forced open one eye and saw white, a white cloud, and he opened his mouth wider to breathe and some of the white cloud caught on his lips.

Feathers! He looked down with his one open eye. Feathers! All over him, all over the floor, in the black ooze. He fell over on his face and whimpered.

Larry Collins strode down De Vargas Street with Mo Bowdre keeping pace a half step behind him. Collins went over to the police car parked along the curb. Two cops were just emerging from it.

"Hey, officer," Collins said. "There's something real

strange back there. In that office. Someone in there is moaning. Maybe you should go look."

"What office?" the cop asked.

"That one," Collins said, pointing.

"That's where we're going. You didn't hear a shot or nothing, did you?"

"A shot?" Mo Bowdre said. "No, just some guy moaning. Sounds as unhappy as the dog that sat on a nail. You better hurry, officer."

The two policemen marched up to the office door and entered. Collins set off down the sidewalk, the big man alongside.

"What do you think of the civilian life so far, Collins?"

"Pretty damn satisfying. Even exhilarating. I feel light as a feather."

Mo Bowdre laughed his snare-drum laugh.

Be sure to read the next mystery
about Mo Bowdre...

THE LETHAL PARTNER

by Jake Page

In this sequel to THE KNOTTED
STRINGS, an arts scene mentor in
Santa Fe claims he has discovered
seven rare Georgia O'Keeffe paintings
dating from the 1940s. As experts
labor to find the truth behind the
paintings, the death toll around Santa
Fe begins to mount. Mo Bowdre is
soon lending a hand in this tale of
black-market trading, stolen paintings,
and mutilation murders.